Praise for *Temple Folk*

Finalist for the 2023 National Book Award for Fiction
***Time*'s 100 Must-Read Books of 2023**

"Aaliyah Bilal's debut short story collection, a finalist for a 2023 National Book Award, offers a vivid and nuanced portrait of the Black Muslim experience. Across ten stories, she introduces characters, often women, who are reconsidering or rediscovering their faith. . . . *Temple Folk* is Bilal's love letter to her community."

—*Time*

"These nine short stories follow Black American Muslims who drift toward and away from their faith, judge one another for immodesty, wrestle with upended family lore, and reflect with ambivalence on the impact the Nation of Islam has had on their lives. . . . Bilal's stories depict characters who serve as sensitive guides to matters of apostasy, racial prejudice, and gender roles."

—*The New Yorker*

"*Temple Folk*'s stories touch on modesty and sexuality, abuse and family, responsibility and faith."

—*The New York Times*

"Bilal's finely drawn and unvarnished character portraits leave much space for readers to reflect on their own conflicting allegiances, identities, and beliefs. These singular stories offer great insight on a community underexplored in literature."

—*Publishers Weekly* (starred review)

"Aaliyah Bilal says she knows that a lot of people associate the Nation of Islam with hate. But in her new collection of short stories, *Temple Folk*, she reclaims narratives about Black Muslims and how they contemplate faith, identity, and community in the US."

—NPR

"A groundbreaking debut collection portraying the lived experiences of Black Muslins grappling with faith, family, and freedom in America."

—*BookBrowse*

"In Bilal's debut, Black American Muslims explore the intricacies of their faith and community."

—*Kirkus Reviews*

"This stunning collection by debut author Aaliyah Bilal features Black Muslims as they reckon with family, faith, and community. A collection dealing with faith of any kind, regardless of the particular religion, should wrestle with the gap between what the characters believe and how they act, and Bilal is a master at drawing those contradictions. The characters come to life in these stories, which are often quiet, but never without an elegant assuredness. . . . *Temple Folk* announces Aaliyah Bilal as a remarkable talent and a writer to watch."

—*Chicago Review of Books*

"*Temple Folk* is more than a special literary accomplishment; it is a gift of glorious songs. The people in the nation of Islam have not appeared very often in literature. Now, Aaliyah Bilal arrives with a splendid and grand collection of ten stories that, with sensitivity and insight and skill, give us a world of people—our loved ones and neighbors—who decided that life might be better in the nation. We have long needed these stories, these songs, and this gift should be praised from as many rooftops as possible."

—Edward P. Jones, Pulitzer Prize–winning author of *The Known World*

"Obviously a student of history, and even more so, a student of the human heart, Aaliyah Bilal lays bare the interior lives of Black Muslims in these ten extraordinary stories. Across decades, generations, and con-

"Aaliyah Bilal is a gifted storyteller who understands how to build a world that feels both particular in its contours and universal in the challenges, triumphs, and yearnings of its characters. The stories that make up *Temple Folk* explore love, faith, loyalty, and disillusionment while offering up gorgeous language and unforgettable imagery. *Temple Folk* feels like no collection I have read before and announces Bilal as a literary talent worth championing."

—Angela Flournoy, author of *The Turner House*

"A beautiful and vivid collection of stories. Aaliyah Bilal is the truth. Grateful for her voice in the world."

—Jacqueline Woodson, National Book Award–winning and *New York Times* bestselling author

"*Temple Folk* is a remarkable debut that does many things at once. It opens the door to a people we barely know, yet opens our eyes to the struggles that make us all human. People surprise and they disappoint. They stumble spiritually and soar morally. They love with all they have and lose all they've got. Put between faith and family, duty and self, Temple folk live through all the ties that bind and break."

—Marlon James, winner of the 2015 Booker Prize

"With her landmark debut, *Temple Folk*, Aaliyah Bilal shines a light on a Black American community that, for all its influence, hasn't been given its due in fiction—the Nation of Islam. The deftness of her storytelling allows total access to characters struggling to practice faith as a means of survival. This is a truly masterful work, full of compassion, humor, nuance, and great insight."

—Emily Raboteau, author of *Searching for Zion*

TEMPLE
FOLK

☪

AALIYAH
BILAL

SIMON & SCHUSTER PAPERBACKS
New York   London   Toronto   Sydney   New Delhi

100 YEARS
SIMON &
SCHUSTER
PAPERBACKS

An Imprint of Simon & Schuster, LLC
1230 Avenue of the Americas
New York, NY 10020

First Simon & Schuster trade paperback edition July 2024

SIMON & SCHUSTER PAPERBACKS and colophon are registered trademarks of Simon & Schuster, LLC

Simon & Schuster: Celebrating 100 Years of Publishing in 2024

For information about special discounts for bulk purchases, please contact Simon & Schuster Special Sales at 1-866-506-1949 or business@simonandschuster.com.

The Simon & Schuster Speakers Bureau can bring authors to your live event. For more information or to book an event, contact the Simon & Schuster Speakers Bureau at 1-866-248-3049 or visit our website at www.simonspeakers.com.

Interior design by Carly Loman

Manufactured in the United States of America

10 9 8 7 6 5 4 3 2 1

Library of Congress Cataloging-in-Publication Data has been applied for.

ISBN 978-1-9821-9181-8
ISBN 978-1-9821-9182-5
ISBN 978-1-9821-9183-2 (ebook)

To my family, especially my parents,
John Bilal II and Doris St. John

It is He who made the stars as your guide through the darkness of land and sea

—THE NOBLE QUR'AN, 6:97

CONTENTS

BLUE

In the early hours before the dawn, the women of the Muslim Girls Training class stood single file on the sidewalk, waiting to board the Trailways charter bus headed to Chicago. A pair of streetlamps at the corner of Prospect and Main funneled soft light onto their frames—dressed in peacoats with long white skirts and head-scarves that matched the light drift of snow. They inched along, moving toward the yellow-orange light that filtered a halo from the top half of the coach. Slowly, they ascended the steps and filed down the aisle to their seats. The others shivered, waiting outside, eager to get out of the cold, eager in the awareness that soon they were headed to the Saviours' Day celebration where they would behold the Messenger of the Lost-Found Nation—the maker of men and reformer of women—the seal of the prophets, up close and in person.

They were greeted at the top of the steps by the captain, Sister Lucinda. She was tall and handsome with café-au-lait skin, a commanding air, and bright, green eyes that looked softly upon the women as they passed. In the singsong voice of a grade-school teacher, she offered each one a greeting of "Salaam," checked her name from the list, and pointed to her assigned seat.

Where Sister Lucinda managed the entrance, Sister Memphis— her lieutenant—was positioned at the rear of the line. She had her hands folded behind her back and paced slow, observing the women. The MGT had their thoughts about her, but fearful of the consequences of exposing them in their rawest form—lest word travel back to Sister Memphis—they were careful to hide their gossip behind half-hearted concern, mostly about her appearance.

They couldn't be all the way sure but said that, from the look of her eyes, something had to be out of sorts with her health. Standing before them that early morning, they bulged uncomfortably as she scanned the women, examining them for undone shoelaces, strange odors, and buttons fastened in the wrong places. Sister Guadeloupe, a twenty-five-year-old nurse in training, said it must have been a problem with her thyroid that set her eyes to protruding that way.

"Nothing that daily glasses of beet juice and a little bit of iodine couldn't help," she said.

Sister Memphis had skin like charcoal, with prominent lips always pursed tight until the moment she started in on some poor MGT. Then she'd expose her brilliant teeth—the canines like little daggers—and her mouth would open wide as a Venus flytrap, ready to snap off their heads at the slightest offense.

The women's anxieties had only multiplied over the last two months since Sister Memphis's husband, James 17X, had gone away. Out on a walk, some of the MGT saw him at the entrance of the high-rise where they lived, loading a Chevy pickup truck with all of his belongings. He caught eyes with them, then shook his head like he'd seen something foul, and that's how they knew his Nation days were over. They couldn't have known the challenges—how over the past months, James had grown more vocal with Sister Memphis in his private denunciations of the Messenger. He said he was ready to leave the Nation for good and asked her if she would leave with him.

"It would just be me and you," he said. "We can go somewhere and build a little house, make us a family. Me, you, and our children, with a clean slate and the whole world open to us."

He was a decent man who liked peace in the home, who sometimes picked wildflowers that grew near the construction site where he earned a living and brought the prettiest blossoms to her. Despite it all, she dismissed his invitation and, quick as mercury, sent him on his way. His going had pained her, though she was not in the least conflicted about her decision to stay.

When Brother James didn't show up at the Temple the following week, the sisters were certain that her husband's departure would turn Sister Memphis's half-beating heart all the way to stone. The theories of the MGT were as ornate as they were plenty, but none garnered enough sympathy to lessen their fear of her, so that standing there in the icy snow, they trembled from her nearness as much as from the bitter cold.

Sister Carol, a twenty-two-year-old new recruit—no more than eight months in the Nation—froze the instant she felt Sister Memphis fixate on her. Eight months was long enough to have heard all the stories and to have witnessed the unfolding of the lieutenant's quick temper. She'd grown so accustomed to the rhythm of Sister Memphis's barking at the women—of having them repeat tasks that they hadn't completed to her standard—that she saw it as a painful inevitability that soon it would be her on the receiving end of the lieutenant's tirades, and there she was, with those strange eyes, gathering her entire person like simple math.

Sister Memphis sensed Sister Carol's nervousness, feeling it pass from the new recruit and filter through the other MGT standing at the tail end of the line. Slowly, she reached for the edge of Sister Carol's headdress, and when the young woman flinched, she stopped mid-gesture.

"Not to worry," a rare, softening lilt rode Sister Memphis's words. "It's nothing serious. Got a bulge in your scarf, that's all. Just doing my job. Everything clean and neat under there, just like the Messenger taught."

Sister Memphis felt a cramp in her abdomen but moved on, applying a moment's pressure to her side. The women turned, peering at her and each other as best they could, trying to understand who this new woman could be and what she'd done with the old lieutenant—looks that Sister Memphis noticed and let slide.

One week earlier, she'd overheard a conversation between the minister and his men about a lieutenant at one of the newer Temples by the name of Morgan 4X. Angry over the poor sales of trout that the brothers were made to cart through the neighborhood, he went upside the head of some lazy, fresh-out-the-joint FOI who refused to purchase the surplus with his own money. No more than a few days had passed between this rather mundane circumstance in the ordinary business of the Nation and the scene that had captured all of their attention—someone had repaid Morgan 4X for his brutality, going so far as to take his life. He was headed home late one night when an unidentified man came upon him and settled the score with the blast of a Model 36 Smith & Wesson straight to his cranium.

The incident sat heavily with Sister Memphis and mediated her actions toward the women. It made her wonder if they might have thought of her, not as keeping order but overstepping bounds, and what kind of revenge they might enact in the instance the sisters deemed she had gone too far.

With the women all on board and no FOI around to secure the bus, as they were already en route, Sister Memphis helped the driver close the under-coach panels where the luggage was stored, then scanned the sidewalk for stragglers. There was a rustling at the side of the Temple that shifted her gaze from the road to the alleyway. With the aid of the faint light she peered in the direction of the sound, trying to make out the figure that, from its raspy crescendo, was clearly approaching. She braced herself, fearing it might be a vagrant or some criminal element, and was relieved to see it was Sister Saundra, a new recruit—a tall, honey-toned wire of a woman, who'd been a student in the MGT class for less than a month.

In the short time since Sister Saundra had come into the fold, Sister Memphis had worked closely with the woman, trying to help her acclimate to the demands of life at the Temple. Despite her greatest efforts, there was little she could do to help motivate Sister Saundra to whatever task was at hand. Whether it was sewing, or learning how to make a whole-wheat piecrust, Sister Saundra seemed incapable of absorbing any new knowledge. She performed her duties with lackluster energy and was immune to any disciplinary measures—the scolding passing through her ears like words uttered in a foreign language. She impressed Sister Memphis as one of the types she'd seen come into the Nation over the years— the sort of people who were moved by the Messenger's words but uninterested in living out their substance. Sister Memphis figured that it was just a matter of time before Sister Saundra, like James before her, would resume her place in the murky stew that was life on the outside, abandoning the Nation like it was nothing more than a child's amusement—a masquerade of votaries.

It took a solid minute before she made her way through the snowfall, at which point it became clear that Sister Saundra was not alone. Sister Memphis had presumed that Saundra was struggling with a large sack of luggage, though she soon realized that the new recruit was tugging at the arm of a girl as tall as her shoulders, who could have been no older than thirteen.

"Sister Memphis." Saundra's voice was filled with syrupy angst. "I tried to make it on time. Swear to God, I did. Would have been the first in the line if I hadn't been weighed down by this little demon. You should honor your mother!" She spoke with more fervor than Sister Memphis sensed she was capable of, yanking at the hand of the child who was trying to free herself from Sister Saundra's grip. The girl would occasionally pause from her tugging and then, hoping to catch Sister Saundra off guard, start tugging yet again. She was poised to run down the street, alone into the dark—willing to contend with the miscreants and users who lurked in the shadows of the Eastside rather than stay with Sister Saundra—as if the woman were not her mother but a miscreant herself.

"This here is Sister Memphis," Saundra said, bending toward the girl. "She the lieutenant of this whole operation and she don't take no mess from nobody, especially not no snot-nosed children! Go 'head, tell the sister your name."

Sister Saundra nudged the girl over and over, and each time the girl resisted, her eyes cutting from one woman to the other like a spirit level trying to find its center.

Sister Memphis stared at the girl, a strange awareness rising within her that she was not going to like this child.

The girl had skin like French Vanilla ice cream, heavy on the egg, with an abundance of freckles that ran across the bridge of her nose—a face as instantly familiar and threatening as a schoolyard bully's. She wore her headscarf and skirt lopsided so that tufts of reddish, knotted hair showed from the edges—like someone who had gotten out of bed and not dressed herself, but instead decided to roll the linen around her body before venturing outside. She puzzled at the way the child's eyes seemed to open no more than the width of a silver dollar, giving her the look of someone who would always be limited by her own cunning, no hope of ever growing wise.

Sister Lucinda called to them from the door, and then marched through the snow to where the group of them stood.

"Is there something the matter?" she said, half-bright, half-concerned. "We mustn't delay any longer. Everyone is here now, and it is time for us to go."

Sister Memphis opened her mouth to explain, but Saundra spoke first.

"Excuse me, Sister Lucinda. This here is my daughter, Danielle. She's going to be spending some time with me and I was hoping that ya'll wouldn't mind if I brought her along to the Saviours' Day."

"But the child won't cooperate," Sister Memphis cut in, her voice heavy with disapproval. "Every time you ask her to do something, she just stands there like she doesn't understand English."

Sister Lucinda looked at all the women and pursed her lips, nodding.

"Go ahead and find yourself a seat on the bus, Sister Saundra," she said. "As for little Miss Danielle, you can sit with Sister Memphis. Keep her in line however you must," Sister Lucinda said to Memphis. "But try not to go too far."

Then she turned to the girl. "Beware, Miss Danielle," Sister Lucinda intoned seriously. "The Temple folk don't play games."

A look passed between Sister Memphis and Sister Lucinda that rehearsed the news of Morgan 4X, though the girl noticed and assumed something menacing. Her eyes widened slightly to regard Sister Memphis, noting her height, her broad shoulders, and the permanent alarm in her eyes, gathering she had the power to take her tiny frame and snap it into pieces, quick and effortless as a twig.

7

And with that, the women boarded the bus and after a long hydraulic hiss, it pulled off into the darkness, inching down the quiet streets with the Temple receding into nothing.

THE BUS MADE a low hum as it ventured west, driving along a two-lane highway cut through endless farmlands that were fallow and snowy in the February cold. There were occasional bumps in the road—clumps of frozen earth the hawk had blown there; bumps that the shocks absorbed, so that the women felt they were being cradled, the gentle rocking motion lulling most of them to sleep.

They were thirty women in total, filling the cabin with the sounds of their snores and the occasional utterances of minds loosed in dreams, all except for Sister Memphis. It was still dark outside, and equally dark inside the coach, save the reading light she had illuminated above her seat. She brought the previous day's newspaper along and had it spread neatly in front of her, silently mouthing the words as her eyes scanned the print. As quietly as she could, she folded the pages once she finished a panel, determined to read every single word and learn what the white man said were the most important happenings going on in the world. She read about the recession, about Richard Newhouse and his crusade to unseat Mayor Daley, how Sheikh Mujibur Rahman's Awami League had just turned Bangladesh into a one-party state. She made a habit of avoiding news out of Indochina, though she was drawn to a story that she read and reread about events unfolding in Cambodia. The Lon Nol regime, with the faltering support of the U.S. forces, was losing its grip on power as the Khmer Rouge blazed a path through the countryside and surrounded Phnom Penh. The Americans had a hand in the devastation—opposing the king for supporting North Vietnam—strengthening the guerilla forces of the Khmer Rouge.

So much of the present devastation, as read the report, was at the hands of Saloth Sar and his band of revolutionaries. They were the ones pushing the people from the capital into the countryside, making farmhands of doctors and intellectuals. She read on. Wherever in the world you went, Sister Memphis considered, you could always count on the white man to act against the interests of the native people. That was to be expected. However, it was the leaders among them who had extended the suffering of the ordinary Cambodians. They were fanning air against the house of cards that was the remains of their country, and whatever followed, she knew, would send the entire edifice of their nationhood tumbling to ruin.

She was reading a passage about the thousands of families lining the roadsides headed to Neak Loeung—the tearful and desperate masses with distended bellies, their hands perpetually outstretched for food, when she felt Danielle's eyes on her. She tried to continue with her reading, but after another minute, Sister Memphis lowered the paper and turned to the child who was scanning her up and down.

Sister Memphis peered at Danielle, who was looking dead set into her eyes, and then she began to speak, her words unusually soft.

"I know Sister Lucinda made it look some kind of way, but I'm a nice lady—it's just that if our people gonna get out of the condition we're in, we need structure. Rules! Order! That's all I do. I don't bite none. Now tell me, what's the matter? Didn't your mother—"

"Saundra is not my mother," Danielle interrupted Sister Memphis, her eyes cutting into her like razors.

Sister Memphis had, by that point, spent enough time in the child's presence to know the two were related. They had the same turned-up noses and the same jolty mannerisms that could only be explained by shared blood.

9

Sister Memphis resumed, "The lady, Ms. Saundra? Didn't she give you anything to do for the ride?"

Just then the girl looked from Sister Memphis and down at herself. Sister Memphis had not gotten over the child's disheveled appearance, though she hadn't enumerated all the out-of-place details that were, then and there, overwhelmingly apparent. The headdress looked like it was made with used dinner napkins—it was wrinkled, stiff, and too small to accommodate the child's unruly, reddish hair. The toga-like skirt had large, yellow splotches as if it had been used the previous night as a tablecloth, before it was hastily removed and wrapped around the child's waist.

"Saundra doesn't care," Danielle said. "Not about me and not even about my little sister."

"You have a sister?" Sister Memphis intoned seriously.

"Yes," Danielle replied, "but she stayed with Nana. I'm the only one that had to go with her. Then she just yanked me off the pallet where I was sleeping and had me put on these clothes."

From the moment Sister Memphis had seen her face through the snowfall, she began to forge an image of Danielle that compelled her to strong memories of her own past. Danielle was a child—innocent and good at her core—who bore the hurt of a no-good family—a feeling she had known all too well.

"That's why I say Saundra is not my mother," Danielle continued. "Nana is my mother, and I'm halfway mad at her right now for making me spend the week with Saundra and her crazy self."

The crashing, raspy sound of their talking stirred Sister Almina from across the aisle. She was still asleep but had turned her head in the direction of Sister Memphis and Danielle, most likely blending the sound of their chatter into her dream.

Sister Memphis switched off the reading lamp and let go of the paper, folding her hands onto her lap so it wouldn't fall. She turned back to Danielle and looked at her in the new light—it was still not quite dawn, though the sky had turned the ultramarine of morning on Neptune.

"She's nasty and sneaky," Danielle went on, "and don't care about nobody but herself."

"Careful," Sister Memphis said, "lest you turn out just like her." Her eyes were soft, reflecting the growing warmth she felt toward the child—this little girl who was midstream through a river she herself had crossed.

"That's how I know this is not going to last," Danielle said finally. "This whole thing with her and these white dresses, it's just a matter of time. One day she'll get tired of all of it and then she will be back on Nana's porch, crying to be let inside. She will leave again when she meets a shiny new man, but in the meanwhile she will eat up all the food and only spend a little bit of time with my sister, and not me, like I ain't even there."

Sister Memphis wanted to hold the child but knew better than to show too much affection. Trying to be helpful, she grabbed a carry-on from beneath her seat and removed from it a brush, a few bobby pins, and a nail file.

"Would you let me fix your hair? I'll just pull it back into a neat little bun so it will lay flat under the headdress if that's alright." She said this, and the child's eyes widened not so much from the offer, but because she was dazzled at the glittery, metal file with the pointed tip and the marbleized plastic handle.

"That's to clean under your nails. You can do that while I get your hair together."

Sister Memphis said this, and the child nodded. With the sun rising at their backs, she grabbed the brush and, with firm strokes, tugged the kinks from Danielle's hair, pulling the mass of her reddish curls into a tidy, braided knot at the nape of her neck.

*

IT WAS IN the fall of '58 that Mr. Chesterfield—the man in the fedora, with the grease-slick face and Perma-Strate roller curls—started visiting 121 Bradley Street. Edith met him some weeks earlier at the Oldsmobile dealership where he had sold her a brand-new Super 88. He told her that a Fiesta Hardtop Wagon was the only car that a woman of her style and taste should ever be seen driving. This prompted her invitations and over a string of Friday evenings he would come over for dinner. Each time he came, she grew more and more certain that, of all the men she knew, who claimed to love her, this was the one who was destined to be her husband.

Mr. Chesterfield lived twenty miles outside of town in a tiny hamlet called Mason with a woman named Vernelle—his actual wife and mother to five of his nine children—though this fact didn't keep him from accepting Edith's invitations. He came over every Friday night and sat at the head of her twin pedestal mahogany dining table, eating oversized helpings of fried chicken, creamed rice, and lima beans while Edith filled his ears with stories. Edith went on about her marriage to her daughter Tiffany's father—a traveling salesman. Tiffany, who sat at Edith's right side, gnawing on a drumstick, listened as her mother went on, telling Mr. Chesterfield that she was but a month old when the salesman died, leaving her alone with her one and only daughter. It was just one year later, after Edith's grandmother Bertha died, that she acquired the house. According to the last will and testament, the home would be hers as long as she agreed to take in Martha—a girl several years older than Tiffany, who Bertha had found on her doorstep one morning, thus explaining how she'd come into the care of an additional child.

"I've been through trials and tribulations," Edith said, "but we do our best to get by."

Mr. Chesterfield laughed and nodded at the stories Edith told, knowing good and well that barely a word of what she said was true.

MARTHA SAT ON the far side of the table and neither smiled nor spoke a word other than "yes" or "no, ma'am," as she was frequently on her feet, refreshing everyone's drinks at Edith's request and cleaning the place settings whenever crumbs found their way onto the white linen.

One evening, when the dinner was over, the group of them migrated to the parlor where Tiffany put on a show, singing and dancing for Mr. Chesterfield's pleasure. Martha played a piano accompaniment, trying to keep pace with Tiffany as she sang off-rhythm and off-key.

Picture you upon my knee,
Just tea for two and two for tea,
Just me for you
And you for me alone . . .

Her voice had an affected sultriness that was uncomfortable to Martha's ears—singing the lyrics as she dragged a white feather boa along the length of her left arm.

Tiffany hadn't bothered to learn the song beyond the first verse, and so she repeated the chorus, but Martha carried the tune further than Tiffany could go. When she sensed a change in melody, Tiffany banged her kitten-heeled foot on the threadbare rug.

"I'd a sang the song half-right if Martha hadn't messed me up!"

Tiffany balled her fists at her sides and looked over her shoulder toward the piano.

"Do it again, Martha, and this time try a little harder to follow your cousin," Edith said.

Martha looked back and met Edith's eyes for a prolonged instant—her expression half accusation, half question—*why would you say that she is my cousin, thereby denying that I, too, am your daughter?*

Martha turned back to the keys as Tiffany counted backward for the downbeat.

When the playing was through and Mr. Chesterfield had finished his dessert and left to go back home to Vernelle, the house came undone—a dissonance returned to the air of every room—as it did whenever he was away. Martha stood over the sink scraping food waste from the dinner plates when Edith walked over and slapped her hard across the face.

"Don't you dare think about sassing me in front of company, looking all sideways while I'm talking like you don't know who's who in this house! Can't make no claims over what goes on in the rest of the world, but in this place, if I say the sky is green, it is; and if I say you ain't mines, you ain't."

Edith raised her hand to Martha yet again, but noticing a hardness in the teenaged girl that threatened to hit back, she restrained herself.

"I want this kitchen and the whole of the downstairs clean 'til it shine, else I got something for you that'll wipe the smirk off your face."

And with that she left the room and went up the stairs.

Tiffany had been in their midst all the while, sitting at the kitchen table, her face hovering over a bowl of cherries, the juice, like blood, dripping from her lips and down to her chin.

"Mama wouldn't be so hard on you if you hadn't turn so contrary all a sudden. Ain't saying she right, but you gone and make life hard for yourself not playing along. I don't know no other colored folks nowhere near this place live as good as you. Ought to get your head out the clouds and stop thinking 'bout what you wish you had and be grateful for what you got."

Martha snarled at this, noting the way Tiffany used the word "colored," pointing it away from herself as if the term did not include her. Tiffany smiled at her sister's frustration, the stain of the scarlet nectar discoloring her teeth. She dabbed a cloth napkin at the wetness that pooled under her chin, then took a single cherry and tried to throw it from an arm's-length distance into her mouth. She missed by several inches and laughed at her own foolish game, and the whole of the house, now settled and quiet, agreeing or indifferent to her delusion.

✳

THE DRIVER MADE it as far as Angola, Indiana, before pulling into a gas station. He parked at the pump as Sister Lucinda stood to speak into the PA system microphone.

"Only twenty minutes to make your ablutions or grab a bite to eat. Then—and I'm serious when I say this—I need you right back on this bus because we will be taking off no later than eight thirty a.m., understood?"

The women stretched, standing from their seats, and slowly filed out of the bus.

After they descended, Danielle nodded at Sister Memphis, then walked in the direction of the bathrooms where a significant line of women had already formed, while the lieutenant remained near the bus to keep the time.

The driver was Mr. Wilson, an older gentleman who was not a

Temple goer, though from his formal appearance, dressed in a suit and tie, he could have been mistaken for one. He ambled off the bus and started his way around the frame, checking the pressure of the tires.

A middle-aged white man in a trucker hat and navy-blue overalls stood several feet away from Sister Memphis, where he began pumping gasoline into the tank. He wobbled on his feet and despite the distance between the two of them, Sister Memphis could smell the stench of Jack Daniel's emanating from his body. He tried steadying himself as he pumped the gas, and every few moments his eyes would close as if he were about to fall asleep.

The driver came around to the tires that were nearest to the tank where the white man stood, and the gas attendant issued the comment, "Looking at the tires, Old Sammie? Causn' they look mighty . . . mighty fine to me." He paused to hiccup, then kicked the tire treads as hard as he could, sending a red trail of the gasoline trickling into the brown slush of melting snow.

Immediately Mr. Wilson stood and walked away, headed back into the coach. The gas attendant turned to watch him go, a look of sadistic ecstasy plastered all over his face.

Martha watched, incensed at the gas attendant's disrespect of the driver. She balled her fists as the attendant removed the pump from the receptacle. When he caught Sister Memphis scowling in his direction, he stopped moving and tried to steady himself.

"'S the matter with you?" He slurred his words. "Look to me like you're . . . like you're fixin' to do something with them hands. Now don't you go studyin' me!" He stumbled yet again, the gas pump wobbling in his hands. "I tell you one thing for sure! I can cause a whole lot more trouble for the likes of . . . for the likes of you than you can cause for me!"

Not wanting to pursue a full-on argument with a drunken man, she refocused on the women who had started their way back to the bus. Danielle was among the last to board, returning not from the bathroom, as Sister Memphis had anticipated, but from the far side of the parking lot, her movements fast and her face pointed toward the ground. Sister Memphis wondered for a brief instant where she had run off to and what she had been doing wherever she went, but settled on feeling relieved, happy that Danielle had returned before time.

With most of the MGT already aboard, Sister Memphis walked to her own seat, where she saw Danielle looking out the window toward the lot.

"What were you doing over there?" Sister Memphis's voice was almost playful.

Danielle shrugged, twirling the nail file in her hand.

"As for me, I just had one of the strangest encounters I've ever experienced with a white man. I swear, it doesn't matter how poor, or how down and out they get, they always trying to show you they're the boss. It's just a shame the brothers aren't here."

Sister Memphis tried not to notice the smirk that crept up the side of Danielle's mouth, as she was merely grateful that the child had mellowed somewhat over the last few hours of their journey. A bit of distance from Saundra and a firm but gentle hand was all it had taken, she thought, to lower the child's defenses and set her on the right path.

Sister Lucinda was last to get on the bus. She climbed the stairs into the coach and took the microphone, which distorted in the moment that she stood there staring straight ahead, looking at nothing in particular. It was a long, awkward pause and made the sisters turn to each other, wondering what was the matter.

Finally, she raised the microphone to her mouth, "Salaam Alaikum, sisters," she began. "I just got off the telephone with Sister Ophelia out of Chicago."

Another pause.

"She just let me know . . . and I'm standing here to tell you that the Messenger made his flight."

In the ensuing years, the sisters would refer to this as the moment when they began to notice the early signs of Sister Lucinda's cognitive decline. First there were the momentary blackouts, which quickly devolved into the complete unraveling of her personality, leading to her untimely death five years later at the age of fifty-one.

The women inhaled at once and a breathless stillness came over them after the captain uttered the words. They made stunned, confused expressions as they tried piecing together the precise meaning of a phrase as vague and shadowy as "the Messenger made his flight." Conferencing with their seatmates, they searched for answers, until the entire bus was animated with chatter; all of this happening as the captain remained standing, completely stone-faced, too consumed with the new voices assembling in her mind to be overly concerned with the noise.

It was only when Sister Loraine—a woman sixty years of age who had been in the Nation since the Messenger was released from prison—let out a guttural scream as loud as a siren, that the captain came back to herself.

"We are *not* going to have none of that, you hear me? Now get control of yourselves!" Sister Lucinda's eyes flashed with a furor the younger members had never seen in her. The young recruits were so stunned by this deviation from her ordinary grace that it silenced all their talking and made them regard her as she came fully into her command.

"We are still the Nation, after all—united and strong. Everything is moving in the right direction. The Messenger is merely, away," she said, though the women could hear the strain in her voice, "having joined the Master where they preside over us all. So we will keep decorum and keep heading on our way."

Sister Lucinda's expression was hard as stone as she turned to sit in her chair, and within a minute, the bus rolled out of the parking lot and onto the open road.

Sister Memphis stared out the window, counting the logs that held the power lines in high, parabolic arcs across the endless fields. She had been so blank, so oblivious to all happenings on the bus and Lucinda's momentary reversion to her old ways in her lieutenant days, as she tried puzzling through it all. The Messenger had taken his flight, she considered. Her mind arranged and rearranged the words, trying to find a way for them to mean that the Messenger had merely packed his bags and journeyed someplace far but reachable. She imagined him on a beach somewhere in Polynesia, sitting under an umbrella on a hot, sunny day, sipping on a cold glass of lemonade. She tried to see him this way but the visions would not hold, each conjuring instantly giving way to leagues and leagues of ocean.

THEY HAD MADE it twenty miles farther down the road when the whooping of sirens and red flashing lights of two cop cars appeared from behind the bus.

As soon as the driver realized it was his vehicle that the police were after, he pulled over. He immediately opened the side door to let two Indiana state troopers in their khaki-brown overcoats onto the bus. Sister Lucinda stood to greet them, and the larger man stayed near the door as his taller, lankier colleague walked down the aisle. The taller man looked menacingly at the women as the larger man, who was clearly in charge, took the microphone.

"Morning ladies," he said, his voice burdened with a heavy twang. "Got a call from a gas station a few miles back saying it was some illegal activity happening on the premises. Man said it was a bus of women just come and gone and to see if they might'a had something to do with it. So if y'all don't mind, we're just going to perform us a little search and get you on your way quick as can be."

The stout officer remained at the front listening to Sister Lucinda's plea that his claims were unfounded, that they were all holy and upstanding women of God, trained to respect the laws of the land. He looked as dispassionate as his partner was eager. One after the other, the deputy yanked the women up by the arm and used his hands to trace the outline of their bodies, looking for evidence of thievery in their eyes though most of the women looked away, their minds too overwhelmed with the news of the Messenger and his unexpected flight to muster a great fury at the officer.

"You!" the deputy said abruptly, pointing at Sister Memphis once he reached the back of the bus. "What's that that you got in your hand there?" he asked, pointing at the nail file which Danielle was handing back to her, raising his voice, eliciting the attention of all the other sisters in the vicinity.

Sister Memphis looked down at the nail file, half in her hand, half in Danielle's. She wanted to respond but didn't, her eyes suddenly focused on the MGT, the ones that were nearby having turned around to see what was going on.

"But she didn't do nothing wrong," Sister Barbara said in her mousy voice, seated in the chair directly in front of Sister Memphis. "She ain't even go in the store like the rest of us."

"I didn't say a god-damned word about going in no store," the deputy barked at the woman. "Station manager said illegal activity! Breaking into old cars! Now show me what it is you got there in your hands!"

Sister Memphis was about to hand over the file, but the boss man called out to the deputy.

"O'Malley!" The officer spoke into the microphone. "It's time for us to move along. I should have known that old drunk fool's always calling about some such nonsense. I'm not trying to raise hell with no whole bunch of ladies clearly on their way to a prayer meeting. We're moving out."

The deputy turned his head, scanning the lot of women. He focused his attentions one final time on Sister Memphis, as if he were considering breaking orders, but he finally relented and turned to leave.

"Y'all be on your best behavior," the deputy said on his way back down the aisle, "lest the law come find you again."

It was only fitting, given the strangeness enveloping their day, that there were no FOI present. They would have stood up for the MGT and at the very least prevented the deputy from manhandling the women like packaged meat. In that moment Sister Memphis felt the first real pangs of grief as she contemplated a world where the MGT would have to move without the Messenger's guarantee that they would always be protected.

A low whimper from across the aisle distracted both Sister Memphis and Danielle and they looked over to regard thirty-year-old Sister Rochelle. In two years' time, she would stand before the congregation of the Mount Zion Baptist Church and offer a testimony:

"I used to sit up there listening to all that yapping, but I didn't believe not a word of what that old man said. Kept the love of Christ burning in my heart like always," she would tell the church folks, but in that moment, still among the sisters, she sat in her own embrace, rocking back and forth to calm herself. Sister Almina tried rubbing her back, but Rochelle flinched from her touch.

The driving resumed, and Danielle started laughing, crossing her arms and shaking her head, and that's when Sister Memphis knew something had happened with her in the parking lot and that, whatever it was, none of it could have been any good. She wondered why the cop hadn't suspected the child and pointed the finger at her instead, but dismissed the thought as quickly as it had formed. What average person would bother a girl like Danielle—her skin like whipping cream—with accusations of wrongdoing? When in the experiences of fair women, she considered, had such accusations ever amounted to anything in the way of hard consequences?

IN THAT DUSTY southern town passing itself off as a city, there were only so many pleasures a Negro woman could enjoy out in the open. One that Edith didn't try to keep secret from her daughters was the elaborate daily ritual of her toilette. She collected potions and perfumes in frosted glass diffusers, arranged neatly on her bedroom vanity. After her nightly baths she'd spend an hour or so dousing herself in fragrance, then blotting her skin with cottony poofs of Tabu Dusting Powder, regular and reliable, like a prayer to God that he would always keep her young and beautiful.

It was this devotion to the maintenance of her body that sent her into a rage on the evening, just an hour before Mr. Chesterfield's next arrival, that Edith found one of the perfume bottles shattered on the floor—the fragrance having already seeped through the faulty wooden planks. She screamed at the sight of the broken glass and immediately set her rage on Martha.

"I was a fool not to lock the door when I left the house! I was thinking it would only be a few minutes, what could go wrong? But I shoulda known you would plant your grubby hands on my nice things. That was L'Air du Temps! Do you even know what that means or how long I had to work to get it?"

Martha stood at the foot of Edith's big brass bed, reflecting. She'd known exactly what her mother had done to get these things, to afford all the trappings of their seemingly gilded life. She thought, finally, that if her mother wanted more L'Air du Temps, she ought to go back to one of the men that bought it for her, then ask him for another.

As if sensing the thought passing through her mind, Edith slapped Martha so hard she tasted blood.

"You gotta get out of my house. When Mr. Chesterfield get here tonight, I want you in the yard and you can stay there 'til he leave."

Edith seethed, speaking the words to Martha while Tiffany— the real offender—stood in the doorway, watching her sister take blows that were meant for her. Martha turned to leave and met eyes with her little sister; they were guilty but furious eyes—eyes that didn't bother to plead for Martha's silence, but that dared her to tell the truth. But what, in this house, was the value of the truth? Martha knew her mother well enough to understand that there was no argument she could make that would relieve the guilt and pain that a lifetime of her mother's cruelty had proved was her birthright.

She sat all night on the back porch, hearing their strange laughter through the paned glass windows, and Tiffany's awful singing once their dinner was through. Martha entertained herself with the night sounds and by looking up at the stars, unaware of constellations, but assigning to them meanings of her own design. She was brought back to earthly concerns when a sense of indignation reemerged and turned her peaceful contemplation back to anger. She wondered what it was that she had done to deserve her mother's wrath and—by natural extension—the wrath of God, to be so despised in the place that was home, by the people who were her blood relations.

When the lights had gone out and her mother had failed to unlock the back door to let her inside, Martha made her way to the front porch. Up there, there was a two-person swing where she could sit comfortably, stretch her legs, and watch the orange streetlight filtering through what leaves remained on the trees. She sat holding herself in the chilly fall air, looking up at the sky, and imagined herself dancing on the farthest star, far enough away that the very memory of her family—of this dreadful place she called home—would be rendered void. Up there she had the power to jump from star to star, each one flashing bright on her landing. She imagined this twinkling effect and the thought lulled her into a light sleep.

Martha was awakened only half an hour later. She didn't hear the goodnight kisses Mr. Chesterfield and her mother exchanged just feet away from where she laid, nor their syrupy "I love yous." It was only the sound of her mother's shrieking that roused her from dozing.

"Why in God's name are you out here?" her mother screamed. "Nearly scared me half to death. Coulda swore you was a homeless come to take me for all I got!"

Mr. Chesterfield looked on—a shadow of a man with the orange streetlight at his back. She only made out a glimmer of his face and saw it etched with disgust as he turned toward the light, headed to his car.

"I don't know how you saw her there," Martha heard Mr. Chesterfield speaking the words to Edith as the two descended the front steps. "I wouldn't have guessed it was anyone there if you hadn't scared me so."

"Who you telling?" her mother said. "The child so black, she blue. Half the time, even in normal hours, I can't tell her from cast iron."

Edith tried to embrace Mr. Chesterfield on the street, but he raised his hat as a gesture of goodbye. She then returned to the house and took a wordless, snarling glance at Martha. The child knew what would happen next. Edith entered the house, closed the door, and fastened the locks behind her.

Martha turned her face and watched the street. Mr. Chesterfield had already climbed into his car and drove to the end of the block, his break lights flashing red like devil's eyes. He made an immediate turn on Hadley Street and Martha listened to the vrooming of his engine, following the sound as it faded.

It was in that moment that she realized she didn't have to visit a distant star to be free of Edith. There were roads and highways, cars and trains that could carry her from this dusty, worthless town to someplace better, and in that moment, she began forming a plan to leave. With the money she saved doing day work after school, she would find her way up north, where no one would have to know from whence she came or the sad life she led there, save the fact that the Temple folk would eventually uncover her place of birth and give it back to her as a name.

"WHAT WERE YOU doing in the parking lot?" Sister Memphis snapped, the previous hours' work of trying to ally herself to the child having dissolved into a memory. "Were you doing what the cop said? Breaking into cars with a nail file of all things!? I swear to God, if it turns out you were doing something illegal, you're going to really have it coming, because I'm going to tell the minister!"

When Sister Memphis was through, Danielle could not help but laugh.

"Ha!" the girl said. "That's some threat! Look at me! I'm scared!" Her eyes were wild with mockery. "Anyway, what's it matter to you? What does any of this matter to you or your minister now that your leader is dead?"

And that was the first time Sister Memphis heard it spoken aloud—that the Messenger of the Lost-Found Nation had not made his flight, but was merely dead, returned to nature like the mortal man the Temple folk were always told to believe that he was not.

"That's exactly what I thought!" Sister Memphis continued. "That's just what I thought! Guilty as all get out! I can see it in your itty-bitty eyes. Now hand over whatever it is you stole!" Sister Memphis stuck out her hand with the palm facing upward, waiting for the girl to comply.

"Hand what over?" Danielle's voice was newly serious. Immediately she grabbed the side seam of her peacoat and pulled the garment tight around her body. "I ain't got nothing to be handing over in the first place. Ain't like I'm the only one on this bus could of done something. There's a whole lot of women on this bus you could be interrogating, but you're here picking on me."

These words made Sister Memphis reflect that maybe the girl was right. Her mind began to follow the possibility that perhaps it was someone else among them who had broken into a car that morning, but Danielle kept talking.

"I know my momma ain't worth a damn, but I got people. They bigger and badder than you could ever dream with your monkey-lookin' a—"

Before Danielle could finish the word, Sister Memphis took both of her hands and—defying the barrier posed by the child's white polyester skirt—grabbed twin patches of flesh from her underlying thighs, twisting fast and hard in an almost complete revolution like burners on a gas stove turned high. The blood came quickly, racing through the fabric like ink on a Rorschach test, stretching outward into the symmetrical pattern of a big red butterfly—a Siderone galanthis.

Danielle sat in great pain but was silent for the stunning abruptness of the offense, and what seemed like the crazed delight that was apparent on Sister Memphis's face. Within a moment, she leapt from

26

her seat and ran to the front of the bus, tapping Sister Lucinda on the shoulder. Sister Memphis leaned over the child's empty seat, watching Danielle gesticulate to the captain, then point back in her direction. She watched Sister Lucinda turn, displaying a furrowed brow that broadcast her clear sympathy with the girl, like she was an angel, as if it were not possible that she might deserve some reprimand.

They stayed there talking for some time, drawing the attention of the other sisters who crowded into the aisle to hear the story and examine the girl's wounds. It wouldn't be long, Sister Memphis knew, before Sister Lucinda would come stomping back to where she was sitting. She would wag a finger in her face and mouth on about the justice awaiting her as soon as they arrived in Chicago. Sister Memphis contemplated this and allowed a fear to come forward, though it never surfaced, not as it would have just a few hours ago, for without the Messenger, what did any of it matter? Perhaps very little, or perhaps it didn't matter at all.

Sister Memphis sighed, looking out the window, a vague suggestion of the Sears Tower and the John Hancock Center visible in the distance through a sea of white. A blinding white; white as the sun beating down on the sidewalk in the summer of 1960.

SHE HAD BEEN in the city for just over a year and already had the hollow feeling of the people she'd come to know there—who spent all their days on concrete, who never ventured past the tenements to see the trees and the lakes beyond.

She dreamed of arriving there and making her way into school where she would study to become a designer, but like so many of the women she'd met who'd made a similar trek from south to north, the most reliable employment was domestic in nature. She was leaving one job, where she cleaned a suite of downtown offices, headed to the next—cooking dinners for the Smith family. The sun beat down on her brow and she could feel its rays pulsating like the rhythm of her heart. It was days like this that made her reconsider her choice to leave home. Back there was hotter still, and unless she wanted to live as her mother did, the work was no more rewarding and no better paid, though there was the land—fields dotted with oaks and pecan trees, the ponds and the streams. She considered it every now and again, going back with her bags in hand and contrite, downcast eyes as her mother let her back inside her childhood home. It was only imagining Edith's face, haughty and disapproving, that kept her in the city, resolved to never give her the satisfaction of knowing her northward ventures had failed.

She walked farther along the street, wanting to sit on a nearby park bench to rest her ankles, though she knew it would make her late. The Smiths were decent—aloof and distrusting (the matriarch always watching her as she performed her duties)—but reliable with their pay, and she didn't want to alter this circumstance by upsetting them with her tardiness. She only paused before what seemed to her an impromptu gathering at the corner of Fifth and Prospect Street. It was a large crowd of regular folks surrounding a small group of men who she saw through the weaving masses of pedestrians. One man stood before the others, and Martha had to move to see him clearly. He was tall and slender, with skin that shimmered like polished bronze. He spoke a flurry of words that captivated the crowd enough to make the people stand and listen.

Walking through the dense crowd, Martha drew the ire of two women whom she'd accidentally bumped on her way into a clearing. They had skin like Tupelo honey and wore cigarette pants with sleeveless button-up shirts and sunglasses—so out of place in that part of the city. The women looked her up and down—showing only slightly more disdain toward her than the speaker.

They scowled as he went on, shaking their heads and even laughing out loud as he made his point. The sight of them, imperious and important-looking, reminded Martha of her sweatiness and generally haggard appearance, and so she stepped away, leaning in closer to hear the suited man speak, when he noticed her. His eyes went wide at the sight of her face, and instantly she was afraid, growing even more so when he pointed in her direction and all the onlookers turned their necks to see.

"This! This right here is the point and the reason I'm speaking. We are living in the wilderness of North America, this land of misfits and misanthropes, got you thinking day is night and night is day. Thinking right is wrong and wrong is A-OK." Some people in the crowd chuckled, entertained by the cadence. "Got you all confused about yourself, making you wish you were something you are not. Walking around, knowing your mother looks like midnight, and won't dare to be seen arm in arm with a woman darker than a rubber band.

"You can follow what the white man tells you to think if you want to, but for me, I'm looking for the real thing," he said, his eyes fixed on Martha. "A real original woman, with none of the stain of ol' master's blood running in her veins. An original woman! Preserved and clean, a taste of chocolate sweetness out of a dream.

"An original woman! I want her hand. The good fruit grows in the darkest soil and not in the sand."

"I *know* that's the truth!" a woman on the far side of the crowd yelled, and tentative laughter followed, but Martha was drawn in, mesmerized by the bronze man who was still looking into her eyes.

"I need an original woman! Blueberry, dark cherry! That's the only kind of woman who's sweet enough to marry.

"A woman held high—righteous, battle ready, sweet to the bone. That's the only kind of woman I plan to take home."

The bronze-colored man went on with his oration, a sonnet of lovely words falling off his tongue, and for a moment, Martha felt she was floating just an inch above the earth, the pain in her ankles gone away. It was not so much that he was speaking the words to her, but the words themselves. Words like keys, unlocking closed-off, hungry, and hidden places, letting in the brilliant day.

She again met eyes with the women who stared her down, their looks now softened, curious, equalized. Perhaps they had noticed how, in those few moments, Martha had turned her face up to the sky, inviting the sun onto her skin. Perhaps they had seen the glint in her eyes of children acquiring new skills like learning to crawl or uttering first words. She was indeed filled with a new haughtiness—the kind that she had always assumed was the sole province of the Ediths and Tiffanys of the world—and it felt healthy and good and right. She would not continue on to the Smith family home. There, they expected the old Martha, and the person walking down the street (headed to this place a man in front of the Laundromat pointed out as the Temple) was someone completely new.

And so she sat toward the back of the bus with her face turned toward the white fog on the window but tilted upward to catch the diffuse gray light, trying to revisit the feeling of that day—a feeling that she would not recapture until six months hence. She did not know it then, though the doctors would soon inform her that she was already three months pregnant with a little girl—a wide-eyed chocolate drop of a baby whom she would name Jamilah, the beautiful.

NEW MEXICO

I.

About two weeks into the assignment at the Mirage Hotel, I realized I was in a place that I would never wrap my mind around. Something about it was always trying to evade my grasp. The strange smells, the native folkways, the cold despite the latitude— all of it threw me and I spent my days off-kilter. Every day was something different.

One time I hitched a ride in a brand-new 1970 Plymouth Barracuda, trying to feel like a Don, when I saw two coyotes stalking a white-tailed deer, bringing up the rear as it lowered its neck to eat a patch of ground cherries. I had the driver slow the car so we could watch the attack and was alarmed as one of the coyotes jumped to face his mate, showing his fangs. The two of them set to brawling. The one caught unaware yelped as the other went for blood, leaving the deer plenty of time to run off in the brush. The yelping stopped and the triumphant coyote rose. He jolted away from the bear grass where he left his brother for dead, making me ask myself where else in nature this sort of thing happens.

The place was strange that way.

It was early on a Friday morning. I was standing on the loading dock near a crew of men carrying crates of produce from a set of refrigerated trucks into the hotel kitchen. I held the push broom given to me by the head butler, a stuffy Brit who called himself Archibald Harrington, and looked out at the sierra—purple, orange, and pink in the dawn. I tried to take in the simple thoughts of a man who does this sort of work in earnest and was briefly entertained by the idea this is how it might feel to live on Mars.

Basil came out some moments later, a kid I couldn't stand but had to put up with. He was new meat at the Bureau—a Harvard grad, tall and blond (just the way the boss liked them), and grossly underqualified for his job. A mix of charm and family connections got him the role and landed him here with me—the presumed sympathetic Black man forced to teach him the ropes. Despite the difference between our exposure to the work, he was appointed to the concierge desk, donning a suit and tie every day, and I had to play janitor, pushing a broom in a navy jumpsuit like I was the upstart, trying to get his feet wet.

He took two cigarettes from his back pocket, lit both and handed one to me.

"Two hours, that's how much sleep I got last night. For Christ's sake, I tried to do the right thing. The one time I'm in at a respectable hour, the guy next to me decides to blast his record collection. And not just anything, mind you. He had to play fado. You hear that shit?"

I shook my head.

"That's one more thing the world could do without. There could have been a whole mariachi band around my bed all night long—with the maracas and that shit—and I would have been fine. Anything but that fuckin' fado. Saddest shit I ever heard. Does Quantico always do this? Make you work in the best spot, then put you up in the worst hotel in the worst part of town?"

I tried to remind him that the job wasn't about creature comforts, and he winced at me. His eyes flashed with the knowledge all white men seem to hold; that all they need to do to get whatever they want is make a big enough stink.

Sour over my response, he came back at me. "You could really stand to unwind a bit, you know. Not take yourself so seriously. There's a pretty Mexican girl, Maria I think is her name? Anyhow, I see her around all the time. You could put a move on her. That'll mellow you out fast."

I flicked the butt of the cigarette out onto the gravel and told him to come to attention. Put a little bass in my voice and in seconds he went from pit bull to plebe.

A call came through at four thirty that morning with news that the Swan was on the move. Reports from the field office clocked her passing through Pueblo, and if estimates were correct, she would be arriving at the Mirage by noon, give or take an hour.

I relayed this information to Basil and made sure he was clear about the mission. He repeated it to me.

"Engage but do not create suspicion, try to get as much information as we can."

I nodded, pleased that some of the details managed to sink into his skull. Then his face went slack again.

"Just one thing. Tell me . . . why would Poole want to bring her all the way down here?"

I sighed at the dumb motherfucker.

"Listen. They have a house in Phoenix, plus the boy was born here. Also, she's traveling with the child this time, not her husband, and by the way, you should know from the material that he goes by Mr. Muhammad."

"But how is the house *hers*?" he said. "I understand that men like that have women here and there, but she's not by any stretch his wife, not his *real* wife. That would be Clara, after all. It just doesn't make any sense. Why, when you've got the whole of the U.S. government breathing down your neck, would you be so cavalier parading your concubines?"

I wanted to answer him but I couldn't.

It had been a year since Veronica left me for dogging her out, dealing me a blow I still hadn't gotten over. In the time that passed, I had come to understand how it was possible for a man to cheat on the woman he loved the most.

When I didn't respond, Basil came closer.

"Maybe you've got a soft spot for Poole; a lot of Black guys do and won't admit it. I guess you've attended enough of their meetings to believe the white man is the devil, too. Is that your deal?"

I told him not to be ridiculous, but he wasn't all the way wrong. In the past year I developed some sympathies for the Nation, just not in the way he imagined. I couldn't say I accepted their beliefs, but despite the things I knew about the organization, I had a chance to see up close and personal some of the good work they did on the ground, cleaning up the neighborhood.

He was laughing, trying to recover from openly accusing me of being a double agent, but I scowled and he backed down.

"I guess you were part of the Chicago operation in December of '69," he came back. "They say you were ruthless against that Hampton guy. It's gotta take a sick bastard to do the work you do and still smile in the faces of the Black Panthers."

It crossed my mind to clock him straight in the jaw, but I heard someone call my name.

"Calvin!" It was Archibald Harrington. "There's been an accident and your services are required in the basement lavatory. Posthaste!"

He was near the swinging doors where the men stacked the

empty food crates, his hands folded at his navel, standing impossibly erect like there was a rod shooting straight up his ass.

"I'll be right there," I told him. He snarled, turned about-face, and goose-stepped back into the hotel.

I looked at Basil. "Is there anything else you need before I go?"

"Not really, but should I come strapped?"

That made me huff and I shook my head.

"Not at all, she's harmless," I said. "We're just observing and taking notes, understood?"

He nodded.

"One more thing," I asked. "This Archibald fellow ... where do you think he's really from?"

"Aw, that's easy." Basil was incredulous. "Parma, South Cleveland, without a doubt."

I folded my arms and shifted my weight, enlightened by the observation. "I would have sworn it was New Jersey, South Orange or thereabout."

"Nah," he came back. "The vowels are more nasal than that. He's definitely a pierogi-eating Midwesterner."

"I think you're probably right," I said, and turned away from him, headed inside. When it came to placing accents, I knew that was a job Basil wouldn't muck up.

II.

In the weeks after Veronica left me, I was a fumbling mess. Turning in my work on time without raising any eyebrows about what was going on in my private life, I could at least function at the Bureau. It was when I was alone in the house that it became clear just what a wreck I'd become. I'd walk through the rooms and catch glimpses of myself in the bathroom mirror looking disheveled and sorry. When I wasn't spinning around in circles, I camped out near the phone like a teenaged girl, waiting on the moment she'd take pity on me and call to say she was coming home.

On one of those early days, when Veronica had first left, a female voice on the other end of the receiver took me temporarily out of my misery. I had missed the sound of a woman's voice in my ear and drank it in, not really paying attention at first to who was calling me and why. I must have sounded like a drunken fool before she made her voice hard and brought me back to reality.

"Mister Calvin Baxter! Are you hearing me?" she said. "To be clear, this is the Halifax County Department of Corrections, calling on behalf of Melvin Jones. He's set to be released early next week and it's important for his rehabilitation that he has somewhere to go."

Her last words shook me out of my stupor. I wiped my eyes and sat upright on my living room couch.

"Don't know why you would contact me on the matter, it's not like I know the man," I said. "Don't they have halfway houses and parks for people like that?"

"Mister Baxter," she sounded furious. "Are you proposing that we release him out on the streets? I understand you must have mixed emotions, not having seen him in over a decade, but he is your father."

Just to get her off the phone I took down the information, but determined I'd let him wait there, expecting me to come, then never show up. I amused myself thinking about the times when I was young and he did the same thing to us, but in the week between the call and the day of his release, my plans started weighing on me.

It didn't make sense for me to feel this way. Despite the short length of time he was in our lives I kept my memories of him;

his brutality came back clear as a just-heard song on the radio. I remembered the gruff sound of his curses as he fought with my mother; the way he left her bruised and bloody in the hallway, then slammed the front door on his way out. All the years, I figured, should have been sufficient practice for him to learn how to take the same blows he dished our way. Why should I pity him?

Somehow I wound up at the gate waiting on his ass. Every other minute I nearly convinced myself to leave, but I stayed put. In due order he came out, stern and grisly-looking in a yellowed T-shirt with jeans that rode up high enough to see the top of his socks— white with two burgundy stripes circling his calves. He walked out and we caught eyes, him snarling at the sight of me. I didn't anticipate he'd be as angry as I was in that moment, nor could I have known that in just a few months' time he would be dead.

I leaned over to the passenger side to raise the lock, but he walked to the back door instead. He knocked and I reached back to raise the lever, thinking this fool expected me to carry him around town like a damned chauffer. He closed the door and there I was, just a few feet away from him. I tried to stop imagining myself turning around and choking him out, trying to think of something to say, but he sucked his teeth, "What you waiting on?" he screamed. "Drive, Goddammit!"

The route into the city was mostly wooded and quiet, though as the scenery became familiar, he started calling things out, spouting "Bob's Big Boy" and "The Chrysler" like a kid looking at Christmas lights.

A few blocks away from my house he told me to move over toward the median. Without putting up a fuss I did what he asked. A young man in a suit and a bow tie was walking along a concrete strip in the middle of the road selling *Muhammad Speaks* newspapers.

"You got a dollar?" my father asked. "I needs me one of them papers."

I reached for my wallet, thinking jokingly that prison had turned my father, a petty crook, into a man of ideas. I pulled out the dollar and when my father reached to grab it from me, I yanked it away. I rolled down the window and motioned at the young man. That's when I realized it was JoJo—a kid who lived a block down from my house, who I only ever saw hanging out with a crew of hoodlums. I narrowed my eyes at him and handed over the money, a gesture that he took in stride. He gave me the paper—cold and succinct like he didn't know who I was—and thanked me for supporting the ministry of the Messenger of Allah.

My father grabbed the paper. "Now that's a real man right there," he said, "supporting his own people, not working for the white man like you doing. They told me in the pen that you Five-O. I can't think of nothing worse for the Black man than working for the pigs."

He flit through the pages, making it obvious he wasn't reading any of the contents, then tossed the paper on the empty seat next to him as we pulled up to the house.

"So this is where you live. Thought that you'd be someplace better than here, with you working for the man and shit."

He got out of the car and didn't even reach for the newspaper.

We walked in the house and I showed him to his room. I planned on giving him a tour of the entire place, but he planted himself on the bed.

"Don't you want to know where the bathroom is?"

He sucked his teeth and looked at me like he was a caged animal.

I turned to leave, and as soon as I passed over the threshold, he commanded me to close the door.

"I ain't a child. I got a right to some privacy, now *get*!"

He said this to me and lay down in the exact position where I would find him several months later—on his side, his feet curled under him, hands near his chin like an infant in the womb.

III.

She made it to the hotel at 1:17 p.m. I nearly missed her arrival. I got caught up in a petty argument with one of the groundskeepers. He was barking at me about a cracked porcelain vase, getting on my case as if I broke the damn thing, when she appeared at the door.

"*Now* what's the matter with you?" he said, then turned to follow where my eyes had wandered. I heard him swallow, then whisper,

"Sagrado santo," he said, "quien es ella?"

The sight of her stunned me. I had to shake my head and squint my eyes to be sure I wasn't messed up in the head. I saw several photos of her in preparation for the assignment, always clad in the traditional female garb of the Nation—long white gown with a fitted headdress flowing over the shoulders and cascading down her back. But standing there, she appeared altogether different. She wore a billowy knee-length dress that revealed her long, cream-colored calves and her hair, a darker tint of blonde, was uncovered. It was long, with manicured curls that bounced in the rhythm of her stride. A bellboy stopped to receive her instructions, most likely to grab her things, and for the briefest moment I caught a glimpse of her eyes—a mix of hazel and green.

She moved a few inches, enough for me to make out the child standing beside her. He came to the height of her torso and looked around, admiring the crystal chandeliers and marble interiors. Though his coloring was closer to his mother's—fair except for his dark eyes and hair—he had the head and face shape of Elijah.

I got on my knees to fix the vase, lest the groundskeeper swipe at me again, but I angled myself for a better view. Basil was tending to her, having what appeared like a very amiable conversation. In the two weeks I'd known him, he'd already made a handful of conquests with the local girls, but I never saw him smile as wide as he did with the Swan.

Her movements were commanding, not those of a woman taught to demure in the presence of men. It seemed so counter to what I'd learned about the Nation, and yet in that moment I understood it must have been this trait that made her so irresistible to Mr. Muhammad. She was finicky with the child. She smoothed his hair over and over so it would lay flat like an old school conk. Frustrated, she finally put a baseball cap over the child's head and made him sit on a bench near the elevators as she continued on with Basil.

This was odd, but not for reasons that seemed to have much value to the Bureau. The Swan was overly conscious of the boy, who, like any Black child, had hair with tight coils—that was just a fact that couldn't be leveraged. My thoughts drifted away from the needs of the investigation, to pondering her choice to stay in a place like this. If she'd been so concerned about what the white folks thought of her son, there was always the Black hotel a few miles away. Why didn't she simply book a room there?

When the bellhop came to escort the Swan and her child to their room, I walked over to Basil. A dumb smile plastered on his face, he looked high as a kite.

Slightly amused that he'd gotten butterflies for a Black supremacist, I asked him, "What's that all about?"

"God, she's a looker. It's all in the eyes, really. I can't say anything good about Poole, but he knows a pretty woman when he sees one . . . I think she's got a thing for me. The way she was looking me over? You could just tell."

That didn't surprise me, I thought. What good-looking younger woman would want to spend all her time pretending to be turned-on by an old man?

"She asked if the hotel still had a personal maid service, someone to look after the kid. Know anything about that?"

He should have sensed how much easier it would be for him to get an answer, but I reassured him, "I'll figure out something."

"Well good," he said brightly. "She asked to meet me later on tonight. Like I said, I really think she likes me. Maybe she'll open up and tell us something useful. You never know."

MY CHANCE TO see her up close would come later that afternoon. I was assigned to man the solarium, which had a large in-ground pool. I was to pick up the dirty towels and replace them with crisp, clean ones. I only just settled at my post when she sauntered in. She was wearing a long tunic like a Moroccan princess, which she quickly removed to reveal a polka-dot swimsuit underneath. The boy was next to her, in a swim cap and trunks. As the Swan reclined on one of the lawn chairs that ran along all sides of the pool, he jumped into the shallow end of the water.

It struck me that she seemed awfully comfortable, milling about in a place where she and her son were the only Black patrons. It was so unusual. In the company of all whites, I could always read the self-consciousness in other Black people. There was always an extra layer of caution in their gestures, but she bore none of these signs. She merely sat there, talking playfully with a woman on a nearby bench, sipping from what looked like a piña colada.

I had been watching her for ten minutes, pretending to be cleaning one of the bar surfaces when her son jumped out of the pool. He had made friends with another kid who came running after him, causing him to fall onto the concrete.

I grabbed the first aid kit and went to the child in the same moment the Swan abandoned her conversation and ran in his direction.

By the time I arrived, she was already squatting with her son, wrapping his knee with a cloth napkin.

"Let me help you out, ma'am. I have some gauze and alcohol here. Helps prevent infection."

Like I was a common thug and not an employee of the hotel, she glared at me for a long moment. "Well, get on with it! Don't keep the child waiting all day."

Pretending I had a clue what I was doing, I opened the box. I pulled out some ointment and a large Band-Aid. The bottle sloshed as I dabbed the brown solution on one of the cotton balls and brought it to his leg.

"Now you be strong," the Swan said to her son. "This boy is going to fix your leg and you'll be feeling good as new."

My ear caught hold of what she said. Though I tried to put it out of my mind, needing to focus on the matter at hand and not startle the Swan, her words confused me.

"That's it little fella," I said, trying to calm the kid down and ingratiate myself to the Swan. "Just a few more seconds and it's over. Now there! All better?" I smoothed the Band-Aid over the wound and patted it for good measure.

The Swan and I stood at the same time. I wanted to tell her my name, but when I stuck out my hand to shake hers, she pulled away.

"Thank you for helping my child," she said, her Nordic eyes glaring at me. "Now I know where to go whenever I'm looking for the help."

"By the way, ma'am," I said, setting aside her contempt for me. "Prime tanning spot is in that corner over there. If you're looking for some sun, I can bring your things over for you."

With that she turned away from me and took the child's hand to where she'd been reclining, grabbed her things, and left the solarium.

IV.

Those first few weeks with my father were tedious. It was interesting to note the things we had in common, the way our bodies jolted when the TV went to static and the way we held our cutlery. Everything else I observed about the man annoyed me, a feeling that seeped into me like a slow venom. He liked listening to his music at odd hours and played the volume so loud it was hard to fall asleep. I had to put a lock on my bedroom door to keep him out of my money, and what little he got he used to buy cigarettes he'd smoke in the house, with booze and tins of canned fish. He'd mix the salmon with onions and fry them into little cakes that stank up the house worse than the Marlboros.

Two weeks into his time with me I came home and caught him having his way with one of the old girls who spent her days sitting in front of the corner store up the street—big, curly wig and round at the midsection, with long, skinny legs like a flamingo. As soon as I opened the door I saw him giving it to Old Gal from the rear— his buttocks taut, dungarees at his ankles—bending her over my couch, no less.

"What in the hell?" I yelled. The thought that he'd been doing this every day I went to work or, worse yet, that I might have been conceived this way turned my stomach worse than the salmon cakes.

A Sam Cooke album was playing in the background. I stomped in the direction of the old Victrola and pulled the needle off the record.

"Didn't I tell you not to be bringing nobody up in here when I'm gone? What you think this is, Motel 6?"

While Old Girl covered herself, scowling at me like I had just barged into *her* living room, Melvin smirked like a man completely immune to shame.

I was about to lay into Melvin but I heard what sounded like gunshots. Instinctively we all fell to the ground. We crouched there for a while, but I looked up and saw yellow dripping down the first-floor window and realized we'd been egged.

I opened the door to the sounds of scattering. Hoping to find some evidence of who had done this to my house and where they ran off to, I looked down the road.

I ticked my head down one side of the street and up to the other, where I saw JoJo. He was standing on the other side of the road in his suit and bow tie, his face half-curious, half-scowl.

I was considering whether to go after him when Old Gal pushed past me. She bumped me on her way down the porch steps and flashed a middle finger as she headed to the sidewalk.

I turned my attention back to JoJo, but he was gone. In just that short amount of time he'd run off. That's when I was sure that, if he wasn't the mastermind, he'd at least been in on the scheme. I vowed then and there that the next time I saw him, I'd make him regret what he'd done.

Fastening his belt buckle and laughing, Melvin emerged from the house.

"You must be popular around this way, seeing how they do you, Five-O. Not one person came to help your ass. Better get the hose," he said, headed down the steps and out of the gate, most likely to make amends with Old Gal. "You don't want to see what happens if you leave that shit 'til it get all crusty."

I cursed him under my breath, then I went over to the side of my house, grabbed the hose, a rag, and a bucket and started filling it with water.

V.

When Basil told me about the Swan's invitation to meet later over drinks, I cleared it with Archibald that I would spend the night working in the bar. I was told I would be assisting Jose Fernando, mostly washing the dishes and cleaning the tabletops.

The work wasn't terribly hard but I hated handling the ice. Jose made it my job to crush it, then scoop large chunks of it into the glasses. I used the icepick like a dagger, imagining it was my supervisor at the Bureau on the other end and I was punishing him for placing me on this boring-ass detail. I'd gotten so into the motion that I failed to notice the moment when Basil and the Swan walked in, having seated themselves in a far corner of the room.

Jose got on my case a few times about slowing down on the ice. He gave me a stern look every time I paused, and I'd start hacking away again, but I eventually stopped just to hear them better. They were looking pretty cozy, and I was sure something important was being shared—all information that I knew Basil would forget. I wanted to be certain that everything was on the record.

After about the third time Jose raised his voice at me, I asked him to let me clean off the tables instead of working behind the bar, and he agreed.

There was a large collection of glass mugs at several empty tables, left there by a group of insurance salesmen who had left just a few minutes earlier. I carried a large brown plastic trough to collect all the glassware. Slowly, I placed each one in the bin and, over the tinkling of the mugs, I tried to make out what Basil and the Swan were saying.

"What I don't understand is why someone as handsome as you would ever have to work at a hotel, however nice."

Basil fawned like a smitten teenager.

"There's a whole lot the world has in store for people like us. People with half your looks and no smarts whatsoever are running companies, heads of state."

She shook her head. "You could be doing more with what you've got."

"I suppose you're right," he said. "I know there's one thing in particular that I'd like to be doing right now."

I nearly threw one of the mugs at him. What a crass thing to say. Anyway, why not follow up with a question? Something that would further the investigation along.

I felt a pause in their conversation and assumed they were sensing me nearby.

I immediately picked up the glasses and walked back to the bar. I watched them intently as I washed the mugs and stacked them upside down on the counter. I had to admit—she was on her game, but there again, she was a secretary to the Messenger. She had to have heard enough smooth talking in and around Chicago to know how to play a man for a fool.

Despite my better judgment, I walked back to the table with the trough. I removed the rag from a small bucket of water and used it to wipe up the alcohol residue.

Hoping that the Swan would be less on edge not seeing my face, I turned my back to them, but I heard her suck her teeth.

"It seems like every time we get a moment alone, that *nigger* keeps bothering us! Come on!" she told Basil. "Let's go outside where we can get some privacy."

The two of them got up, and Basil gave a shrug, following her lead.

VI.

The illness was sudden, declaring itself just a week before Melvin died. I was sitting in my own bedroom—the only place where I could find any peace, when I heard him screaming. I rushed into his room and found him moaning like a walrus, doubled over in pain, the floor around him covered in vomit like watery oatmeal.

"Help me, would you please help me?"

The immediate impulse I had was to spit on him, but something magnanimous took over. I left the room to the sound of his wailing, called an ambulance, and came back with a bucket of hot, soapy water to clean up the mess.

Gingerly, I lifted him out of his own filth, sat him on the bed, and removed his shirt, which had been soiled with puke.

As I wiped the floor clean, he sat heaving.

"I bet you happy," he said through winces. "Bet you happy to see me helpless, at your mercy. You been dreaming 'bout it your whole life."

I had nothing to say to that, just continued wiping up the mess. I helped him sponge down and gave him a clean T-shirt to wear. His body was tense, him jerking away from my dabs, but he didn't tell me to stop.

When the medics arrived, I told the EMT what happened as he examined my father's chest.

"Seems gastrointestinal," he said. "But he's letting me touch his abdomen without wincing, so the symptoms must have gone away. I can still take you to the Emergency Room if you like. Completely your choice."

My father was resolute. "No, I'm alright. I been through worse, nothing I can't get over with some rest."

And with that the EMT packed his tools and the crew of them left.

I managed to convince the old man to take some medicine, and the pills knocked him out cold. That left me a few blissful hours to feel like I had the house to myself again. I still had no notion how soon this wish for solitude would come to pass.

I was sitting on the couch, enjoying the silence of my own house when there was a knock on the door. I rose up, fearing it would wake my father and fill the house with his aching moans.

"And what the hell do you want?" I opened the door to the sight of two young men, no older than fourteen, in suits and bow ties, standing at my door. I was perplexed. I knew the Nation sold papers on the street, but I hadn't realized that they had started going door to door like the Jehovah's Witnesses.

One of them started talking with his face pointed at the ground before the other one told him to speak up. "Look in the man's eyes," he said.

"We came by this afternoon to apologize for what we did to your house."

I took a step back, my mind racing as I put it all together.

"We made a change in our ways. The Black man should not treat another Black man like the white man treat us. We the original people of the planet Earth. We got to stick together."

"Sir," the other one piped in. "We just wanted to know if it was some way we could make it up to you? Maybe wash your car?"

I thought about it, then shook my head.

"Maybe another time. Just keep yourself out of trouble, you hear?"

In that moment both of them turned to the street, shaking their heads at someone in the distance.

I looked past them and saw JoJo standing just beyond my gate, his chin up and hands at his back. I realized he had been there all along.

He waved at the boys and they walked toward him, bouncing as they went, like a weight had been lifted from their shoulders.

JoJo sent up a call and the boys started marching down the street, like they were heading into a hopeful destiny. JoJo followed behind them, though he turned his head in my direction and gave me a military salute. I would recall it all again in New Mexico. Staring into the murky trough water after Basil and the Swan left me at the bar, I thought of JoJo. He was someone with an essentially good nature, who could be moved by fanciful notions of a glorious past to compel his sense of virtue. I was glad it was a hardened man like me who'd experienced this and not him. It was one discovery I highlighted in the record of our time in New Mexico and delivered to the Bureau on my return. The Swan, mistress of Mr. Muhammad and mother to his illegitimate son, was a passing woman; soldiering for a cursory kind of freedom, wrought in the lie of white superiority we thought they all opposed.

THE SPIDER

It was Brother Lateef who decided to convene the purchasing committee's second quarterly meeting at the Best Western downtown. He talked about the merits, saying that we, as a group of men trying to improve our business prospects, would never get very far until we started looking the part. The others quickly agreed, as they were, generally speaking, awed by every word that fell out of his mouth. He was a gruff figure in the days of Malcolm and the First Resurrection—one of the Messenger's most formidable goons—and carried out of it the same fearsome profile he honed in the Nation. Since it all fell apart, he transformed himself into a textile merchant and found some success selling Members Only jackets in the dying days of disco. He drove a long, shiny Buick and had a house in a rich suburb, which was sufficient to earn the respect of the men in our collective. They didn't seem to share my suspicion that his holdings were exaggerated and most likely, Brother Lateef was a man living dangerously outside his means. But I was never the type to talk in whispers and didn't want to be accused of starting a fitna, so I went with the flow, satisfied at the very least that he had the assent of the majority.

The first thing I noticed was how drab the room appeared from the inside. It was small and dark with composite wood paneling on the walls and a single fluorescent light that buzzed every odd second. The men who arrived before me sat around three skirted tables arranged in a U formation that ran the length of the room. The smallest table was at the front, dressed with a tiny microphone stand and a brown glass vase with a single plastic rose dangling over the lip. A large painting hung prominently on the wall behind it that disturbed me to view, though I couldn't pull my eyes away for longer than a few seconds. It was one of those corporate monstrosities, chaotic in effect, like the thoughtless finger paintings of a small child. The thing looked like it was made with grenadine, melted chocolate, and a smattering of contempt for all the normal people who don't have patience to try and understand that shit.

The hotel staff placed a pitcher of water on each table next to a small stack of translucent cups. I couldn't help but shake my head at that. We would have been better off, I figured, taking Imam Saleem's suggestion and just staying put at the Temple. The kitchen sisters would have at least given us some fruit punch and sugar cookies. Hell, had we asked nice enough, they might have made us some fried chicken and potato salad. If we were trying to throw money around like Rockefellers, why not put it in the building fund or pay zakat? But I was a one-man HVAC operation, with little more than a truck, some tools, and a house I was just three mortgage payments away from owning outright. As far as those brothers were concerned, I was too ordinary, based on outward appearances, to be an example.

When I entered the room, I fell into a lively conversation that I could hear all the way out in the hotel lobby. The brothers were in an uproar over something that unfolded a couple of nights prior, and that was on the lips of all the Temple folk in the hours hence.

I learned about it in real time watching the ten o'clock news, sitting on my living room couch, drinking the ginger beer my wife Sadaqa just pulled out of the fridge for me. At the tail end of the broadcast, the TV voices went from monotone to bright as the state lotto flashed sparkly colors across the screen, ready to call the day's numbers. Instead of a thousand balls tumbling inside a clear plastic globe, there was a live-action shot of a small camera crew approaching a house I instantly recognized as Qasim Abdur-Rahman's—a taxicab driver, longstanding member of our committee, and Brother Lateef's number two in command.

A woman in a long red evening gown, looking like Veronica Lake, stood beside a man in a tuxedo who knocked on the door. Qasim opened it, sure enough, clad in a black kufi and a long black thobe, having most likely just finished up his nightly Quranic recitation. His jaw was tight, eyes bulging with anger. I'm sure he thought it was a couple of the local hoods looking for late-night kicks at his expense.

Qasim's grimace sent a flash of terror through the announcer's body, though he quickly regained his composure.

"Are you Mr. Abdur-Rahman?" he said with radio verve.

Qasim looked back at his wife and two daughters. The camera poked into the living room, showing the women all seated together on the couch, hijabed down like a gaggle of nuns. He returned his alarmed gaze back to the camera.

"Yeah, that's me," he said, "Something I can help you with?"

"Congratulations!" The suited man's voice bore the singsong cadence of Ed McMahon's. "You didn't just hit the right number, my friend. Today you struck gold!"

The woman in the red gown simpered as she handed Qasim an oversized check with the words ONE MILLION DOLLARS typed in big bold print across the front.

Brother Suleman reenacted Qasim's shock, the way it morphed into elation as the news registered across his face.

Everybody laughed at that and so did I, happy for the moment to be thinking about something other than this ugly-ass room and the fact that there were no decent refreshments on hand, not no Nilla Wafers or nothing.

"Then he had the nerve to look right in the camera like a deer in headlights," Suleman squealed. "That's when it had to cross his mind that all of us was watching. Just goes to show . . . It's always the holiest of holy's out here backsliding on the low, violating the commands of God." Then Suleman pointed at Qasim's closest ally in the room, the only one among us who wasn't amused. "Nah, Brother Larry, how does it feel knowing that your home skillet ain't nothing but a low-down, gambling *kafir*?!"

We got out the worst of our laughter by the time Lateef entered the room. He walked in slow, carrying a large white board under his arm. He motioned for a couple of the brothers to help set it on the tripod at the front of the room, and they leapt from their seats to do it. Behind him entered another man who none of us had ever seen. He was clearly of Mediterranean descent, dressed in the guido fashion—slicked-back hair, colorful Cosby sweater underneath a black leather jacket. He lugged a large sack over his shoulder like an olive-skinned Santa Claus and sat it in front of that painting as Lateef began the meeting.

"Alright, alright. Now that we're all here I figure we get right down to business. That's so often the problem with these endeavors. People out here too busy investing in foolishness and we don't end up getting nothing accomplished. Well, those times, brothers, are coming to an end. We have a perfect leader in the Messenger's son, who is guiding us on the straight path, al-Hamdulillah, teaching us the way business is really supposed to be done."

A takbir went up in the room, and faint calls of "Allah-hu-Akbar" followed.

"So with that being said, I'm going to hand over the floor to

Brother Firdus Alam, who's going to tell us all about his company and how we can get a collaboration going."

After a light applause the man stood. He made a long du'a in Arabic that felt like he was showing off, then he launched into his presentation.

"Brothers," Alam began in a deep, guttural accent, "it is my pleasure to be with you tonight. On behalf of Arabia Enterprises I'm very proud to present an opportunity to your collective that will bless you personally and professionally, Insha-Allah. First, imagine a world of thriving Black business, safe streets where children can play without fear . . ."

That was the moment when I started to check out. Imagine a world? This the type of stuff that you say when you don't know who you're talking to. As the descendants of slaves, we were already steeped in imagination. It was imagining a better world for our people that led many of us out of the church and to the Messenger, and when he died, it was imagination that made us follow his son from the Nation to the worldwide ummah. If we could only pass on one thing to our children, it was imagination. What he was saying was old thought. Later for the platitudes; what we needed was a plan to enact our designs and make them real.

I started to think about the beef stew and mashed potatoes Sadaqa said would be waiting for me when I made it home, when Brother Iklas, one of our youngest members, walked in the room.

"Nah, look who it is showing up late," Suleman said.

Iklas settled into his seat, opening a briefcase to pull out a pen and notepad. He looked up from the riffled pages, acknowledging the comment, though he did not respond.

"With all that ed ju ma cation," Suleman said, "a brother like you surely got more important places to be than here, building up the community with an *insidious* group of people like us."

I always cringed when Suleman misused words like a regular Don King, thinking it made him seem smarter. I wonder if he ever had an inkling that the effect was the opposite; that every time he said one of those out-of-place, million-dollar words, he sounded dumb as Billie Buckwheat.

"Alright now, hold on," Lateef interjected. "We got to focus on the matter at hand." He turned to Iklas. "This committee applauds your efforts for self-improvement, getting your degree. It ain't no detriment to our work. This here is Brother Firdus and he joined us tonight to talk about some leather tanneries in Fez, Morocco, where we're trying to do some business. He was just about to show us some of the beautiful things they make over there, isn't that right?"

"Oh yes." Firdus rushed over to the big cottony sack he'd brought in earlier and pulled out several women's purses, wallets, and belts. He sent them around the circle for us to get a good once-over. "We have all kinds of skins, cow and lamb. Whatever your customers could want, we can make."

It was just like Suleman to talk trash out the gate. He tried to start a tow truck company a couple of years after the Messenger passed, raised a whole lot of money in the community trying to get it off the ground. He wore a chip on his shoulder and gained over a hundred pounds ever since the thing fell apart, and to see Iklas— the youngest member of the committee, working on his master of business administration with so much sparkle and promise, moving about life with a sense of real possibilities—must have hurt his pride something deep.

He sat there with his arms folded, studying Iklas with a smirk on his face, while the rest of us examined the goods being circulated around the table.

"The proposition is very straightforward," Firdus said. "We produce quality goods like the ones before you and sell them to you in bulk for you to then market to consumers at whatever price you desire."

Iklas raised his hand and Brother Lateef nodded for him to speak.

"Good evening, brothers." Iklas said it real formal, talking like the kids in my high school days who used to get called Oreos. "This all sounds interesting, Mr. Firdus, and the goods seem high-quality. I know we're trying to pool our money to make this happen, but if I'm going to participate, this is not good enough."

"Come again?" Lateef said, looking to Firdus like the kid was speaking a foreign language only the Mediterranean man understood.

"For instance," Iklas began, "in the model you've presented us, there's no skill transfer component. We could easily sell your bags, Mr. Firdus, but it would be much more beneficial to the community if your plan included some means to teach us how to make the bags ourselves. And pardon me for going on . . . while I agree that warehouse space is essential, shouldn't we be thinking about manufacturing, too? And then buying a space instead of renting it?"

That's when I piped in.

"I like the way you think, lil' brother, but we have got to be reasonable. Think about scale and capacity; start where we are and build from there."

Iklas glared at me in a way that made the room contract, though I assumed he was offended that I'd used a diminutive when addressing him.

Before I could apologize and try to smooth things over, Suleman jumped in. "Ain't nobody trying to start nothing with you, *lil' brother*." He put emphasis on the last two words. "Yeah, I said it. I called you lil' 'cause that's what you is! This brother was trying to help you understand the thought process, and here you go blowing things out of proportion."

He was standing by then, pointing at Iklas from across the table, the irony completely over his head. Brother Shuaib, who sat next to him and was himself a father of seven boys and a bailiff in the municipal courthouse, gestured for Suleman to calm down, but Suleman shooed away his hand. I looked to Lateef, waiting for him to intervene, but he was studying Firdus's reaction—frozen as it was, holding a brown leather belt in one hand and a woman's clutch in the other.

"Nah, that," Suleman went on, "is why we should only let established businessmen up in here and not no children."

"Bit of a stretch, calling yourself a businessman," Larry said, still sour over the wisecrack about Qasim's big payday. "Everything you ever *done* fell apart. Probably got too much street left in you to act civilized."

It was in the split second before Suleman cocked his fist and sent it crashing into Larry's jaw like a steel ball through a wall of bricks, and all of the other brothers scrambled from their chairs to break them up, that I decided it was time to go.

When I walked in the door, Sadaqa was smiling in the kitchen, ladling chunks of stewed meat, carrots, and gravy over a buttery mash. I passed the kitchen without a word, and headed down the hall.

"You're just going to walk right by me and not give the greetings?" She sounded equal parts curious and upset as I opened the door to the basement. "Omar!" she called out to me, "your food's going to get spoiled. Don't nobody like mashed potatoes on the second day."

"Just wrap it in some plastic and leave it on the table for me," I said.

Those were my last words to her as I went downstairs. I turned on the TV to watch the last of the Knicks game and fell asleep. I didn't even catch the score.

∗

AFTER EVERYTHING THAT happened, people went on about their business like the events of that night amounted to a whole lot of nothing. Somehow, despite the commotion, we signed a small purchasing agreement with Arabia Enterprises and sold just enough bags and belts to turn a profit. Because they thought the partnership was going to put us on the map and make us all into millionaires, a couple of the brothers went sour on the whole endeavor. That struck me as wrong-headed. In the end, we did alright by the deal.

I recall telling Larry, once his wounds had healed and he started showing his face at the Jummah again, "At least we ain't in the red."

The one thing I hadn't gotten over was the matter of Iklas. Anytime I went to the Temple or was anywhere downtown he always came to my mind. I regretted everything about that night, especially where he was concerned, and chided myself that I hadn't stuck around to be sure he made it out okay. I spent enough time with the rough-and-tumble brothers from the FOI to know that life wasn't for me. Despite our effort to be different, based on the look of things, we seemed to have turned out a whole lot like them.

In the late spring I got a call to go fix a broken air-conditioning unit out near University Park. After a morning of work installing a network of vents at the School of Arts and Sciences, I took my lunch break at the Montego Bay Jamaican Eatery on Plessy Street. I was about to bite down on a beef patty when Iklas walked through the door.

"Brother Iklas," I said, and it made him look over from the ordering line. At first his face registered alarm, like the sight of me had brought something traumatic and ugly to the fore of his mind. "Got a minute?" I asked, gesturing for him to come sit at the table with me.

Bob Marley died only a couple days prior. The restaurant played his albums on a loop in the background, "Three Little Birds" was spinning when he finally walked over and laid his satchel on a nearby seat.

"So what's new with the MBA student?"

"MBA graduate."

"Now how do you like that? Al-Hamdulillah," I said. "That's excellent. Excellent! Please. Lunch on me. Or better yet, I haven't even touched the food. We got beef patties, rice and peas, cabbage sauté . . . Plenty to go around."

"I can't do kidney beans, brother," he said, "but thank you for offering."

"Since when?" I said jokingly. "Coulda swore I saw you tearing up some chili at the Temple a couple years back."

"I'm just trying to eat to live, that's all," he said.

That made me tick my head back and narrow my eyes at him. Last I heard of our people swearing off kidney beans, we were under the Messenger's orders. It was a rule I hardly heard spoken in the six years since he passed. I wasn't sure if he was showing his smarts again, letting me know he was aware of the strict dietary rules we used to follow in the days before the change of the guard, or if there was some kind of strange medical situation at play. I let it go.

"So what's your plan for yourself now that you're done with school?"

Iklas nodded thoughtfully. "As for what I want to do career-wise, that's something I'm still trying to figure out. I'm applying for some office jobs, doing the responsible thing like all the other working stiffs out here. What I really want is to do something meaningful. Something to help the Black man get a foothold in the world."

"A lot of time has gone by," I said. "It should have happened sooner, but I just wanted to take the opportunity to apologize to you on behalf of all the brothers. What happened that night was a disgrace, plain and simple, and I know I didn't help matters. I always shake my head when I think about the kind of example we are setting for the next generation. In your position, I would have left, too."

At my urging, Iklas took a bite of one of the patties. When I finished talking, his jaw slowed. He swallowed the food hard, then reached for a paper napkin out of the dispenser to wipe his mouth.

"I want to thank you for saying that and for this kind gesture . . . you inviting me here to eat with you, but I'd rather put it all behind me. As far as I'm concerned, that night couldn't have unfolded any differently than it did. You see"—he leaned into the table—"in my conception of things, the fish stinks from the head, not the tail."

"You talkin' bout Lateef?" I said, incredulous. "I mean, he got some space to grow. A little proud, no doubt. A little boastful? Maybe . . . But he means well. All them brothers do. We just learning as we go, that's all."

Iklas shook his head. "No," he said. "The very top."

"You mean the Messenger's son?" I nearly choked on the patty.

"Did you hear the Saviours' Day address?" Iklas's eye widened. "The one this year?"

Back in February there were all kinds of rumblings at the Temple that Brother Minister had spawned a second resurrection, reviving the Nation before a huge crowd in Chicago. I pretended not to care, but when Sadaqa brought home a VHS cassette, I sat and watched the address. He had a phalanx of mean mugging soldiers standing at his back while he talked about the need to recover what was lost. He said that after forty years of illumination, a time of darkness had befallen the Nation and a spider had come. He spun his web in the night and made it so that the weak could not escape its hold. Once the flies were caught, the spider moved in, injecting them with venom, then devouring his prey—the pitiful ones who didn't understand that Islam as practiced in Arabia and proffered by the Messenger's wayward son was not suited to the needs of the Black man in America.

"So you're with the calypso singer now." I laughed a little, though I felt a tug in my heart in saying the words. I studied his eyes. I once read intensity there and would have to fight not to see him in the cultish light with which I regarded myself and the other Nation followers from back in the day.

"Now that's a leader if I ever saw one," Iklas said. "He knows what the Temple folk really need to hear. Not all of this wishful thinking . . . us trying to curry favor with white Arabs, but making real progress."

Immediately I thought of Fard, who we were taught to call our "Master," and the whiteness of his skin—the only man more exalted in the Nation than the Messenger himself.

"I know what people say about Brother Minister," Iklas went on, "calling him the David Duke of Black America, which is just ridiculous. He's strong and principled and a moving orator. Unfortunately"—Iklas cocked his head and his voice shifted downward—"you can't say the same thing for the Messenger's son . . . Stuttering and all that . . . he's about as articulate as a brown paper bag. When the Shepherd doesn't know the way, the flock will stray."

"You got to do what you think is right. Every man got the right to decide his own destiny." I echoed the words of the Marley song that had just started playing.

"You know you could always rejoin," he said, full of enthusiasm. "The Minister is always talking about how he can never have too many soldiers."

I'd just finished my patty and was dusting my hands free of crumbs.

"Youngblood," I said, "I respect whatever choice you choose to make for yourself, but understand, I've been down that road. Them was some crazy times and I'm not interested in going back—"

"But you wouldn't be going back," Iklas interrupted. "You would be moving forward with competent, intelligent leadership. We are putting together a new plan and a new approach, with the most articulate Black man in America at the helm!"

I was going to say more, but in my peripheral vision I saw a man I immediately recognized as Mister Softie, a panhandler who always happened to be standing at the intersection of Main and Prospect whenever I was on my way to the Temple. I used to smile at him and give him my spare change when I was feeling generous but stopped the practice all together when I looked in my rearview mirror and found him pissing on my tires.

Mister Softie turned from the line and looked right at me. He stuck out a hand, then, registering who I was and what he'd done to my car, he diverted his attention to Iklas.

"Brother! Could you spare a dollar? Help me get something to eat?"

Without looking, Iklas reached into his back pocket, pulled out his wallet, and handed Mister Softie a five-dollar bill. "Take this, man," he beamed and riffled through his wallet again. "And when you're ready for something more, please reach out to my organization. We'll be there to help clean you up and get you where you need to go."

Iklas handed Mister Softie a business card—all red with a white crescent moon and star on the upper left corner.

"Aw, thank you, brother." Mister Softie revealed a yellowed, snaggletooth smile. "Imma call you, sure thang."

"Be sure to do that," Iklas said, getting up from the table.

"Well, it was good to see you again," he said to me. "Let the brothers know that we're back, and this time we're moving forward with a vision to really help the people get ahead."

I watched him through the glass window as he walked down the street, and a kind of sadness I hadn't felt in years revisited me. I held on to a certain view of the Nation so I would never forget what it had visited upon me, and that had nothing to do with Brother Iklas. Might things be different this go 'round? That was entirely possible, but like Brother Minister said, a man should try his best not to get caught in the spider's web, and as best as I could tell at the time, it looked to me like he was spinning one of his own.

I looked back toward the pickup line and saw Mister Softie inching toward me, his plastic wrapped feet rasping against the tiled floor. "You don't be coming to see me no more," he said. "You think I wasn't gonna find you? Can't get but so far before I find you!"

Immediately the restaurant owner emerged from the kitchen, raising her voice as the man hurried up to go.

The bells on the door jangled as he left, then the owner had another outburst, talking to her staff.

"Jah know me tiyad fi tell you," she said. "You cyan 'low the waste man dem fi a bother the customa! If a never fi big puppa Jesus and me sister Pearl weh dead, me would abandon the lot of you wit a dried-out coco bread and a one-way ticket back to Kingston!"

She sent the dustpan clattering to the ground, mumbling under her breath and began sweeping up a scattering of debris. It was all dirt with bits of food waste and scraps of paper, including the red and white NOI business card that Mister Softie had torn to shreds while standing in the line. She bent down to brush the mound onto the tray, then dumped the contents in the waste bin.

CANDY FOR HANIF

Sister Norah was first to arrive that Friday morning in preparation for the Jummah dinner. After leading Hanif, her adult son, to the boiler room where he did janitorial work with Brother Akil—the grounds engineer and weekday muezzin—she set upon completing the first of the day's tasks—reading any notes that had been left overnight in the suggestion box. It was an idea the shurah board had come up with years earlier. So that the believers could feel they had a say in the workings of the kitchen, a small metal container had been hammered onto the back of the service door, with a loose stack of white leaflets in a separate bin attached to a stout yellow pencil that dangled from a string. It was a system that had never fulfilled its intended purpose—the rare comments always involved complaints of matters unrelated, like the excessive height of the trough that was the women's wudu station or the air-conditioning, which was in a constant state of disrepair. But, reliable as usual, she carried out the chore in spite of precedent, always eager on the off chance a relevant comment had been received.

Standing on her tiptoes, Sister Norah fumbled inside the box, where she found a single anonymous note written in a messy cursive script. She walked into the kitchen, flipped a switch to illuminate several panels of lights that turned on one after the other, like a trail of falling dominoes, then leaned against one of the stainless-steel prep tables to read what it said.

"Beautiful Jummah dinner," it began. "Kitchen always coming through, but Sister Lunell," the note went on, "when you gonna bless us with that good old, smothered steak? The folks are waiting. Please put back on menu."

Sister Norah winced at the card. She read and reread it to be sure she had understood the contents, then felt dizzy. Trying to catch her breath, she rested her elbows on the table and leaned her face into the palm of her vacant hand—the note having triggered another of the waves that she had of late grown accustomed to—the surge of strong emotions always cresting unannounced.

It had only been three weeks. Just three weeks since Sister Lunell had stood—in her command—at the ten-burner gas range, stirring a large pot of field peas mixed with onions and turkey necks, the back of her one free hand resting on the broad curve of her right hip. Three weeks since she last heard Lunell's wry laughter and peered into her luminous, knowing eyes.

"I'm so happy, child, I could jump," Lunell said. "I don't know, I just feel young again. I would say young as you, but, child, look at you? I'm probably younger."

Sister Lunell Uqda was a powerful Temple presence—a master cook of savory foods who had run the kitchen since the last days of the Messenger. She worked with a small group of her contemporaries—Beverly, Cheryl, Anna, and Mattie Johnson—creating wholesome meals for the dinner crowds week after week. The team was reliable and efficient—qualities the women feared would be compromised when, ten years after the fall of the Nation as they knew it, Sister Norah came to them one day, a small photo album of her ornate confections in hand, asking to join the sisters in their work. She was upbeat and insistent, but

Beverly, Cheryl, and Mattie Johnson declined on account of her lack of training.

"She didn't come up the MGT way like we did," Sister Cheryl had said. "What if she can't keep up, then we all get rained on by the Imam? People got patience for a whole lot of foolishness, but you can expect the folks to raise hell over a bad plate of food."

This line of argument kept her off the crew for the first few months of inquiries. That was, until Sister Anna decided to retire after thirty years of working for the city government, moved out West with her daughter, and the kitchen suddenly found itself in need of a baker.

They welcomed Norah with some begrudging, but quickly came to respect her for her eagerness, skill, and dedication to the work. It was the kind of respect that gave Sister Norah the space she needed to figure things out on her own. Instead of step-by-step instructions, they left recipes for her to follow—simple things like sheet cakes, blondies, and monkey bread, asking her to bake test batches on Wednesdays so that her contributions were practiced and reliable in time for the Jummah. They preferred this to hands-on instruction, not wanting to intimidate Sister Norah, or make her feel they were ganging up on her because of their seniority. She was only thirty years old at the time of joining, a full twenty years younger than Sister Cheryl, who was next in the stair step of ages that topped out at Mattie Johnson's sixty-five—a situation that was ripe for conflict, though their strategy succeeded, helping her integrate into the flow of things at a comfortable pace.

Sister Norah was not bothered by the separation. Except for the focus demanded by the work itself, her mind was always elsewhere, consumed with private circumstances that her presence in the kitchen was intended to help her escape. She had led a quiet life at the fringe of the Temple as the wife of Idris Mubarak, a man many years her senior, who passed away just a few months before her first petition. After caring for her husband, who had succumbed to lung cancer—the product of years of cigarette smoking that not even the Messenger's program had helped him curb—Sister Norah was left alone to pick up the pieces of her life, all while raising their cognitively delayed, special-needs son. What she hoped for was community—a way to lighten the load of her grief and socialize her son, whose quirks and eccentricities seemed to grow more pronounced each day.

It was only Lunell to whom she'd developed anything bordering on a close relationship. Just four years after Sister Norah had joined the kitchen to make the cakes, cobblers, and fruit cocktail they served the children after T'aleem, Sister Lunell had experienced a similar fate when her husband, Brother Benjamin Uqda, suffered a massive stroke that left him paralyzed on the left side of his body.

For the past six years, when she wasn't at the Temple, Sister Lunell was "shut in" as she called it, taking care of Brother Benjamin. She spent her days and nights tending to his most basic needs, emptying his bedpans, and preparing his sponge baths, until the day his heart finally gave out. In the few months that had passed since Brother Benjamin's death, Sister Lunell had wasted no time. She moved herself into the Joseph Bradley Senior Living Center, started wearing colorful, younger-looking clothes, and used the money from Brother Benjamin's life insurance to purchase a brand-new Cadillac Cimarron in light-blue metallic with a cheetah-print cover on the steering wheel.

"It's going to be a whole new world from here on out," Sister Lunell had said. "No more thankless nights caring for a man who never did more than the bare minimum for me. It's just going to be me in a caftan on a beach somewhere, looking out at the sea."

This should have been her clue.

It was later the same night that Sister Norah got the call. The staff at the Joseph Bradley Senior Living Center had found Lunell unresponsive, splayed out on her living room couch, just hours after serving her last Friday meal. She recalled it all in the moment at the prep table, the waves of grief carrying her, but this time with a newborn sense of indignation. Announcements had been made and a sparsely attended janaza was organized for the following Monday, so there really was no excuse. It was nothing but shameless ignorance, she thought of the note, that someone could know the kitchen well enough to call the women staff by name and yet be unaware that Sister Lunell Uqda—the Temple head chef for over twenty years—was dead.

How heartless and uncaring—the thought coursed through her mind, cycling over and over to suppress another thought, one that had tried rearing its head over the past few days but that had only, in just that moment, come to the fore—she could point the blame at an anonymous note, though it was only to mask her own feelings of guilt.

After Brother Benjamin fell ill, Sister Lunell started reaching out to Norah—owing, she supposed, to Lunell's notions of the burdens they had in common.

Sister Norah had also been saddled with an ill husband, though she'd spent the last ten years of her widowhood focused on doing what she thought was best for Hanif. She refused to put him in a school—not trusting the white folks in charge to do right by her one and only child. Sister Norah chose, instead, to take sewing work in the home, where she could keep a constant, loving eye on his development. For outings, she brought him along for her weekly sojourns to the Temple where, despite his erratic behavior at home, he was reliably cordial and quiet. When it was just the two of them, he could be easily distracted by the goings on in his mind—a flash of something menacing triggering his alarm nearly every waking moment—causing his head to tick back and forth, chasing the specters that danced around him like Stevie Wonder. At the Temple, he was grounded enough in reality to lay the plastic tablecloths before the Jummah dinner and take out the trash at Brother Akil's behest. When there was time to observe him at work, Sister Norah would pause to watch him through the service window, and it made her smile. She took joy in his productivity, happy that, for at least a few hours each week, their lives could feel easy and normal.

"You better put that boy in a home and go about living your own life," Sister Lunell had said to her. "They got some good places out here, you know. You can go and check on him from time to time, make sure he's getting what he needs. You too young and beautiful to be thinking that caring for that boy is all God got planned for your life. Don't you lie to me, now. I know what it's like. Child, I can't even imagine the type of shit he must be putting you through."

Lunell was not at all off base in her assumptions, though Sister Norah would eschew her concern, shaking her head each time at the slightest suggestion of leaving him in anyone else's care.

Hanif had, indeed, given Sister Norah more than her fair share of trouble. There were too many opposing forces raging inside him—he had a mind like a child's, though his body pulsed with hormones that deepened his voice and made dense muscle of his limbs, communicating in all the ways a body does that he was a full-grown man. It was an inner conflict that often pushed him to acts of violence. On a regular basis, from the age of eighteen, he punched holes in his bedroom walls and broke any glass plates, bowls, and cups he got his hands on, so that Sister Norah had to replace her dishware with all plastic items. She would come upon him in his fits of destruction, frown with disapproval, and then he'd wilt, crumpling over his bedside like a cornered five-year-old, full of remorse over the damage he caused.

A week before Sister Lunell's death, Hanif—in the grip of one of the epic battles that were constantly playing in his mind—had, on an impulse, pushed her in the path of the 31 crosstown bus on their way home from the Sunday T'aleem. The scene arrested traffic for several minutes, the driver descending from his Plexiglas cubicle to check on Sister Norah and make sure that she was okay. He reached over, full of fury, ready to subdue Hanif until the authorities arrived, but Sister Norah put up both hands in a panic, explaining her son's condition, trying her best to keep the man from calling the police.

"Please don't hurt him," she said. "He's my son. It's just something in his head and he can't help it."

She spoke these words to the driver, the same as she'd always told Lunell. The obligations and emotions attendant to motherhood were quite different than caring for a husband, so that while their experiences with caretaking did overlap, there was not enough symmetry for Sister Lunell's advice to feel entirely pertinent to her own life.

Or so she'd led herself to believe. Now, she sat with the memory of how these constant refusals of support had been received by Sister Lunell. Norah didn't think the guidance was prudent but was always grateful for Lunell's interest, and even when she didn't take her advice, she had always listened, but her poor communication of these subtleties filled her with shame. It was nothing less than ungodly to show so little care for the doers of good, and this awareness tore at Norah's heart, as she contemplated the idea that Lunell had gone to her grave without ever getting her just rewards. She had never heard the full summation of the beauty and wisdom

Norah saw in her, as she had never taken the time to express the magnitude of her respect.

There was distinctive chatter in the multipurpose room alerting Sister Norah that the other women had arrived—first Mattie Johnson followed by Beverly and Cheryl. The sound of their shoes on the clay tile forced her to stand upright and tidy her appearance.

They were upbeat just after the janaza and had carried the same spirit with them into the kitchen that morning, their voices chipper as they rehearsed the day's menu—baked ziti with chicken piccata, garden salad, and Sister Norah's own cream cheese lemon pound cake.

"I can hardly wait for that cake," Sister Beverly said. "If it's any luck, I might get me two pieces!"

Sister Norah saw her own reflection in the half-dull work surface. Despite her effort to regain composure, her face sagged around the cheeks and eyes like a drowsy Shar-Pei, giving her the appearance of someone much older than her own age of forty-one.

The women gathered around the table and, at the point where they were going to pray Al-Fatiha before starting preparations for that day's meal, Imam Saleem appeared at the door. He walked into the room, smiling hard in just the same way Brother Masood, the snake, had done two weeks earlier. He had come in a similar fashion, striding into the kitchen, just days after Sister Lunell's janaza, asking what the sisters were going to do with the kitchen now that the "brains" of their operation was gone.

They refused the proposition he set before them, allowing his new business venture—the Johnson and Sons Fish Company—to share space and profit for that week's Jummah dinner, though he'd shown up anyway late on Friday, boasting a crew of five men. They parked a food truck in front of the Temple and sent a young man in an all-white smock out onto the sidewalk, ringing a small bell and singing to welcome customers.

"Johnson Sons does it right! Johnson Sons, fresh and light!"

They had sold several brown paper bags of trout and fried whiting sandwiches before the sisters caught on. Sister Mattie Johnson, alone, went outside to confront Masood, but it was only the police officer who came riding through on his motorbike asking to see the vendor license, which he failed to produce, that finally sent Johnson and Sons on their way. With no intervention from any of the Temple folk, it made the women suspicious that perhaps the Imam was in on the scheme and had come that morning to seal the deal, robbing them once and for all of their position.

"Come on now," started Sister Cheryl. "Imam Saleem, please don't go doing us like the brothers. Did you catch wind of last week? Got these big honking men trying to take our jobs, and no one coming to our defense!"

The Imam put his hands up to calm her down, and all of the women fell silent.

"As-Salaam Alaikum, sisters," he began. "I know it's been a hard couple of weeks since all that happened with Sister Lunell. Beautiful woman, right there. Bold and outspoken, no doubt, but she dedicated many precious years to this place. I just can't imagine how you must be feeling."

All the women, save Sister Norah, stared the Imam square in his eyes—a cold reaction to a tender sentiment, Norah thought. Between them, they had spent sixty more years on Earth than she— time that had robbed them of a tolerance for open signs of grief. There again, they weren't alone. Death, among the Temple folk, was always treated like a silent parade, always marching but with little fanfare and barely any visible signs of mourning.

"We're making it just fine," Sister Mattie Johnson replied. "Just taking things as they come."

"Then for Brother Masood to show up like he did? That was

just adding salt to the wound, and trust me, I'm with you," the Imam said. "It was not in the best interest of the Temple to have folks leeching off our customer base. But for all that you've been made to endure, it hasn't shown up in the food. Everything was beautiful last Jummah, al-Hamdulillah."

The sisters all nodded, grateful for the acknowledgment, but wondered what it was that made him linger in the room.

"And with that said," he continued, "I'm standing here today on behalf of the shurah board just to thank you for keeping it together in the wake of such a terrible tragedy, and then again, for all the years of service you have given to the Temple. God knows this place wouldn't be half of what it is without your contribution, so without further delay, I wanted to present you with this token of our gratitude."

He went into his suit and grabbed a large white envelope from the inside breast pocket. Sister Beverly was first to reach for it, taking it from his hand, then immediately opening the seal. She struggled pulling out the thick cardstock from the golden interior and read the ornate cursive writing aloud once it was freed.

" 'The Spirit of the City,' " she read slowly and deliberately, " 'welcomes you on an evening cruise of haute cuisine, music, and magic city views.' "

She and the other sisters looked from the card to the Imam, whose expression was suddenly gleeful, his hands splayed at the sides of his face like fireworks.

"It's an all-inclusive, two-hour journey up and down the river," he said. "Me and Donna went awhile back and had ourselves a good old time. You'll get to see the city like never before."

Something akin to an electric surge traveled through Mattie Johnson, Beverly, and Cheryl, their smiles turned up high, as they clapped in excitement.

"Oh, Brother Imam," Sister Beverly reacted. "This is so generous, really, but it's four tickets in here, and you know Sister Norah. On account of Hanif, she don't hardly go nowhere."

Sister Norah felt herself about to speak, the refusal fully formed in her mouth, but the sisters stopped her with a uniform glare of disapproval.

"Not this time, sister," Cheryl shook her head. "Who would ever think I'd be in a position to tell a young person like you to go have some fun; we're not making no excuses today. It's just"—she turned her gaze to Imam Saleem—"we need to find a solution for Hanif, find someone to watch him who Sister Norah can trust."

She stopped speaking and everyone turned to see Brother Akil walking from the boiler room toward the men's wudu station at the bottom of the stairs. He paused midstep as Imam Saleem called him over, then turned toward the kitchen, his tool belt jangling heavily with every stride. A tall, slender man, he easily rested his fingers on the upper casing of the door, swinging in and out of the room, asking if something was the matter.

"Aw, nothing serious," the Imam replied. "It's just that, given everything these sisters have been through recently, and to honor their service to the community, we wanted to treat them to an evening out on the town. Only problem is, Sister Norah can't make it unless Hanif has someplace safe where he can stay."

Brother Akil turned it over in his mind for a brief moment, then nodded.

"It's no problem for him to spend a few hours with me. No problem at all. I was going to be here anyway, doing some touch-up painting in the upstairs office. I never seen him handle a paint roller, but if he don't take to it, I'll find something else for him to do. You should go on and have yourself a good time, sister." He looked, wide-eyed and insistent, at Norah. "Just keep in mind, I got a hard stop at six thirty. Made a commitment to my own kids that night to take them to the Skate Palace, if you understand. But up until then, don't even worry 'bout it."

Though Sister Norah was inclined to say no, she thought again about Lunell, and something in her relented.

"Okay, I'll go," she said, "just as long as he stays with you, Brother Akil, I trust he will be okay."

"Atta girl." Sister Cheryl smiled, clapping her hands. "Now it's time for you to start doing some living!" She said this as Sister Beverly gave a hoot, pulsing her hands in the air, and Mattie Johnson started shaking her shoulders. "Look out, now," she said, "'cause Spirit of the City, here we come!'"

THE NEXT DAY at three p.m., Brother Rashad, owner of "Back in One Piece" Limousines n' Things, LLC, arrived at the Temple in a Lincoln town car to pick up the sisters for the 3:45 embarkation. They were all gathered in the bathroom lounge, prettying themselves like teenage girls on the way to the prom. Sister Beverly stood gap-mouthed and wide-eyed in the mirror, applying mascara, as Sister Mattie Johnson helped Sister Cheryl with her dress, fussing over the few gold lamé panels on her skirt that refused to lay flat.

Donning an all-cotton, olive-colored shalwar kameez she'd purchased at an Eid-al-Fitr bazaar several years earlier, Sister Norah was dressed more plainly than the others. If not for the shimmery scarf and pearl-drop earrings Sister Beverly forced her to wear, Norah might have appeared like she was getting ready for a good night's sleep rather than a dinner cruise. She refused the lipstick Sister Beverly had offered her, but accepted a light spritzing of Shalimar. She had turned a few revolutions, letting the particulates fall on every inch of her clothing, when Rashad knocked on the bathroom door, announcing it was time to leave. They exited quickly into the multipurpose room, and he gave a high-pitched whistle.

"Looking beautiful, ladies, al-Hamdulillah. Now it's time for us to get a move on."

The women walked toward the front door, though Sister Norah turned to catch one last glimpse of her son. He was in the boiler room, but his back was turned, facing Brother Akil, who was teaching him how to paint. Brother Akil made his motions, then handed the cylindrical roll to Hanif, who mimicked the act, smoothing an even coating of white paint on a large piece of particleboard. She saw the smile growing on Akil's face, proud of what her son had learned, and it made her heart happy. If only he had a man like that in his life every day, showing him the way to go. He'd be so much better off, she thought, then turned to leave.

The women had been talking, enjoying the Motown playlist that Brother Rashad piped into the back of the limousine. They were sipping sparkling cider from tall plastic flutes, when he pulled up to the waterfront and pointed out the *Conduit*—"the premier sailing vessel of the Spirit fleet"—bobbing on the waves. Their banter slowed as they took in the ship, not knowing what to make of what they saw. The place where the hull met the water was rusted orange, with large colonies of barnacles growing all over its sides. A greenish-brown film covered all the windows, giving them a dull appearance that, along with the rest of the *Conduit*, begged to be scrubbed with several applications of ammonia and rinsed clean. As if they were contemplating not going in the end, the women lingered in the car, but Brother Rashad snapped them out of their daze.

"Alright, ladies," he said. "Time to go have some fun." He hopped out of the car and walked around to let the women out onto the sidewalk, holding the door and steadying them, grabbing their hands as each one issued forth. With everyone out, he tipped his hat and walked around the car, headed back to the driver's seat.

"I'll be right here at six on the nose to come and get you, Insha-Allah. Now y'all go on in there and have yourselves a good old time."

The women walked slowly toward the dock, when a young man approached them from the side. He was stooped in his bearing, leaning over a single makeshift crutch, trembling as he stood. He was dressed in layers of sun-bleached rags that seemed excessive given the mid-summer heat. His face, like the overcoat he donned, was caked with dust, turning what must have been his honey-brown complexion all the way to mocha, the heavy scent of urine wafting off his person, churning their stomachs.

"Spare some change to help the homeless," he rasped, wobbling on his crutch. "I need some money so I can buy me a sandwich."

The sisters pressed on, suddenly eager to make it to the boat, though Norah lagged behind. She went into her purse, pulled out her wallet, and gave the man a five-dollar bill. She placed the money in his hand, and he smiled a tarnished smile.

Beverly and Cheryl stared at her blankly, as Sister Mattie Johnson gestured for her to come along. In their looks, Norah saw pity mixed with disdain, mostly directed at the young man, and some for her as well.

Once Norah had rejoined the group, Sister Cheryl intoned, "The Messenger said 'do for self.' A dollar ain't gonna help him none, and five is going to encourage him to keep doing what he doing, and not what he ought to do—go get himself cleaned up!"

Though Norah paid the criticism no mind, the other sisters let the words linger, unchallenged, as they joined the line of other passengers waiting to board the *Conduit*. The man was noticeably young and clearly needed the support of a loving mother. She imagined the woman that conceived and carried him, who cradled him in infancy, feeding him from the stores of her own body. Presuming she was alive and in her right mind, it would horrify that woman to see her baby boy in such a state, subject to the casual cruelty of the average passerby. Five dollars was but a small sacrifice to make, her way of expressing her own mother love in the unfamiliar and uncomfortable absence of Hanif.

Once the women made it to the front of the line they were greeted by the maître d'—an older man with wiry, gray hair who donned a crooked bow tie, inch-thick glasses, and a scrooge-like frown. After finding their reservation on the list, another man in a suit and tie, who seemed just as unhappy, led the women from the boat entrance to an expansive dining hall. As he led them to their table, he offered them no greeting, his gaze perpetually directed to the threadbare carpet.

They were seated in a corner near the stern of the boat—a space very close to the droning engine that, even docked, churned so loudly they had to raise their voices in order to hear each other speak.

It had taken twenty more minutes before the other passengers were seated, at which point the muffled sound of what must have been a safety announcement was piped into the room. The words were too indistinct for anyone to heed, nor did the staff much seem to care as they walked about, placing wicker baskets full of dinner rolls on each table. When theirs arrived, Sister Beverly reached under the burgundy napkin to grab one and quickly withdrew her hand.

"They ain't even warm," she said to the disapproving stares of Mattie and Cheryl.

A group of five men in black shirts and trousers emerged from a side room, assembling behind a drum kit and several guitars situated toward the rear of the large parquet dance floor. As the engine groaned and the vessel began to pull away from the dock and into the river stream, they tuned their instruments, and after a brief countdown, began playing a rather uninspired rendition of "Maneater" by Hall and Oates.

"How you figure they get away with this?" Sister Cheryl asked. "What these tickets must of cost? Eighty? Ninety Dollars? Either the Imam and his wife . . ." she started to say, but Sister Mattie stopped her going too far. "Either something's up with their judgment or this place done fell."

The dinner was served shortly thereafter—Salisbury steak with mashed potatoes, carrots, and a thin gravy covering it all. The women held hands as they said a brief prayer over the food but only pecked at it, the senior sisters commenting on everything about the meal and how much better they could have done things compared with the *Conduit* staff.

"It ain't but fifty people on this boat," Sister Cheryl went on. "Wallahi, I could cook a meal for that many people, hands tied and blindfolded."

They went on that way, filling up on cold dinner rolls with hard butter and the lemonade iced tea, which everyone agreed, including Sister Norah, was the best thing they were served that evening.

"And to think," Sister Beverly said, "these folks are making real money in that kitchen back there and this is what they choose to serve a paying customer."

Forty-five minutes into their set, a petite woman who the keyboardist introduced as "the Incomparable Stacy Pham" emerged from a back room to modest applause. She wore a red mini dress and silvery stiletto heels, smiling brightly at the crowd despite the lukewarm reception. A glittering microphone in hand, she waved it, beating out a rhythm, counting in the band as they struck up a version of Sade's "Sweetest Taboo."

"Ooh, girl, that's my jam," Sister Cheryl whispered the words to Norah, then started wiggling in her seat. The Incomparable Stacy Pham sang with the full-bodied voice of a Broadway starlet, ending each phrase with a rattling vibrato that was not unpleasant, though it overshot the mellowness of the original song. She swayed and danced, pointing accusations at various men in the audience in a way that was on the one hand sensual and on the other, humorous enough not to make their wives and girlfriends uncomfortable. It didn't take long. A few couples left their seats at the start of the second verse. They two-stepped under a stagnant disco ball and among those remaining at their tables, all of the people who, by their looks, were just as disappointed as the kitchen sisters with the meal, were at the very least swaying to the beat, something like pleasure creeping onto their faces.

The rhythm picked up as the singer launched into a high-octane version of Anita Ward's "Ring my Bell," and no longer able to resist, Sister Cheryl got up from her seat.

"You don't understand," she said. "This used to be my song. Come on, little lady." She reached for Sister Mattie Johnson's hand. "You ain't too old to cut a rug."

The two of them got up, and soon Sister Beverly joined them, all three women spinning along with half the other dinner guests, who also made their way onto the dance floor. They formed a small circle on the edge of the parquet, not far from the table where Sister Norah remained in her seat.

Sister Norah couldn't bring herself to dance with them, when, as usual, her mind wandered toward Hanif.

She thought about her son and what he might be doing in that moment, considering it was the first time in years that she'd ever been farther away from him than a single room, and her eyes traveled from the sisters to the nearest window.

The *Conduit* was still close enough to land that she could make out the faces of all the tourists and others traipsing up and down the promenade, enjoying the sunny warmth of an afternoon in summer.

The promenade ran along Canal Street—a one-way artery that pumped traffic from the northwest into the heart of the city. Given the many pedestrians there were on that day, the lanes moved slowly, so it was easy enough to make out the people as they waited in their cars. A few hundred yards from the dense traffic of the promenade, Sister Norah fixated on a single car, a black Mercedes sedan with tinted windows at a red light. It looked like it had just been polished and shined, and she was very clear in the moment that it was the fanciest car she had ever seen, fancier even than Brother Rashad's fleet of limousines. The car door opened and a man got out, though the person who emerged did not look at all like the kind of person she assumed would be riding in such a vehicle. Could it be? No—it couldn't. How could he get from one side of the promenade to the other, and so quickly? How could he have changed his clothes? What kind of person begs the unassuming for things they don't really need? Were these the right questions even? Norah considered. The sisters already suspected the man and had warned her against that kind of almsgiving. Her lack of certainty about his true identity was suppressed at the mind's insistence— suppressed beneath the verdict of her own credulity, as she had come to the realization that, with the least effort from anyone who tried, she could always be deceived.

She tried to play out the chain of events, to see how, with the benefit of hindsight, the sham unfolded, but her mind wandered from the beggar, returning her thoughts to a reexamination of the traffic stop one month earlier.

In actual fact, the incident had unfolded very quickly. She landed in the street and a confrontation ensued between Hanif and the bus driver that resolved itself within two cycles of a stoplight. This would make for an official recounting, though to Norah's mind—having nearly met her end—it had all unfolded like flip-book animation, the frames slow and steady as a viewfinder, flashing one after the next. First comes the push, then the fade. She blinks. The tire treads stop inches from her frame. She blinks. The driver, on the street, reaches for Hanif. She blinks. The driver stands above her, her hands stretch upward blocking a view of his face. She blinks. The driver, back in his chair, looks to where she's standing on the sidewalk, his eyes narrow with concern. She blinks and the driver is gone.

That is how she remembered it, but what, in her recounting, had she failed to see? What details had she hidden from herself that, in the present moment, were laid bare? She cautioned the driver not to bother with Hanif, and turned to her son as if she had not seen the truth in his carriage—the way he stood, arms at his side, head cocked at an angle, his eyes wide with, was it delight? A childlike fascination sparkled around him as he fixated on his mother, as if she were no more to him than a spectacle, a soda volcano or a paper airplane—a honing experiment in his craft of destruction that had nearly taken flight.

She tried to bring herself back into the moment, to partake in the joy of the kitchen sisters, who swayed on, dancing to the music, or to at least feel within herself that she was the Norah they'd always known—quiet and compliant, at peace with the weight life had settled on her shoulders, but she was overcome with a new awareness. She might have collapsed in tears if it was sadness that

she felt, but she sat in stillness, her eyes staring at nothing in particular. Nothing, that was, except the kindling flame of her own rage.

When Brother Rashad returned to pick them up, he asked them
how it went, and despite the bad food and the engine noise and the
poor facilities, the sisters were enthusiastic.

"That one Asian lady," Cheryl chimed in, "she could really sing.
Had me all the way shook. I mean, that woman could blow! I had
to get up on my feet and do a little dip."

"Count on a woman," Lunell had always said. "Ain't we always
the ones, got to make sugar from shit?"

"And how about you, Sister Norah?" he asked again. "You're
being awful quiet back there. Did you have a good time as well?"

It took a moment for her to shake herself from her wandering
thoughts, and after a nudge from Sister Mattie, she finally spoke.
"Oh yes," she said. "It was a very nice time. Sorry it had to end."

By then Brother Rashad had arrived at the Temple. He opened
the side door for the women to exit, and slowly they headed toward the entrance, all of them except Sister Norah, who stood frozen on the sidewalk.

"Something the matter?" Sister Cheryl turned around to ask,
and all of the women paused, looking back at Norah as she uttered
her question. "I'm sure Hanif can't wait to see you."

"No," Sister Norah replied. "It's just that . . . I promised him I
would get his favorite candy from the corner store and I completely
forgot. I don't want to disappoint him."

"You mean the Quick and Save right up the road?" Brother
Rashad inquired, patting the sweat from his collar. "I can take you,
if need be. Have you right back here in no time flat."

Sister Norah shook her head, and her entire body rattled, con-
vulsing at the offer.

"It's alright, don't worry." The words came out groveled and sloppy. She was already headed down the block as she spoke, the sound of her voice fading with each step. "I'll be back," she said. "Please tell Brother Akil I'm sorry." She had to yell it as she turned, stumbling on her way down the sidewalk.

She walked at a clip, her feet pounding the pavement as if she were late for an appointment, her thoughts cycling the words "Candy for Hanif . . . Candy for Hanif " in the rhythm of her stride. "Soda pop, lemon drops, Candy for Hanif." She was so focused on her meditation that when she came upon the Lucky Seven Convenience Mart, where she always went for his Airheads and Jolly Ranchers, she walked right past it, crossing the street at the red light farther down Main.

She was still thinking of candy when she made it past the intersection, walking through the bus depot where for years she traveled the same route with Hanif in tow, taking him from home to the Temple and then back. She knew the streets so well, knew them in such detail that if there were a filled pothole or a trash can just slightly out of place, she would index the change. It was the landscape of her entire adult life, one she relied upon and took for granted, one she expected to provide for all her needs, as if no place else existed, as if no place else could do the same. She looked out at the streets that she once considered to be the only place she'd ever have a life, though in that moment the entire city looked to her like a cage, placing limits on what she could know of the world. She felt the weight of her soul's exhaustion as she crossed yet another street, passing the city buses as they came and went. The 11 and the 87 sat at the edge of the lot, their doors opened, with long lines of commuters waiting to board. All of them were people like her, she figured, all of them going from home to work, then home again—a dance headed nowhere. She cycled the thought, "Dance headed nowhere, dance headed nowhere," the new meditation having replaced "Candy for Hanif" as she raced across the next intersection, on her way into the Greyhound station on Weston Place.

"Where you headed, ma'am?" the agent, a cinnamon-toned, middle-aged woman with a frizzed-out Jheri curl and what seemed like a dozen gold rings on her fingers, asked, her face bent over an old CRS machine.

"I don't know," Norah said shakily. "Someplace as far away as possible, someplace near the water, as fast as you can get me there, please," she said. She spoke the words almost plaintively, as if money were not enough to make the transaction go through, as if the teller, unwitting, though increasingly suspicious, might intervene in her newborn scheme and compel her to stay.

"Okey dokey," the woman said flatly. "Someplace far away . . . leaving as soon as possible." Sister Norah bounced, her nerves on edge, as the teller clicked away—the keys fluttering like the sound of hot grease in a cast-iron skillet.

"And when will you be returning?" the teller asked, and Sister Norah glared at the woman.

"A one-way ticket, then," the teller said, rolling her eyes. "Someplace near the water. Alright, got you covered." She clicked a few more buttons, then fed several white cards through a Microline printer, which made zipping sounds as the paper inched into then out of the ink roll.

"Alright, ma'am, here you go." The woman stood from her seat. She ripped the ticket from the receipt and used a marker to highlight the bus number, the departure gate and time, leaving in just a few minutes. Sister Norah fumbled, her hands trembling as she removed her wallet to pay the fare.

"Take your time, ma'am, I ain't judging," the teller said. Norah took the ticket and handed over the money.

"Good luck to you," the teller finally said. "When you get where you're going, I hope you find whatever it is you're looking for."

Sister Norah turned away, miffed at the teller's presumptuousness, walking in the direction of the echo that filled the terminal, announcing her bus number and gate of embarkation. There was a short line at the number 44, and she rushed to it. In a short while she was on board.

Sister Norah settled into her seat toward the middle of the bus and was pleased with how few people had elected to ride on that day. It would give her space, but to do what? To think about the sisters? The Temple? Hanif? Or maybe the question the teller posed—and what was she looking for? That was something worth considering, but her mind went blank. Norah was tired of all the questions, and so she thought of nothing at all, save the simple stimuli of being there—the navy-blue upholstery of the seats, the faint smell of bleach, the driver calling out to the few passengers there were, welcoming them on this multi-stop bus service with a final destination to Miami, Florida.

JANAZA

I made it to the Everlasting Arms Mortuary that Friday afternoon, only to learn that I'd shown up on the wrong day for the wrong thing. Early that morning, just half an hour before my departure, I got an email from the Temple listserv my mother signed me up for years earlier, saying the man I grew up knowing as Captain Michael 2X was dead. In my haste to leave home, I must have skipped over the details. I had thought, based on the Islamic custom, that the captain would be buried the very same day. I only started to question my thinking as I walked up the block to the funeral home—a gray stone mansion at the corner of Western and Twenty-Second Street. I was brushing off my suit, wrinkled from the long drive south, and noticed that all the other men out front were dressed casual. When a grave-looking man in a kufi and a long beard, who must have been the Imam, handed me a booklet titled, "Principles of the Burial Ghusl," I realized my mistake. The first surprise in a day of odd occurrences—I learned I had shown up for the washing of the body, a full day before the actual funeral was set to occur.

I was confused and a little upset by the mix-up, and sat myself on the parlor stoop, just feet away from the small crowd of men who'd been waiting to be let inside. I pulled out a chocolate bar I had bought a few exits up the interstate, the likes of which I hadn't had in years—chocolate and peanuts mixed with caramel. I was halfway thinking I should leave, maybe head to the Crosswinds Casino another hundred miles south, but stayed put, fumbling with the pamphlet the Imam gave me. I cracked the spine and spread it flat at the gutter to a series of photographs of an actual washing. On the left-hand page, the corpse, its face and private area covered in white gauze, was bathed in a mixture of water and camphor. On the opposite page, the orifices—nostrils and ears—were packed tight with small tufts of raw cotton.

Inside the wrought iron gates of the mortuary grounds the other men stood closer to the street. I hadn't paid them any mind, until one began talking loudly about the circumstances of Captain Michael's death.

On the previous night, the captain corralled all of his and Sister Frieda's children to celebrate her birthday at the house on Euclid, where they'd lived for as long as I could remember. After all the food was out and she blew out the candles on the cake, Captain Michael stood to speak. He addressed each of their children and the grandchildren. "I know how it looks, with all the changes this family been through in recent years. I just want y'all to hear it from my mouth." His voice started to wobble. "That Sister Frieda, your mother, is the only woman that I ever . . ." That's when he grew dizzy. It was only the stumble that followed that alarmed anyone, but before they could react, the old man fell to the ground, never to rise again.

"From Allah we come, and to Allah we return," said the Imam, his head tilted up, speaking the words into wisps of passing clouds.

A small, younger man in a T-shirt that said G-Unit—Get Rich or Die Trying—piped in:

"Y'all don't think it's strange that a powerful brother like the captain would drop dead like that?" The crowd groaned, but he went on. "Tell me that don't sound like some CIA shit to you."

The Imam flashed him a wincing glance, and the young man raised his arms in mock surrender.

"That's the way to go, though," another taller man said. He had a pronounced Adam's apple that rose and fell like it would pierce his throat, the high pitch in his voice making it obvious that he was just as young. "CIA, FBI, whatever . . . but riding out unsuspecting? Sound like the jackpot to me!"

That was all it took, and their conversation turned into a shouting match—just the sort of thing that would send Vanessa's eyes spinning around in their sockets. I saw her in my mind—arms crossed, the flash of her diamonds, a manicured ponytail wagging as she shook her head no.

"That's why those folks are in the state they're in, stuck in the ghetto like they are. My heart goes out to them, really it does. It's just a shame they can't be more like you . . ."

She preferred her antics on daytime TV. I imagined what she might be doing at that very moment—probably sitting on the living room couch, glued to the soaps, or some talk show while painting her nails with layer after layer of shellac—imagining that day was like any other and I had simply left home early, headed to the office.

The thought of her rattled me somewhat and put me off the rest of the candy bar. I wrapped up the remainder and stuffed it in my suit pocket, where it melted in the early summer heat, leaving a brown-burgundy stain on my white button-down, just over the heart.

Above the shouting of the men were the sounds of children being let go from the Our Lady of Peace Day School just beyond the caged basketball court that sat between it and the mortuary. Their voices were all treble as they poured into the streets of the Eastside, competing with the subwoofers on the cars that swooshed up and down the streets blasting hip-hop beats with the bass so loud it rattled your insides.

The argument morphed quickly to a chorus of "Salaams" and "Welcome, my brothers," which made me look up and notice—surprise number two—it was James Shabazz walking through the gate; a man I hadn't seen in forty years. We were classmates at the University of Islam—not the best of friends, but close enough to know something of each other's essence.

Despite the ways my mother tried to shelter me from the world, I saw very early that James was headed for a life of trouble. I went off to college, and between my freshmen year and graduation, only the worst news followed any mention of his name. According to my mother and the flock of Temple women who fed her gossip, he dropped out of school and was in and out of jail for a string of petty crimes. By the end of my first year of law school, my mother sent me an article about a man from back home, with the same name, who was charged and convicted in a double homicide.

A glance at the artist's rendering of the courtroom scene—the man's hard stare, mouth pulled tight, chin up high to expose a broad neck that did not connect with the torso but meld with it, had convinced me that it was James. And then a sudden understanding. Though criminal law was not my focus, it was clear to me that this was the crime that would put him away for the rest of his natural life.

He was talking with the other brothers when a space cleared in the small crowd, and that's when he noticed me.

"My eyes have got to be foolin' me," he said. "Harold, is that you?"

A feeling of gratitude came over me at first. During the telling of the tale about Captain Michael's death, a couple of the men had begun to regard me with a mix of curiosity and derision, perhaps because I was in their midst and refused to make myself familiar.

I smiled at him, thankful that the recognition helped justify my presence. It was only an afterthought, the idea that I was talking to a man who wasn't supposed to have ever left prison except in a body bag.

Though I tried not to show it, I fretted for a moment, standing before him as he put out a hand to shake mine. Then he smiled and pointed back at the others with a glass bottle of coke to extend his reach.

"Y'all, check this out. This right here is a 1974 graduate of the University of Islam, top of the class. Go 'head on . . . Tell 'em what you made of yourself."

Not letting on that, as far as I was concerned, as of that morning the statement was only true in the past tense, I said, "I practice law."

"Ha ha!" James said. "See? That's what I'm talkin' 'bout! Take heed, young men. This right here is what years of clean livin' will get you."

I smirked at that, amused by the flattering portrayal of my life. The reactions that followed among the others present were tepid and filled with the disdain I sensed moments earlier.

Mr. CIA Conspiracy, the bullhorn among them, narrowed his eyes and raised his chin to get the measure of me.

"Alright, then," his young voice rasped. "Good to know you making a way out here, brother. Hopefully you've seen fit to bring some others of the brown persuasion up with you."

I always hated the use of that term "brother" at the end of a phrase. The clipped way it's said makes the word feel like a salve of politeness that is meant to disguise tensions boiling under the surface.

And that was all it was, more or less. The rest of them looked at me like I was a meteor landed to Earth and went back to their conversation. Then James and I turned to each other with the weight of forty years falling like an avalanche in the space between us.

"Time is something else," he began. "She leaves some of us alone and others"—he pointed to himself —"get torn to pieces. You looking good, man." He patted me on my side. I was a bit gray around the dome but still trim, with the few pounds I put on in my midsection hidden by my suit.

As he sat down, I registered that he was shorter than I recalled. James Shabazz wobbled, lowering himself, probably due to injury or just because he'd gained so much weight. He was bald except for a ring of salt-and-pepper hair that circled his crown like a half-eaten doughnut. It was a far cry from the muscle-bound young man I remembered. I was surprised that I had even recognized him. He still had a command about him and those cagey yellow eyes, which made clear that while the vessel had changed, the man inside was the same.

"Well I'll be damned," he started, "of all the people I thought I might see on a day like this, you just about the last one come to mind, I swear 'fore God . . . You gonna get that?"

My phone had started to buzz in my pants pocket, and I let it go on without answering. I waved my hand at the question like shooing flies.

"I thought it'd be a hundred years before you'd come back around here, not after the way they pushed you out."

The story of my departure from the Temple, "the reckoning" as my mother liked to call it, became part of the Temple lore in the months following—a playbook of what not to do when confronted by our leaders. She used that term like a time stamp, interspersed between complaints about why over the years I never came home to visit.

One week after my high school graduation, a hold-back meeting was convened. After the customary announcements and debate, just before Brother Minister dismissed the crowd, Captain Michael called my name. I walked slow and calm to the front and once I'd turned to face the audience, he stood from his seat and pointed a finger at me.

"The other day, one of the brothers saw you hanging 'round on the corner of Western and Thirtieth. They didn't say you was doing nothin' wrong, still at the spot selling papers, but Johnny and Thomas found their way into Lorraine's House of Wines and Spirits when they should have been at your side. You was the oldest out there!"

Then he turned to the crowd.

"One person going right don't mean nothing if his brothers is going left. He supposed to be the example, top of the class, but you ain't heeded the lessons you learned in this place."

The room was thick with all their indignation. A string of hollers went up in the crowd, gritty like they were ringside, and not inside a holy place.

I just stood there and took it, but his anger had contorted his face in such an exaggerated, cartoonish way that, despite an effort to suppress it, I couldn't help laughing.

A burst of air went through my nose and made a crackling sound like tires on gravel. My head leaned forward and I cupped my face to make it look like a sneeze, but the bemusement I felt made my eyes bulge, and it must have given me away. As I tried to regain my composure, I felt the razor strap on my back. Normally they saved this kind of punishment for school hours, so that only our peers would see us bent over and wailing from the blows, but this time he did it there, standing in front of everybody—child and parent alike, and no one said anything to convey that this kind of brutality on the body of a young Black man was wrong.

I shuddered at the memory.

"What bothered me at the time," I told James, "was that my

mother didn't stop him. After the fact she told me that I had embarrassed her, shown my contempt for the 'original woman' who bore me. She said I needed some kind of male discipline after my father died and that's why she allowed it, but the damage was done, and when it was time to leave the University of Islam, I never looked back.

"But my mother passed. It's been a few years, God rest her soul." I sighed and shrugged my shoulders. "Ever since then, you could say I been in a reevaluation space, trying to see the good the way I couldn't see it before."

"Nah, man," he came back, "wasn't nothing good about it. Them brothers spent all that time trying to convince us the white man was the devil, but I'mma tell you I ain't never seen nothing worse than what we went through, and I seen a whole lot."

"Then I guess the question bears repeating," I said, my suspicions on high alert. "What made you come out here today?"

James flinched like my words were a mosquito come buzzing in his ear.

"When it came to the likes of you," he said, "Brother Captain acted like he was doing a service, trying to keep you on the straight and narrow 'cause your pops wasn't 'round. But with me, I think he saw me as a knucklehead wannabe. Tore me up just for looking sideways, just 'cause he could. So it's real simple. I want to be able to say that for once in my life I stood over the man and he couldn't do nothing back to me."

We let the words hover in the air and took a moment to notice a kid, bouncing a ball alone on the court, and the eerie, off-meter song of an ice cream truck winding through the neighborhood.

"I'm not trying to get you riled up," I started, "but that's not what I mean."

"Some years ago," I said, trying find the right words, "I heard you were in prison serving life behind a murder."

James had just downed the rest of the Coca-Cola and choked a bit on the last gulp as I finished talking. It seemed like he was recalibrating, trying to find his balance, and made a face like he was in pain.

He spoke softly and I had to lean in to hear.

"You was lucky getting out when you did. If you stayed through the change, you don't know what would have happened. We was just talkin' 'bout Thomas, wasn't we? Did you know he died in jail over all that confusion, went all the way crazy at the end. We was so caught up on the Messenger, couldn't half of us do right without him giving the command."

James sighed. "So when we found out what happened in '75, my world broke apart. If it wasn't for that man, I would have left the Nation much sooner. I was already on the edge, and when he died, that's when I started to stray for real."

James told me that he fell in with some kids around the neighborhood and they broke into houses and stole cars. After about a year of that, he got picked up and sent to prison on a charge of forgery, but one or two bids, he said, was enough to convince him to iron out his life for good.

And that's where he stopped. As we sat, he looked out over the crowd of men and at the kid on the court, tapping the empty bottle against the palm of his hand, still waiting to be called inside for the washing.

"But there was an article in the paper my mom sent me," I said. "The guy had your name . . . I mean, he even looked like you."

James sucked his teeth and his expression, once forlorn, was suddenly as fierce as I recalled in the days when we were young.

"Of course I saw that paper. You don't think I saw it? People been telling me 'bout it ever since the story came out. Don't forget we talkin' 'bout a sketch artist. You know how they do. As far as they're concerned, we all look the same."

I wanted to come back with some kind of rebuttal, maybe prod him again about the name, but his furrowed expression seemed genuine and it stopped me from asking.

"You don't have to tell me. I know how it goes in the courts. Didn't mean to get you so upset," I said. I noticed a light breeze in the air and the afternoon sun brightening around us.

"Since you've gone ahead and corrected the record," I said, "tell me . . . what has kept you busy all these years? Ever get married? Have kids? How you earn your keep?"

James shook his head. "Never married. No kids, at least not that I know of." He paused.

"As far as work go"—he cocked his head—"I do a lot of different things. Some plumbing, some construction sometimes. But nowadays I ride the trains. Up and down the East Coast, sometimes I'll go inland, but mostly around these parts. I don't know why, man, I just don't like to stay in one place for too long. I get restless, you know."

And just as quickly as I convinced myself that his was a case of mistaken identity, my suspicions, once scattered, began reassembling.

"So when'd y'all get together?" James asked.

I was still fixated on the case of the two murdered women from years ago, and the unresolved matter of James's innocence, so the question threw me. He must have sensed my confusion, then pointed at the band I wore on my left hand. Immediately I started to fumble with the ring.

"Never mind, player. I got you, ha-ha!" He laughed. "You gone and sit up here talking to me about skipping out on a bid? Truth is . . . there's more than one way to be on lockdown. But I understand. Goody-two-shoes like you went and did things the right way. I respect you for that, man. I do. I always thought, you know . . . that you was the type to marry a vanilla girl. Never could see you with nobody chocolate, not the way you used to be."

"Is that what you thought?" I asked, and he nodded, waiting for an answer I wouldn't give.

"I wonder what Ms. Johnson would have thought of that," James said, calling my mother by the name she gave the kids when we were away from the Temple.

"I may be X over there, but at my house you will call me Ms. Johnson."

"She was a tough one," James said. "Everybody knew you had to come correct with her, and she was smart! I guess it runs in the family."

"I can agree with that," I said. Despite the things I may have felt back in the day, she always found a way to be right in the end. "That goes for Brother Captain, too," I went on. "After all this time, I guess I've just come to accept that, sometimes on some things he was just right. No, he wasn't perfect, but you know how it goes. And I guess that's the real reason I'm here. Plus, the news made me think of his wife. I can't imagine how she must be feeling."

For whatever reason, the comment made James suck his teeth.

"From what I hear," he whispered, "that woman probably happy as a thief on a crowded train."

I chuckled at that, trying to envision Sister Frieda—who would tell us in her tinkly little voice that we were descended from kings, and who gave us butterscotch candies from the large coin purse she always carried—as the kind of person to revel in her husband's death.

"Your phone, man," James said again, noting the third or fourth time it had buzzed since we'd been seated. "You sure it ain't nothing wrong?"

"Man, it's plenty wrong," I said, "but nothing I can help. From now on she's gonna have to figure it out all by herself."

I said this without thinking too much about my audience, and when I looked up, I noticed James glaring at me. That's when I tried to bring the conversation back.

"We had it pretty bad, no two ways about it," I said. "But you got to give it to the captain. You can't say he didn't know what we would be up against out here . . . And then I guess, I'm proud of him for standing on principle, for not seeking approval from white people. He never deviated from that."

I recounted the times Captain Michael would gloat about how, being an army man, the state he had hated would be forced to salute him in death.

"Not no more." James shook his head. "Looks like I got to be the one to tell you."

"After some kids around the way got killed by the police, the captain was talking at a whole bunch of rallies. He was speaking like he used to, saying the white man is the devil and all that stuff we heard coming up. He said that law enforcement officers were all in the Klan and that we needed to rise up and overthrow the government, or some shit like that. It was all over the city. I guess, with the bad press and whatnot, he got all of them honors stripped. It wasn't formal at first. Just a bunch of military types on the TV talking 'bout he was a disgrace, pledging they wouldn't work a funeral of a man like that. And it turned into one of those things . . . death by ten thousand tiny licks. All that commotion, then boom— it was done. His wife may get a flag if she's lucky."

Somehow, learning about this filled me with rage. This outcome unveiled a disregard of reality so profound that even I—someone who had suffered at the hands of this man—found it absurd. And the truth we all failed to acknowledge was this: organized Black hate was neither harmless nor trivial. James knew that; I knew that—but its large-scale victims were not white. They were we— the children of the Nation, and all our forebears who led us to their ranks.

That's when I started to feel impatient. In the course of the afternoon I had psyched myself up and decided that yes, I did want to help with the washing after all. The euphoria I felt about this decision began to wane as I started to consider just how long we'd been waiting to get inside.

As soon as the thought crossed my mind, I could make out a string of loud voices growing louder still, coming from inside the parlor. The front door swung open, and James and I had to move out of the way as a host of men spilled onto the sidewalk in the throes of a full-on argument. I couldn't quite understand them, until a high-pitched voice pealed over all the others.

"Enough! That's about enough!" the woman shouted. "I won't tolerate not one more minute of all of this back-and-forth."

The woman wore a knee-length black dress, and had shoulder-length, curly blond hair. She was tall with fair skin and green, penetrating eyes that made her look even angrier.

"I want to thank you all for coming out, but unfortunately there will be no washing today or any other day, for that matter."

The crowd gasped. James and I stood to get a better view as some of the young men gathered around her.

"But, ma'am," one of them said. "Brother Captain was a Muslim. This is what he would have wanted."

The Imam added, "It's an obligation of the faith. Please, ma'am. Try and think of his children."

That made the woman's eyes fill with rage before she screamed at the Imam.

"I am the wife!" she said, spacing out each word. "Mike chose me! It's my right to decide what to do with his remains. Why is it so hard for you to get that through your head?" She poked at her ear over and over like pressing a defective elevator button.

I was shocked but I couldn't focus on the issue at hand, as I'd become aware of a man in the background in a white lab coat. He had cocked his left hand to fidget with the cuff link on the right, and was staring at me. His eyes and entire face disturbed me; it was filled with sick fascination, a Don Cornelius–type of stare. I wondered if by his glance he was imagining me as a client laid out on the cooling board. Perhaps he was envisioning my insides, wondering just where along the neck he might choose to bleed me, to fill me with formaldehyde, or what shade of brown would be necessary to erase the gray hue of death from my skin.

"I'm sorry to have wasted all of your time," the woman went on. "My husband will be buried in accordance with my own faith tradition. The funeral services will be held one week from today at the Trinity Episcopal Church on Larchmont and Fifth Avenue. If you wish to come pay your respects, please give me your contact details and I will send further information. *That* is my final decision."

That's when the scene collapsed into a shouting match. When the woman said, "Back the hell up or I'm going to call the cops," the crowd hushed and shifted into several smaller conversations before all the men scattered. I wondered what my mother would think of this—how she would feel to know that the man she let teach her son about respect for the "original" woman had divorced his wife of many decades and, in the final years of his life, gone on to marry someone who was neither Black nor a Muslim.

"Hey, man, I'm 'bout to go," James said. "I ain't trying to get caught up in this."

He pulled out a pen and a piece of paper and scribbled down a phone number.

Just as he was about to hand it to me, he jerked the leaflet away again and gave me a sly look.

"You don't take me for a fool, do you?" he said. "I mean, I didn't go to MIT or nothing like that, but I know a con when I see one going down, player."

A lump formed in my throat and I could feel the *thud thud thud* of blood pulsing in my temples.

"Try to put one over on any of these boneheads if you want," he said, "but I know what you're up to."

I was getting ready to ask him, in language I knew he'd understand, just who the fuck he thought he was talking to, but he interrupted me.

"Don't do it," he said. "Whatever the problem, she was your choice. You want to throw all you got away so you can end up like Brother Captain? Just think about it."

I LEFT SHORTLY thereafter. I was shaken by the events of the day and totally creeped out by Don Cornelius. I didn't want to stick around a whole week for the ceremony; or have to watch Sister Frieda sit on the back pew of an organ-filled sanctuary while some preacher spoke over the body of a person they'd never known, who never believed in the Father, Son, or Holy Spirit.

I climbed into my car, my clothes smelling of the city, sweat, and melted chocolate, my stomach grumbling for food. I hit the highway, intent to make a stop at the Dairy Queen before I got myself in gear to go back home. I finally looked at my phone and found no less than fifteen missed call notifications from Vanessa. I felt a tug of something on seeing them, but I wasn't sure which side of my thinking was pulling harder—the side that said by heading home I was doing the right thing, or the side that said the home I claimed up North was never really mine in the first place, too much flash and not enough soul. Driving up to the exit, I thought about what my explanation would be for having left so early and come back so late. I thought of what it would take to break the coldness that would hover for a period of days before things went back to normal, thought of the narrow values that had contented me for so long in my old life and that I would need to readopt to try and be happy there again. I saw the northbound traffic pointing to a dark corner of sky, and the sight of it filled me with dread. Without thinking, I made a U-turn and found a path back onto the open road headed southwest. The engine shifted gears automatically as I reared up the hill onto a stretch of road so steep it erased all sight lines and the earth itself seemed to fall away. The brightness filled my eyes and I stared into it, willing myself not to flinch from the glare. I cracked the window, tugged the band off my finger, and tossed it in the median, and then I pressed harder on the gas.

WOMAN IN NIQAB

The day after my return home from Egypt I sat with my mother and her sister Linda, telling them about my time over there. I mentioned things I thought they wanted to hear. The Sphinx, I told them, wasn't as big as it looked in the glossy magazines. Compared to the great pyramids on the far side of Giza, it was kind of petite with round, nubile features. The atmosphere was light. Except for prayer times when the adhan would drift up from a thousand minarets and hover in midair like a chorus of ghosts, the cities were filled with happy sounds—children laughing in the streets, the striking of hand drums, and the rhythmic clapping of distant celebrations. All of it was covered in a haze of golden dust that primed everything for memory like the sepia tinge of old photographs.

We were in the Temple after the Friday prayer. We sat at the end of a long table in the downstairs multipurpose room eating the roast beef, stewed cabbage, and apple cobbler the kitchen sisters worked all morning to prepare. My mom and aunt ate their food as I went on, looking up occasionally to show they weren't ignoring me.

"That all sounds very interesting, Imani," Aunt Linda said, "but I want to know the real story . . . like that right there." She pointed a plastic fork at my uncovered hair. "Is that something you picked up while you were in Cairo?"

It was an interesting question coming from her. Temple women had certain standards of dress that my aunt barely fit. She had pretenses to good taste, though her clothes always made her look like a Midwestern stage mom. Her version of covering involved stuffing her dyed blond hair into a bedazzled baseball cap, which she wore along with shimmery tracksuits. Her lips were always painted fire-engine-red—a big taboo—and she never removed the polish from her claw-length nails at prayer times, as was the custom. My mother played by the rules, donning West African head wraps and floor-length skirts under loose-fitting tunics. It might have been something to quarrel over, but Aunt Linda was a full decade older than her and, as with most things between them, the younger rarely said a contrary word.

The truth was that Aunt Linda didn't expect real answers when she asked kids questions, and while I was seventeen—a rising senior in high school and not quite a child anymore—I knew my aunt wouldn't care about my reasons. My mind was made up—I was determined to stop covering and there wasn't anything she or my mom could do about it.

I sort of shrugged, took a bite of cabbage, and scanned the room. The Temple women sat at the other tables, some coddling infants, while others walked around in long, delicate fabrics of colors, brilliant as the striped shades of test-screen TV. The men traded "Salaams" in jeans and T-shirts with kaffiyehs draped at their necks, while the city professionals talked business in suits and Jinnah caps. Food smells blended harmoniously with the sweet scent of musk wafting up from incense burning in the Temple bookstore. It was the usual parade of characters, though not so usual beyond the Temple walls, and I marveled at it—so much so that for a moment I could almost forget the weight of air at our end of the table.

My mother was silent. She sat, shaking her head, looking from me back to the sickle cell anemia pamphlet she was pretending to read. She'd been acting strange since the previous afternoon when, driving up to the airport arrivals hall, she found me standing on the curb with my hair braided into two long plaits at the sides of my face—the first time since puberty that I'd ever been outside without a headscarf.

On the drive home from the airport she talked mostly about my father, whom neither of us had seen or heard from for a solid month before my departure. Only days before my return home she started making plans to meet with a lawyer. "You know he still thinks I'm totally clueless about everything," she said, "but as they say, whatever's done in darkness always comes to light."

SHE DIDN'T FIGHT me too hard on the hair stuff the first night; my mother had been too preoccupied with the state of her marriage for that, but it was the constant staring of the Temple folk that Friday at my uncovered hair—particularly by Imam Saleem (the last good man on earth as far as she was concerned)—that pushed her over the edge.

It placed my aunt in the unusual position of mediator between us.

"That's just what you get for sending her to that lily-white school out in Grantville. You should have put her in the Clara Muhammad system, but no . . . Does Dawud know about this?" Aunt Linda asked, and my mother shook her head.

"He has yet to call and even acknowledge that his daughter has made it back to America," my mother said, eyes still glued to the pamphlet.

"You may have an easy time with your mom and me, but wait until he sees you. He's going to lose his mind." Over a period of years I watched my father morph into someone I couldn't recognize. He loved music, and could talk for hours about Coltrane, Monk, and

Charlie Parker. "With Monk," he would say, "people dogged his technique, but they weren't looking at the essence of what he was doing. You don't need to prove nothing to no one when you've got the essence down pat."

After a while his vinyl album collection began to disappear. His conversation, once full of reflections, turned into lecturing. He started wearing a thobe every day, then grew a full beard and dyed it orange. And in the months before he left home, my father stopped coming to Temple all together, preferring the immigrant spaces where, as he liked to say, traditions were more pure and closer to the true source of the religion.

"He doesn't want to see me." I blurted out the words and Aunt Linda peered at me as if longing for an explanation, though she stopped short of asking.

Then she went on to talk about . . . who knows what? I saw her mouth move and her wagging an index finger in my direction, though whatever followed blurred into a muddle of shadow and sound.

✳

I TRAVELED WITH the Luqmans—a Temple family my parents were close to before Mr. Luqman found a new job and moved them all to Philadelphia. When she heard about our situation, Mrs. Luqman begged that I come along with her and her two daughters, telling my mom it would help get my mind off things.

We were reunited in JFK's international terminal where our flights connected East. I remembered Mrs. Luqman just as she appeared, broad shouldered and stately, like Leontyne Price. She wore a long black dress, a tightly wound turban, and large pearl clip-ons. She held me close on first contact—the way people do when comforting the bereaved. I shook hands with her daughters— Sumayyah, just a toddler when I last saw her, was now eight years old and bubbly; and Amatullah, who was my age, though more subdued than I recalled. She stood to greet me at her mother's command, her eyes down cast, then plopped immediately back into her seat. Mrs. Luqman peered at Amatullah, though she resumed skimming a copy of *Vogue* magazine, lifting the pages so high that she couldn't see her mother's face.

"I know you're going to simply love this life-changing trip," Mrs. Luqman said, loud enough for her daughter to hear. "From everything your mom says, you're a most deserving girl."

On the plane ride over Mrs. Luqman said, the treble in her voice worn off by drowsiness, "I'm not sure if your mom has told you, but a lot of what you're going to hear about Egypt is going to be totally wrong. They're going to tell you everything but the truth. Everything over there was built by Black people. Like the whole world, they're just ashamed of their African roots, that's all."

When we landed in Cairo she said, "Of course they would call this place the Heliopolis Airport. If it came from Greece, it must be something to hold on to."

Sumayyah bobbed ahead of us, practicing the Bangles' "Walk Like an Egyptian" dance, completely unaware of her mother, while Amatullah dragged her luggage along, hearing everything but saying nothing.

This is Cairo.

Our tour guide was Mr. Abdel Messeh—a slender man with a sunny disposition who wore a gold crucifix around his neck. He greeted us with a cheerful "Salaam," and as we ventured into the city, he pointed out all the interesting things we saw along the way. He spent most of his time answering Sumayyah's questions, talking about the walled-off City of the Dead and helping her decipher Arabic numerals. "The same as in English if you tilt your head," he said.

When we arrived at our first place of residence in Ma'adi, we were greeted by a large group of children. They had been playing on the street, though when our tour van pulled up to the apartment building, they stopped their games and crowded near the door.

They looked at us blankly for a moment before one little girl, who was Sumayyah's height, waved at us. We all smiled at them and immediately they all smiled back. Another girl who was slightly older-looking approached Sumayyah as if inviting her into their game, before a tall man in a white turban and long gray thobe emerged from the building, making the children scatter.

Mr. Abdel Messeh told us that he was the manager of the building. "Call him *boab*, always *boab*. If you need anything at all while I am away, please let him know."

The boab lived on the first floor with his children and his wife, Khadijah, who came up morning and night to prepare our meals.

The flat was opulent in a way that one couldn't gather from the façade. It had marble floors throughout, with high ceilings and two large bedrooms. I assumed Mrs. Luqman would mention something about the European look of the place, though she said nothing at all about it. Instead she inspected the flat, smiling broadly. "This is what a dollar gets you outside the U.S. of A.!"

"I should apologize for my mom," Amatullah opened up in our shared room. "I try to tell her how ridiculous she sounds, but she's too stubborn to listen."

I told her it didn't bother me, that I was just happy to be away from home doing something other than thinking about my parents.

Amatullah nodded mournfully and paused from unpacking her things. Then she perked up. "I wonder if, in a weird way," she said, "you feel free. I mean, without your father around telling you what to do all the time."

She couldn't know the ways I vacillated between pure rage and the hope that somehow my parents might save what they had built together. Amatullah still had a mom and a dad living under the same roof and could persist under the adolescent notion that she might be better off if the people who secured her life simply weren't there. "No," I said. "I can't say it feels that way."

Amatullah looked at me like I misunderstood. She riffled through her luggage and lifted a large pile of scarves that had been folded into neat little squares. "I mean free from *this*," she said, shaking the scarves until they lost their form and fell messily onto the bed.

I didn't respond and she filled the emptiness, sitting on the bed, looking at her hands.

"I can't wait to go to college," she said. "I'm going to move so far away from home that my parents will never even dream of coming to visit. They're so full of it."

Just then we were called to dinner. I had time enough to unpack some of my things, wash up, and consider that Amatullah was like the other girls I knew, who as soon as they left home abandoned everything connecting them to the Temple. That, I was sure, was someone I would never become.

This is Cairo.

Khadijah prepared a lavish meal for our arrival. She stood nearby as we ate, laughing heartily when Sumayyah turned away her portion of ful medames, and blushing when she went back for second and third helpings of the excellent koshari.

She asked us, "Are you family from Egypt? You grandmother? Grandfather?" All of us were cinnamon in tone and looked like the people we'd seen. Maybe it was reasonable to assume we might be from the region, though I knew better than to answer.

Mrs. Luqman was quick to say, "Yes, we are Egyptian. We are all descended from the people of ancient Kemet, Hotep!" She made a big circle with her arms like holding all of Black America and Egypt inside.

Khadijah laughed, totally oblivious to her meaning, which made Amatullah cover her mouth to chuckle.

I pointed at the baladi breadbasket, which we'd emptied within minutes of sitting down to eat.

Khadijah sent me downstairs to the boab who, when I showed him the basket, walked with me the short distance from our building to the local baker's shop.

WE STOOD THERE waiting for the artisan to complete our order, when a little boy with skin like night approached me from behind.

"Hello, mum," he said in perfect English, a hand outstretched, his eyes waxing like tiny moons. I really liked Egypt though I would never claim it as my own. In that moment with the boy I felt a strange connection, a kind of instantaneous identification; the sort of familiarity that the Temple folk spoke about after visits to West Africa.

I reached into my purse to grab a few coins, when the boab moved in front of me. He forcefully shooed the boy away and sent him running down the street. The boab frowned as he watched him go. He muttered a string of words; one sounding like "Sudani" and then something else said in scathing Arabic that I didn't understand. He shook an angry fist in the air until the boy disappeared around a corner.

THIS, TOO (I learned), is Cairo.

✳

A BOOMING VOICE from the foot of the stairs made all the Temple folk turn away from their chatter. It was Brother Mustafa. He wore inch-thick glasses that made his eyes look like tiny pebbles. In a voice raspy from years of selling T-shirts on the street, he announced that the shurah meeting would be starting in a few minutes. Anyone concerned with fundraising or helping to organize the Temple's 12-step outreach program was encouraged to come. A small trail of people followed him from behind, but most stayed and the room returned to a hum of conversation. As he spoke, I scanned the room looking for Sister Abdul-Mubarak, one of the Temple seniors who approached me weeks before when she had learned about my trip. She told me that she'd been on the pilgrimage but always wanted to go to Cairo. I bought her a scarab jewelry box from the Khan el-Khalili souk. I carried it with me to Temple that Friday and was hoping she would appear so I could give it to her and see her smile in gratitude.

"I remember the Luqmans," Aunt Linda said, through chews of gravy-dipped roast beef. "I know they are decent people, but was Mrs. Luqman too strict? Sometimes when parents are too strict, the children go in the wrong direction."

Mom and I traded a brief glance. I knew in the moment that, like me, she was thinking of Aunt Linda's sons—my cousins Saeed and Kareem. I thought of the times years back when she would chase them around the house with a leather strap when they punctured her waterbed or tore strands from the beaded curtains hung at the mouth of her kitchen. It had been years since I'd seen them. Each time I begged my mother to let me visit my cousins, she said that where they were was no place a girl like me should ever go. I looked again at my aunt, though her glance did not betray any sense of irony.

"You know what I read the other day?" Aunt Linda went on. "A girl—twenty years old—in school here in the city was out running with some girlfriends one night and got assaulted right in the middle of the street. Yes, child! Her girlfriends were in sweatpants. She was the only one in a tank top and biking shorts. You see that? Dress like that out here and you'll pay for it one way or another."

A woman in full niqab entered the multipurpose room from upstairs. I watched as she walked around, never settling in any of the chairs. She didn't stand in line to wait for food. She moved from corner to corner of the room, then disappeared behind the curtain to the women's bathroom.

"Excuse me." Aunt Linda tapped me on the shoulder. "Can I distract you for a minute? What would you tell that girl who was assaulted? Is there something she could have done to avoid that situation?"

"What about the guy that assaulted her," I said, though I was still thinking of the woman. "Isn't it his fault?"

"What your aunt is trying to say," my mother interjected, "is that hijab is a protection for you."

Then Aunt Linda said, "Hijab says to a bad man, 'This girl's off-limits.'"

"But what about when it doesn't?" I asked.

My mother looked at me confused, though Aunt Linda wore an expression like she'd been called out of her name. She then proceeded to rattle off a list of things she'd do if her kids ever "talked back" to her, which began with "they'd be the youngest patients up at Dentures Direct because I would have knocked the teeth right out their mouths . . ."

Just then the Imam's wife walked by. Aunt Linda noticed and her expression changed from a snarl to a smile. She pursed her mouth and nodded. "I'm doing fine, sister. I'm just fine. You know . . . just trying to stay on the straight path, Insha-Allah!"

✳

THE DAY BEFORE we caught the train headed up the river delta toward Alexandria, Mr. Abdel Messeh moved us from Ma'adi to an apartment in Zamalek, which was closer to the railway station. The new place was on a tree-lined street with large apartment buildings that seemed plucked straight out of Paris. Moving into that night's dwelling was unremarkable, except that seconds after disembarking the van, a woman in a full covering appeared at some distance down the road—a woman who, in the aftermath, none of the Luqmans claimed to have seen.

The others lugged their bags into the marbled foyer of our temporary residence as I stood and watched her in silence. The sight of her standing in the street puzzled me. All of my exposure to women in niqab taught me that they were always tended to; that you'd never find such a woman in public without a male to accompany her. They were the aristocrats of the Arab world who would never dare spend time in public and suffer the indecency of being seen by everyday people. And yet there she was, a hand clutching a purse at her side, her head ticking hurriedly back and forth.

A car disturbed the quiet, vrooming past me in the direction of the shrouded woman. It stopped before her. I saw her duck into the vehicle and watched the car pull off before she even had a chance to close the door.

I HAVE TRIED to make sense of what I saw that afternoon and have constantly returned to the same conclusion—but no, it couldn't be. That was fantasy—just the sort of thing the Temple folk would call a perversion of reality. She was probably an extremely pious woman. More than likely that was her husband, a brother, or an uncle just swinging by to pick her up, except that his driving was hurried, with a bit of swerving and lots of jerky stops and starts. I looked again down the road, just as Mrs. Luqman called me inside, but the car was gone as if it had been a desert apparition—there, and suddenly not there.

We stayed in Alexandria for only two days before our trip to Luxor, and got to see the rebuilt library, eat fried squid, and watch the cold Mediterranean waters crash onto the rocky shoreline. The city was sparse with people, and Mrs. Luqman allowed me a bit more freedom than usual. I explored the side streets and the markets and I took tons of pictures.

Back at the hotel I sat on the bed, scrolling through the frames, when Amatullah came into the room to say that someone was on the phone for me.

"Hey, baby girl." It was my father. "It's been a long time since I'd heard from you, so I had to track you down. I saw Brother Luqman, who came to town the other day and said my baby was in Egypt. He gave me the number to the hotel. I figure I'd try calling since I haven't heard a peep." I should have felt upset at this—how was it my obligation to reach out to him?—but I let his voice wash over me, appreciating the notes of concern. "How are you enjoying Egypt?" I told him everything was fine. I told him I missed him and wondered when he was coming home.

"I'm just glad you're having fun," he redirected. "That's all I want for you. You know, I don't know what you heard, but I have a feeling there's a lot of misinformation going on about why your mother and I are having problems these days. I wanted you to know that I personally don't want to end the marriage, your mother does. I've just been growing in my deen, and that's where she and I disagree."

"Mom is in the deen too," I said. I immediately regretted the smallness in my voice. Then I asked him, "Dad, have you been talking to another woman?"

The phone seemed to go dead for an instant. I heard him sigh.

"Imani, it's not that simple. Let me explain because it's difficult for a young person to understand. As a man, this deen gives us certain . . . rights and responsibilities. First, there's nothing incorrect going on between me and this woman."

I felt the receiver slip as my hand grew sweaty.

"She's a real believer, very deep in the deen. She knows three juz of Quran and makes all of her prayers on time. Honestly, I think you would like her."

I asked him if I knew her.

"Maybe, but I don't think so," he said. "She wears a full covering, so if you've seen her you probably wouldn't know it."

And then I lost it.

"I can't believe," I said, "that you would call me after a month of not reaching out, just so I could co-sign your affair. And that woman!" I choked up. "You think I'm so impressed that she wears niqab? Don't you know that prostitutes wear the veil over here?"

I said this emphatically and he was silent. I went on, talking about Mom and her suffering before I was interrupted by the male voice of an automated Telecom Egypt phone operator saying that my call had been disconnected. No one could coax me out of the room that night, not after what my father did, and not after I'd cursed him on the basis of something I didn't know to be absolutely true.

The next day I tried to go back to normal, covering my hair for the rest of my time away, but the cloth always shifted out of place. I waited for the Luqmans to make their connection in New York, and when they disappeared down the boarding dock, I removed the scarf in a single tug and told myself it would be forever.

*

AUNT LINDA AND my mother were off on a tangent when Sister Abdul-Mubarak appeared at the Temple entryway, headed for the dinner line. They didn't notice me smile and wave at her. They didn't see her look back at me smiling, nor did they see her smile turn into a squint, then a frown. She was with a group of pioneer sisters—women who lived in that space since the days of Malcolm, who were present for the breaking of the ground beneath our feet. I knew then that she would not draw close enough to say hello, much less accept the gift.

I COULDN'T FINISH the apple cobbler. I reached for one of the braids and immediately moved my hand away upon feeling it. How strange: the way something so plain and unassuming as a braid could feel so unseemly. Just then the woman in niqab reemerged from the bathroom. I stared at her, intent to make out her features through the small patch that exposed her eyes. We traded glances for a prolonged instant before she exited the building through the Temple front door.

"But what are you going to do about people who think you're, you know, out there?" Aunt Linda said. I heard the screeching of a folding chair in a far corner and the mute sounds of shoes on linoleum. "No offense, Imani," she said to me, "you're young and you're curious, but Sheila, you're not just going to let her go out with people thinking she's a bad woman."

Mom shifted in her seat. She put the pamphlet down and peered at Aunt Linda as if she were looking at something far away.

"Your mother's not going to tell you this, but you're going to be walking around one day and it's not going to matter that you've been to Cairo or Alexandria or to the moon and back. Those people are going to think, 'Who would let their daughter be so loose?'"

"Just what are you saying about my child?" my mother said, her voice curled with newborn incredulity. "I know you're not calling her a—"

"Now don't go putting words in my mouth, Sheila," Aunt Linda interrupted; her voice shook in a way I'd never heard before. "You know I would never speak an insulting word to my own flesh and blood!" They whispered, but in whispering, their words came out hissing and sharp. I looked around, hoping that no one nearby would sense what was really happening.

"Get your things," Mom told me. She grabbed her purse and turned again to her sister. By then there were a few eyes on us. Aunt Linda lowered the bill of her cap until it pointed to the ground.

"If you are so worried about what these kids are up to these days, you should start with your own. Maybe then they would be out here with the rest of us and not down in Lorton. Come on, Imani." My mother started for the door. I followed her, but not before an even deeper shame came over me. I looked back to see Aunt Linda hunched over her cobbler, staring into it, poking the contents with her fork like she was searching for an answer.

The drive home was mostly quiet. There was only the sound of the engine and tires on asphalt and the rasp of my own fingers scratching the side of the scarab jewelry box. The rosy light of dusk illuminated the sky. It made me think of the end of summer. There were four more weeks of vacation before the start of my senior year of high school, and yet I was already missing fireflies and eight o'clock sunsets.

"Penny for your thoughts." My mother's voice was soft, coaxing.

I told her I was sorry. That I felt like I had triggered a falling-out between her and her sister.

"Girl?!" She was teasingly flippant. "We'll be back to normal by midweek. Don't you even worry about that. After all the things your aunt has said and done, she should be relieved I didn't really give her a piece of my mind."

The tightness in my shoulders, which I didn't know was there, seemed to release.

"I changed my mind," I said. "I'm going to start covering again."

My mom wrinkled her nose. "Are you doing this for me? I'm not going to force you. The last thing I want is for you to hate me."

"Only at the Temple," I said. "I just don't think that I can cover outside anymore."

We passed beyond the city limits and approached a grove of trees that always signaled the nearness of home. The pink residue of day sped farther toward the horizon and all else turned a royal azure. Venus and a crescent moon appeared in the eastern sky. "Honey, I think I will learn to be okay with this choice. I should have defended you, but I know that covering is a protection. I know it is. I guess the only thing I don't quite understand is, what happened?"

That's when I looked to my mother, took a deep breath, and began to tell her everything.

WHO'S DOWN?

Back in the days when my dad (budding freedom fighter that he was) decided he needed a diet to match his far-out politics, he made the choice to become a vegetarian. He gathered the whole family and made an announcement about it like it was some great big event. Everyone cheered him and so did I, but I saw his designs coming undone at the inception. He quickly went off all the hippie spots—places like Green Valley Grocers and the Smiling Buddha— saying that their staff members were always uncomfortable at the sight of "a brother" hanging around all that produce. "Like Black men don't care about having clean arteries," he said. After a final visit to another place called Cafe Pangaea, he told us about a confrontation he had with a female patron. She had approached him to say he hadn't put the bamboo fork he used to eat a tofu curry into the right recycling bin. "That's when I told her," Dad said, "when you're ready to talk about the Native American genocide and slavery, then come bothering me about some damn cutlery."

About a month into his walk on the healthy side of life, he told me about a new place he recently visited called Lotus on the Nile. It was run by a group of Black Hebrews he'd met long before his lifestyle change—all vegetarian by dictate of faith. It was a grocery store, take-out spot, and a restaurant all in one, with remixed soul-food favorites served hot. I was a rising high school sophomore with a kick-ass metabolism, totally in love with burgers, fries, and milkshakes. I couldn't see myself on the veggie kick like my dad, but I'd decided that going with him might be the best way for me to sample his new lifestyle. "It's a real nice place; you'll like it," Dad said. "Plus, they are committed to the struggle. They know what's going on out here and they found a genius way to fight on our behalf, feeding good food to the people to help us survive."

The shop was located in an old strip mall nestled between a massive beauty supply store and a church called the Alpha and Omega Apostolic Christian Outreach Ministries, Inc. We swung open the door to a scene of patrons milling about and workers locked in rhythm, filling orders for the lunch hour crowd, the savory aroma of southern foods greeting us as we entered. The women among them looked like us. They wore hair wraps and long dresses as they lifted heavy trays of food onto steaming chafing dishes. The men wore what appeared like oversized white kufis, as they tidied display tables piled high with goods—marking the fresh breads, pecan tarts, sweet potato pies, dehydrated kale chips, and bags of dried pulses and grains with price stickers shaped like the Star of David.

One of them paused from dusting a display of ten different kinds of liquid castile soap to greet us.

"Salaam Alaikum!" Dad said back to him with a broad smile. Immediately I made a face at him, and he made one right back at me, saying, "What's the matter?"

"Dad!" I whispered. "What if they get offended when you say that to them?"

"First of all," Dad said, " 'Salaam' means 'peace.' And the other thing is, when you look at the big picture, whatever our religion, we're all brothers. It's all love, baby girl."

Dad and I both grabbed trays and waited in the long serving line. When it was his turn, a woman with a nose ring and several gold-capped teeth made him a plate of mashed potatoes, steamed broccoli, a big slice of veggie loaf with a single ladleful of mushroom gravy on the side. I ordered the collard greens, the vegan mac and cheese, a small bowl of lentil soup, and just to see how it measured up, a big slice of their sweet potato pie.

We sat in an adjacent lounge where there were dining tables arranged around a large stage lined with adverts of poetry readings, lectures, and homemade herbal remedies. They were posted under a wall-mounted TV that droned in the background, playing the day's news. Cheezing like he owned the place, Dad looked around between each forkful.

"Something I regret in life," he began, "is that you and your siblings never got to see Shabazz Bakery in its heyday. I mean, it was still open when y'all was little, but you were too small to remember. Boy, that was something right there.

"It was a clean-cut, no-nonsense operation. Them brothers made the most delicious food—cream cheese danish, crullers with icing, and the best damn navy bean pie you ever had in your life. Not the kind they make nowadays with all that nasty custard inside.

"I used to make deliveries for them and work the cleanup crew after school when I was coming up. And they paid me every Friday, right on time. It wasn't a whole lot—just enough to do the little bit that I wanted, like going to the movies. All of them were able to raise families from their work in there, and that wasn't no small thing. Some of them brothers spent time in the joint. It's hard getting a good paying job when you got a criminal past, but they were able to make it happen.

"No matter what anybody says about the Messenger—talking 'bout he was a two-timing so-and-so or a false prophet—he did a good thing for Black people. He taught us self-reliance, self-respect,

AND how to make a product so good that people keep coming back for more," he said, taking another bite of his veggie loaf.

One of the waiters was making the rounds, going from table to table to chat with the customers, when a news report flashed across the TV screen. Dad and I both stopped to watch. He shook his head and folded his arms at the chyron:

GAZA IN TURMOIL: 1 ISRAELI, 20 HAMAS MILITANTS DEAD

The images were awful. There were scenes of young men, bent over and bloodied, laid out on stretchers, being carried through chaotic streets in search of medical care, women crying hysterically over the blue-faced corpses of their children, and huge crowds of men with their fists raised as they voiced their anger in chants, their eyes glued to the camera lens. A map of Israel then appeared on-screen to show where a few recent bombings had occurred, with the Palestinian Territories highlighted in yellow—the West Bank looking like a kidney-shaped hunk of Swiss cheese. That's when the waiter made it to our table to ask how we were doing.

"Everything is just fine, thank you, brother," Dad said, returning his gaze, albeit briefly, to the screen. He sucked his teeth.

"It's a shame what they're doing to those people," he said. "Running them out of house and home. I mean, some of them are probably descended from the first followers of Jesus. Where are those folks supposed to go?"

The waiter bent down to hear him better, though after Dad spoke, he stood ramrod straight.

"Something wrong?" Dad said to the waiter.

The young man hesitated, but finally he said with resolve, "That land is our land. It belongs to the Israelite people. You've probably never been over there and seen how they behave. We are trying to make a better life for everyone, and they just don't understand."

I could tell Dad was stunned. Whenever I said anything he

thought ridiculous, like the time, many years before, I flirted with the flat Earth hypothesis, he would go to great lengths until I changed my mind. Instead of showing anger, he became very inquisitive and eager to listen, asking the waiter, "So you've been over there, have you?"

"Yes, sir," the waiter said. "Actually, my family lives there most of the year on a kibbutz. We come here in the summers to help manage the shop and visit relatives."

He went on to talk about his pride at having just completed military service after finishing a business degree at the University of Tel Aviv.

"I've been on the front lines fighting for our country and I will continue to defend Israel until the day that I die."

Like a psychotherapist trying to understand the intricate thought patterns of a new patient, Dad folded his hands in front of him and nodded.

"And what do you have to say to the point about the Palestinian people having lived on that land prior to 1947?"

To that, the young man closed his eyes and recited:

"And Hashem said, I have surely seen the oni ami, which are in Mitzrayim, and have heard their cry by reason of their nogeism, for I know their makhovim; and I am come down to deliver them out of yad Mitzrayim, and to bring them up out of that land to an eretz tovah, a spacious land of milk and honey; unto the place of the Kena'ani, and the Chitti, and the Emori, and the Perizzi, and the Chivi, and the Yevusi."

Probably because not he, nor I, had any idea what the young man had just said, Dad made no reply. The two of them just looked at each other determined-like, the way we used to do in grade school when my friends and I got tired of playing spades at the lunch table and decided to amuse ourselves in a staring contest.

After a beat, the young man unlocked eyes with my father.

"Sarah!" the waiter called out, turning to an older woman who had been wiping down the empty tables with greenish, soapy water on the opposite side of the room. She squinted, pushing her glasses up the bridge of her nose to see what was the matter.

"Would you mind changing the channel please, ma'am?" he asked.

"Yes, sir," she replied. She walked to the stage as the waiter left our table without so much as a "thank you" or "goodbye." The broadcast went black of an instant with the last frame—a split screen of two talking heads, mouths open, their faces contorted by anger to the point of ghoulish exaggeration—searing itself into my memory.

A moment later the TV flashed to life again. On what looked like the peak of a sand dune, a collective of kufi-clad musicians in blue and white kaftans were animated mid-gesture, bouncing happily to the music they made. They strummed guitar, struck tambourines, and raised them to the sky in praise. One of the men, the only one in shades on that summery day, played a sassy riff on the saxophone. He tilted the horn up and down to the rhythm like a rearing horse, while everyone else sang the hook of the song:

"I'm finding a way back to Zion/ I'm finding a way back home. I'm finding a way back to Zion/ To the place where I belong . . ."

WITH HIS PLATE half-full, he slid the Kangol hat back onto his head and told me, "Honey, it's time for us to go."

When he opened the door on the passenger side of the car for me, I knew something was up with my dad. It was a gentlemanly prelude to a string of curses and insults he muttered at the steering wheel on the way home.

"What in the hell was that?" he said, and "Can you believe this foolishness? . . . Talk about somebody lost in the sauce . . . I mean, that kid is out in the stratosphere, the twilight zone, even . . . I've never seen how *they* behave? What kind of ignorant somebody comes out the mouth saying something like that? If it wasn't for our people fighting against that foolishness in this country, brother-man wouldn't have the freedom to take his butt overseas where he can pretend to be something that he ain't . . . Chump! . . . Then he gonna say that's our land . . . Almost took me out when he said that mess . . ."

I nodded, offering the occasional "mm-hmm" so that Dad could feel I was listening. My mind, however, was drifting to other thoughts.

Once when we were smaller, Dad made my siblings and me listen to one of the last Saviours' Day speeches ever to be delivered by the Messenger.

". . . Don't he know when they say 'our land,' they don't mean a land for Black people? . . ."

In the speech, the Messenger talked about the need for the Black man to seize opportunity in the wilderness of North America.

". . . I mean . . . What about the Ethiopians? They've been Jewish for centuries . . ."

Despite the oppression of the Black man, the Messenger said it was still possible for him to claim his rightful place as an owner of American soil.

". . . They got more of a claim to be there than members of some cult that fooled the Israeli government into believing they were real Jews . . ."

A piece of the dream could be ours, the Messenger said. After all, he went on, the Native American "wasn't doing nothing but hunting and fishing" in this open country—not maximizing its potential for commerce and wealth creation. That was one of his final addresses—telling all the constituents of the Nation they had the potential to be masters on the land, of a semblance but not identical to the ones our forebears had known in slavery.

"... Come to think of it ... I knew a woman ... Told me she met the founder of the Hebrew Israelites himself ... Back in those days he was chasing women all over the South Side of Chicago ... Now people talk about the man like he's divine—"

"But why do you care so much?" I interrupted my father. "You know," I continued, "there was an article a couple weeks ago in *Time* magazine saying stress impacts health outcomes for Black people worse than alcohol, cigarettes, and butter combined."

That made Dad quiet down and take a breath, which surprised me because he'd always been such a pro at spotting my lies. Dad sat there in the driver's seat nodding, grasping his chin with his free hand, mulling over what I'd said, and I suppose it was the magazine reference that made me sound halfway credible.

Even though I suspected it was for the best, I felt bad about manipulating my father, and in that moment I realized something; I did not believe in God. As quickly as the revelation came, it dawned on me that I had never believed. I'd always questioned the claims of religion, though the day's events had finally given me my reason. No loving God, I reckoned, would allow a recounting of his miracles to render some human beings more worthy of home than others.

"You know, I think there's something to that," Dad said. "Tell you the truth, I could feel everything happening in there was starting to affect my pressure."

In the months and years that followed, he would pick up on my newfound discontent at prayer times, my disinterest in Jummah, and unwillingness to cover my hair. But that afternoon he praised me as his smart baby girl, having no clue that those few hours had changed me forever.

I'm not sure if anything I said that afternoon really helped my dad in the long run, but I noticed a difference in him after that day. Though he hated giving up on a well-run Black business, he never mentioned Lotus on the Nile again.

The end of the diet stuff came later. After two more weeks of Mom's spaghetti squash casserole and cabbage soup, Dad cornered me on my way to Johnny's Burgers and Fries, asking me to please bring him a Bambino Supreme combo. Two beef patties well done on an onion roll. No sauce, no lettuce, no tomato. Extra pickles on the side and a slice of real Wisconsin cheddar cheese melted on top.

NIKKAH

On her first and last courtship outing with Brother Salahudeen Mubarak, Qadirah sat looking from him back to the timepiece in her lap, counting the minutes until she could finally leave. The evening started off well enough. He chose the Kandahar—an Afghani restaurant in the heart of the city—a place with soft music, low lights, and cloth napkins arranged like fans inside all the water goblets (much nicer than the greasy spoon Khalil, the miserly personal injury lawyer, had taken her to a few weeks earlier). On her arrival, Salahudeen, a tall, rotund man with a bright smile and a prodigious but well-kept beard, presented her with a bouquet of pink carnations and held the door as they entered from the waiting lounge. The rest was all downhill. She barely uttered a word all evening as he dominated the conversation, moving from topic to topic with the bewildering speed of a marble knocking about the insides of a pinball machine. She was particularly alarmed as he carried on, complaining about all the crazy women he'd met of late.

After more than a year of searching for an ideal mate, he bore the aura of a man who was embittered by the effort. The women he'd met thus far, he said, had standards that were plainly un-Islamic and too heavily influenced by the dictates of the world.

"Y'all be wanting a man to give you material things, not looking at a brother for his development, trying to see where he's headed. A

lot of y'all living for the dunya more than the promise of the hereafter. If you're trying to live that dunya life, better have your own
dunya cash, am I wrong?" he asked, and Qadirah shook her head.
It was merely convenient that it appeared like she was agreeing
with him; the gesture hiding her certainty that he was not the kind
of man who was suited to be her husband.

He had a respectable job, working full-time at a mall kiosk,
selling prepaid cell phones and other small electronics, and in his
earnest preparations to become a husband, he started a "side hus-
tle," as he called it, selling incense and oils. The waiter, Kamyar—a
tall man with a Freddie Mercury mustache and a permanent, curious grin—stood above them, scooping the leftover saffron rice
and kofta chalau into Styrofoam containers as Salahudeen twirled
a miswak stick over his molars, going into detail about his foray
into the industry. He only started the gig a few months earlier and,
in that short time, had gotten his sales strategy down to a science.

"I load up the bike with my briefcase and fill it up with product, then head from all the barbershops to all the beauty salons in
a twenty-mile range of the Eastside. If I'm on my game," he said,
"I can make three hundred dollars a day. Total that up with what I
make at the shop? That's a life right there, sister."

She enjoyed his descriptions of the fragrances—the talk of
patchouli, of cinnamon and amber notes. But it was his incuriosity
about her perspectives that had tipped the scales. He'd shared so
much, yet seemed to pay so little attention to Qadirah, much less
the matter of their compatibility. How could he gather whether or
not she really was about "the dunya life" (she wasn't) or if she even
liked the smell of Nag Champa that he claimed as the best scent
ever created by man?

"So as you can see, I'm getting myself together. The only thing
I'm missing is my own little lady, somebody to take my house and

make it a home. And what say you, Ms. Qadirah? You trying to get married?"

"Before you answer," he added, "I got you a lil' something special."

Salahudeen pulled the miswak stick from his mouth—a speck of minty saliva landing in Qadirah's right eye—as he went into his satchel. From the zipper cavity he removed two vials of perfume, both amber glass, tall and skinny with rollerball applicators. He placed them on the table before her, one at a time, and with her good eye she read the names. Oud Swag was the first.

"But this one right here is my best seller," he said. "It will get you all the way right." She made an alarmed expression as she examined the label of the second vial. A SEDUCTIVE BLEND FOR INTIMATE MOMENTS read the caption that was printed under the name, BUMP-N-GRIND SATIN PANTY DROPPER.

"Oh my!" she said. "Thank you so much. What a thoughtful gesture." She said it through a forced smile, and Salahudeen nodded with pride, looking into her eyes like he saw his future there; like he was certain that, in his eyes, she saw the same.

"HE GAVE YOU *what*?"

Qadirah returned home later that night and told her roommate, Ihsan, all about the encounter.

She plopped onto the living room couch and took a breath, went into her purse, and pulled out the vials. She handed them to Ihsan, who covered her mouth to stifle laughter.

"But that wasn't all," Qadirah went on. "He took up the entire two hours talking about himself, his family, his deen. It was all *me, me, me*. I barely said a word all night. I honestly don't know if he learned anything about me other than that I'm five foot four inches with hazel eyes and a registered nurse."

Ihsan put a hand over her heart to try and slow her breath.

"Astaghfirullah, God forgive us," she said. "Truth be told, you and I both know that Salahudeen is a good man. No kids, no other wives, comes from a two-parent home. I know that was on your checklist, right? I'll grant that he's a little bit awkward, but he was probably just trying to impress you."

Qadirah chuckled at Ihsan's explanation, though she also felt it pulling at her heart. It was just like Ihsan to be the voice of reason in all things, as she always had been going back five years to when they first met.

They were nursing students at the same university, though the two had never spoken until Qadirah's junior year, when she first tried attending the Jummah prayer. She was standing at the front gate of Masjid al-Noor, a golden domed edifice across the street from the campus, when Ihsan approached her on the sidewalk.

"Sister," the voice said with the protective cadence of a concerned auntie, "you trying to pray in *there* for the Jummah?" Qadirah turned and saw it was Ihsan—a student one year ahead of her, who she'd always admired for the beautiful scarves she wore on the rare occasions she saw her around campus. "Them folks will have you praying in a cold basement, looking at the Imam on a tiny little TV screen, unless that's what you're after."

Qadirah was merely exploring at that point and didn't have a preference either way, though it was the brightness of Ihsan's smile and the genuineness of her interest that caught her ear and pulled her away from the gate.

"There's another place not too far from here," she said, pointing farther down the road. "We can get there in fifteen minutes, walking, if you want to go. We may miss the first part of the khutbah, but you won't have to sit in a cold basement, that's for sure."

On the walk over, Qadirah learned that Ihsan had grown up on the Eastside and attended the Temple all her life. Qadirah shared her own story about growing up the only child of Mrs. Almina and the Reverend Dr. Melvin Johnson, having spent all her formative years behind the walls of the Bedford Estates, a wealthy suburb northwest of the city.

Ihsan oohed at this revelation, and it made Qadirah wince.

"Please don't act impressed," Qadirah said. "That's just what they want. You see their big houses and cars and think, 'This must be the good life,' when it's anything but."

"If that's how you see things," Ihsan said, "then we're headed to the right place. The Temple doesn't quite compare to Masjid al-Noor on the outside, but it makes up for it with the people. Girl, you don't even know! I just rescued you. Could you imagine, your first Jummah in that place? They would have sent you running out of this deen before you even had a chance to enter."

Qadirah spent the next few hours among Ihsan's people. The two of them arrived in time to sit with Ihsan's mother, Mrs. Hajar Muhammad, as Imam Saleem launched into the body of the Friday address, titled "The Importance of the Middle Path."

"We come to this place," he said, "because we want to live a life of moral excellence. We come because we want to associate with people who are trying to do the same. But what we're not going to do," the Imam went on, "is go to the extreme. When we are extreme with anything—extremely godly, extremely generous—it usually means that something else in life is suffering. No, brother, we don't need to always enter the room with the right foot. No, these sisters don't need to be dressed like they're living in Iran after the revolution. There is no compulsion in religion, so says the Quran, and surely Allah speaks the truth."

They enjoyed a brief dinner of barbeque beef ribs with sides of candied sweet potatoes and baked macaroni and cheese while

Qadirah sat chatting with Nazeem and Basma—friends of Ihsan's (one a law student, the other a fourth-grade teacher) whom she'd known since they were little kids. She enjoyed their easy laughter, and the signs of genuine concern they showed for one another. It was only Basma's recognition of Qadirah's true identity that had slightly upset the pleasantness of the afternoon.

"Pardon me for asking," Basma started off, "but are your parents the pastors at Solid Rock? I knew I saw your face somewhere! I be flipping through the channels sometimes and I see that show they have. What's it called, *Town Square?* Anyway, they had Al Sharpton and Johnnie Cochran on there one time, I remember. And that's when . . ."

Basma stopped talking when Ihsan shook her head, nodding toward Qadirah, whose face had lowered at the mention of her famous parents.

"Not right now," Ihsan had said. "She's checking us out for a minute and probably doesn't want to talk about that while she's here. Basma's cool," Ihsan whispered to Qadirah, "just a little eager sometimes. She doesn't mean you any harm."

Ihsan's reassurances put her at ease, and Qadirah began in that moment to feel comfortable at the Temple and looked forward to her next visit, hoping that she could go in Ihsan's company and that the two of them could become better friends. Over those few hours she developed an impression of her as a wise and sturdy woman—a feeling that remained, stretching out over the years.

"Give him some credit," Ihsan said, still talking about Salahudeen. "It would be hard for any man to feel he's got a shot with you."

"I just can't see myself settling down with someone who doesn't have any interest in me as a person." Qadirah shook her head. "And then the Bump-n-Grind Satin Panty Dropper? That was way too forward for a first date."

"Well, don't forget that he's a man," Ihsan replied. "Those things don't make him a bad person, they just make him human."

She smiled, returning her attention to the piles of documents surrounding her where she sat on the floor. How time had flown, Qadirah thought; how things had changed. In the years Qadirah had known her, she came to regard Ihsan as the most sincerely devoted practitioner of faith that she had ever known. It was the consistency in the way she lived out the letter of her belief—stopping classes to observe prayers and doing so surreptitiously, without the need of other's affirmation—that had compelled Qadirah from abstract curiosity about Islam toward a full embrace of its tenets. In Ihsan's practice, Qadirah saw a living example of the faith that swam in her own heart—the hope to experience the love of God beyond what she saw at the Solid Rock Ministries. But something in Ihsan's words excusing Salahudeen's behavior felt related to the major changes unfolding in her own life.

In two months' time, Ihsan was set to wed Iqbal Abdullah, a third-year cardiology resident at the Holy Cross Hospital—a tall gentleman with broad features and an alluring baritone voice— who Qadirah introduced her to only ten months earlier. Ihsan's evenings were now filled with planning. From coordinating the purchase of and move into their marital home, to determining the seating arrangements for the banquet to follow the marriage ceremony just weeks away, she was joyfully consumed with tablecloths, place settings, and the overall creation of her new life—a life no longer guided, Qadirah thought, by strict adherence to the word of God, but one that was compromised by new fantasies of marital bliss that would find her on the other side of her vows.

"Maybe he's not the one, so be it!" Ihsan said, her head still bent downward at the stacks of papers. "Insha-Allah you'll meet the right person and it will be everything you'd ever hoped."

Qadirah took in Ihsan's words. She noted the way Ihsan's nearing nuptials had altered her friend, changing her tone from cool and resolute to laissez-faire. She only ever felt delight in Ihsan's presence, though the altering circumstances of their lives had introduced new emotions. Qadirah was still seated on the couch, looking into her empty hands, though what coursed through her thoughts, she knew of an instant, were troubling and consuming pangs of envy.

She got up some moments later, headed to her bedroom, and sat in front of her desktop computer, and that's when the idea came. Her email provider, with its snooping ways, learned the desires of her heart and suggested a string of dating websites for her perusal. She overlooked most of them, having heard bad things about MuslimMingle.net and IslamicLoveConnection.com, with their sign-up fees and impossible-to-follow message boards. But when she looked into her inbox and saw the advert for NikkahNetwork .com, she recalled Sister Jamilah talking about having met her husband, Shareef, there. They'd been married for nearly a year already and seemed genuinely happy together, she considered. That was all it took. She clicked the link, filled the input form, and in seconds an email landed in her account with further instructions.

The process required downloading special software and, once it was all set up, a messenger icon appeared in the application bar at the bottom of her screen where, as long as she was signed in, she could receive alerts that would chime a melody like the song of a snake charmer every time a note appeared.

Qadirah spent the first half hour setting up her profile, fretting over what details to share and which photo to choose. She ultimately settled on an overhead selfie. She smiled bright and wide-eyed, with a multicolored scarf to contrast with her caramel-brown skin, holding a white flower at her chest, which is how she derived her screen name, DaisySalaam88. With the information fields completed to her liking, she sighed, leaning back in her swivel chair, hoping for the odd chance that someone interesting might see her online and strike up a conversation.

Within a minute, to her surprise, a notification chimed, with green and white lights flashing at the bottom of her screen. She clicked the tab and saw it was an instant message from a man named Rehan. From his avatar, Rehan appeared tall and slender, his cinnamon skin and glossy black hair contrasting with the brightness of his eyes and smile. She assumed his origins were South Asian, perhaps he was from Pakistan or maybe somewhere in India or Bangladesh, with parents who had found work in healthcare or the tech industry and had come to raise him in the US.

"As Salaamu Alaikum, beautiful sister," his message read. "I just wanted to take the time to introduce myself."

Immediately Qadirah blushed and her heart raced. An ellipsis appeared, the tiny dots flashing varied shades of gray as Rehan typed his next message. What luck, she thought. Someone's coming to me, and so soon? In the ensuing moments, their life flashed before her eyes. She imagined meeting him, of learning he was maybe a doctor or a lawyer, determined to buck traditional expectations of marriage within his ethnicity and pursue an educated and devout Black American wife. She imagined how their children might look; saw them in seersucker dresses and overalls, running up and down a sunny beach somewhere, their luscious and unruly curls bouncing with every step as soft waves lapped their tiny feet. She wondered what languages they might learn and the eclectic array of their holiday meals—the buffets comprised of dhal and chicken dumplings, black-eyed peas, and lamb biryani with chapati bread next to mounds of collard greens braised with smoked turkey.

Finally, a second note appeared:

"On behalf of the entire team here at NikkahNetwork
.com I would like to welcome you to our site. We hope
you'll take advantage of all the features it has to offer,
from instant messaging to our monitored game rooms, all
designed to help you find that special someone. Peace be
with you, and thank you again for signing up with Nikkah
Network, where true love is only a click away!"

"Oh perfect!" Qadirah said it loud enough to get Ihsan's attention, who called out in reply, asking if everything was okay.

"Not to worry," Qadirah said aloud, but too softly for Ihsan to
hear, "just catching feelings for a heartless, soulless bot is all."

She got up from her computer, made her Isha prayers alone,
and got into bed, letting the static play on the radio to distract from
her thoughts and help her fall asleep.

✳

QADIRAH'S RELATIONSHIP WITH her parents first seemed to rupture
on the night four and a half years earlier when she told them about
her decision to convert to Islam.

She laid out her rationale, talking about the Temple and all the
pious and kind people she met there over a few months of regular
visits, going on for ten minutes about her strong resolution on the
matter, how she'd made the decision and couldn't be persuaded to
change her mind.

When she was through, her parents sat still for a prolonged instant, though it was her mother who broke the silence, filling the
two-story living room where Qadirah had made the announcement
with a burst of laughter.

"Oh, don't be ridiculous," she'd said. "You wouldn't dare
do a thing like that after all we've taught you and done for you.

Melvin"—she turned to her husband—"do you hear this child? Better talk some sense into her before this thing gets out of hand."

The reverend sat motionless, not responding to Almina's outburst, but stared intently at his daughter. He asked if this was a firm decision, and Qadirah nodded.

"Well then," the reverend said, "I suppose there isn't really anything we can do about it. 'To you be your way and to me mine.' At least I think that's what their holy book says, anyway."

Qadirah left the family home that night, driving back into the city, proud to have taken a stand and grateful that, at the very least, her parents hadn't disowned her as they'd always threatened to if ever she stepped too far out of line.

It was the following week when she finally understood how much the announcement of her conversion upset her parents, the day she tuned in to the radio broadcast of the sermon her father delivered at the Sunday service—a fiery jeremiad about the fate of backsliders and the hypocrites in and around the church.

"Some of our children are out loose on the street, some of them have lost all faith in God, and some of them are turning to the Moon God. I'll tell you what I know," he said. "The Moon God may clean you up. It may set you straight, but it won't—I said, it *won't* save your soul!"

Qadirah gasped over the last words. So says the reverend, she thought. The reverend who, just weeks prior, stood before the Channel 5 news cameras and encouraged the public to forgive Jeremy Samuelson—the college sophomore and son to the lumber magnate who went viral, chanting on film that Black men would never be welcomed in his fraternity.

"You can hang them from a tree, but they'll never pledge with me," Jeremy said.

The reverend, who brokered a faith-based arbitration between

Robert Lowell and Martha Jackson, Lowell's secretary, who alleged that her boss had repeatedly groped her in the office? The reverend who argued on Lowell's behalf, discouraging Ms. Jackson from filing suit in court?

The reverend, who . . .

Qadirah was fifteen years old when it became clear to her that there was something off about her parents and their marriage. There had always been gestures of normalcy—the hand-holding and flowery words that made them seem like an ideal match in the eyes of the public—though Qadirah had always noted a mechanical coldness that hovered over her parents like unchanging weather, the strangeness coming more clearly into view when she learned that she was conceived from infidelity.

It was common knowledge that her father was married before, and she heard it mentioned in casual conversations during choir rehearsal or at their Wednesday night Bible study, though she was fifteen years old when she got definitive proof of the affair.

With her parents out for a long day of filming, Qadirah wandered into her mother's closet, as she often did, to spend at least an hour trying on her designer fashions. She dressed herself in a black slip dress made of delicate silk, and adorned her neck with a long strand of pearls. She wore a pair of her mother's red-soled, black patent leather heels and grabbed a long fur stole, which she draped across her shoulders, though it kept coming loose. While searching for her mother's favorite crystal brooch to secure the stole, she opened the lid of an old Chanel box, but instead of jewelry, she came upon a collection of letters, yellowed with age, each one addressed from the mother to the father. She might not have bothered reading them at all if the items that fell out of the envelopes were not pictures of her mother dressed in a manner that she'd never seen. The honorable first lady was not clad in one of her characteristic St. John suits, but donned a fitted white tank top that broadcast her petite bust and the curves of her mahogany thighs and buttocks, all of her exposed parts glistening with oil. She faced forward, her hazel eyes staring hungrily into the camera lens with a finger planted between her lips, the feathered ombre of her dirty-blond dyed hair making a short trail down her back.

Qadirah sat stunned under the bright chandelier lights of her mother's dressing room, reading the accompanying notes, the earliest written only five months prior to her birth:

My Endless Love,

When will it be finally over? I am being as patient as I can, but you must understand my position. It was always supposed to be me, Melvin. You are like David in the Bible, come back to everything you used to know, coming back to me after years of wandering. Get rid of her however you must, but remember: your life is with me and very soon we will be three. For now, here's a little distraction. A kiss to you, until we are together again.

Qadirah read the words over and over and then she looked into the mirror. The dresses, shoes, and other ornaments that once delighted her suddenly felt uncomfortable on her skin and she was repulsed by the sight of herself, from her clothes down to her hazel eyes, just like her mother's, staring back at her. Her mind was a scramble of complicated thoughts, though her mother's associations rang true—if the reverend was David, then the first lady was Bathsheba, and theirs was a marriage forged in adultery.

When her mother returned later in the evening, Qadirah came

calling, finding Mrs. Almina in the home office where she was sorting through mail.

"Hey, Ma," Qadirah started. "Could I ask you a question?"

Her mother nodded, a serious look come over her face.

"I just wanted to know," Qadirah said, almost whimpering before she found her nerve, "was Dad still married when you started sending him half-naked pictures? Do you think his first wife knew you two were involved?"

She finished her questions as her mother's eyes flashed with fury before they went back to their ordinary ice.

"Oh no!" Almina uttered with feigned shock, her head ticked down as she started riffling through her purse. "I forgot all about your father's suits at the cleaners! Now how in the world is he going to have anything to wear in time for the Boulé?"

The denial reminded her of a pattern of lies and obfuscations that were the lingua franca in their home, and she knew in that moment that her mother would not entertain any more of her questions.

The days and weeks that followed passed as if nothing had ever happened. Her mother made small talk, troubling Qadirah over her grades, cooking her breakfasts, shuttling her to ballet, tennis, and piano lessons, because nothing on a surface level had changed— nothing except for her parents' newfound unwillingness to discuss their past with any candor, and the key-code lock that her mother installed on her closet door just days after Qadirah's discovery.

That the reverend could champion forgiveness for the likes of Jeremy Samuelson yet speak with such contempt about the Temple folk and their "Moon God" reflected a contradiction in her parents' core theology—the presumption of God's forgiveness despite one's blatant misdeeds. She saw a kind of bankruptcy in their ability to excuse racists, abusers—their own infidelity—all while condemning those who one could presume as moral, except that they held different religious views. The stark incoherence of their faith and their actions stood out to Qadirah and hardened into an understanding. While the seeds of discord had been sewn much earlier, it was the sermon itself that marked a perfect prelude to cut all ties with the pair. From that point on, they needn't any longer be worried about her salvation, Qadirah thought, but ought to be concerned with their own.

So it was with some shock that, just a few days after her outing with Brother Salahudeen, she received news that her mother had called the house phone.

"I didn't know you were talking again," Ihsan said after relaying the news, which made Qadirah grimace. "Whatever the case, she sounded really eager to talk to you. Maybe you should give her a shout."

Qadirah considered the news, wondering why her mother was reaching out after months of no contact. Over the years since she ceased regular communication with her parents, the reverend regularly forwarded her the church newsletter and inspirational Bible quotes, though she always sent them, unread, to her electronic trash bin. For the past three months, however, the messages had stopped, though Qadirah didn't think much of it. She had kept up with the reverend and the first lady, occasionally watching their weekly talk show, and aside from her father's new stutter, everything seemed normal in their world. She knew that if it were serious, say, that if the reverend was in an accident, she would likely hear about it on the news, and sparing any such incidents, whatever her mother called to talk about couldn't have been very important at all.

She went into her room, sat at her computer and googled Almina Johnson + Solid Rock Ministries. Under the news tab she saw an advert for the Sixth Annual Women of God weekend retreat to be held in Tampa, Florida, later that summer. Her mother, who would give the keynote address titled "A Woman of Solid Virtue," had her image photoshopped in the corner of the electronic flyer—dressed in a white blazer and oversized pearls, her arms folded as she smiled, dead eyed, at the camera.

Qadirah assumed this might be why she'd called, and immediately rolled her eyes, feeling sorry for the women who planned to attend. They would spend thousands of dollars between travel expenses and registration fees to hear her mother speak on a topic on which she had no intimate knowledge or experience.

She remained seated there, thinking about her mother for a few minutes when the Nikkah Network instant messenger sounded. In the past few days since her date with Salahudeen, she received a few such notifications, presumably from men who wanted to get to know her, all of them dispiriting. First there was Shahir, a man twice her age who asked her repeatedly to send full-bodied photos of herself, and another man whose avatar was a picture of Anthony Quinn in *Lawrence of Arabia* and who claimed to be a wealthy oilman, descended from the house of Saud, who promised to make her his bride if only she sent along her banking information.

For whatever reason, she clicked the flashing icon and noted it had come from someone who called himself ArikTheRevealer.

"As Salaamu Alaikum, Ms. DaisySalaam," his message read. "Is that your real name, Daisy?"

Qadirah huffed, mildly amused. There was always an angle with the online crowd; they had gimmicks and salutations so out of the ordinary that it was hard to take them seriously. She navigated from the messenger to his profile photo; he was slender and pale with alert eyes and short, dark hair with a stern expression on his face. Very Jon B., Qadirah thought. Very vanilla soul.

Qadirah returned to the messenger, cautious but curious.

"It is my name, yes," she wrote. "Why do you ask?"

"I assumed," Arik continued, "that you chose the name because of the flower you are holding in your profile photo."

"Mere coincidence," Qadirah typed. "Anyway, why should I tell you anything about me when you haven't shared anything about yourself?"

"I am Arik," he replied. "I am thirty years old. I am a graduate student studying history at the University of Pristina in Kosovo. Is that good enough?"

"You claim to be the Revealer? Is that not one of the names of God?"

"I see your point," he replied. "It is immodest; I must beg your forgiveness. It is because of my work. I am drawn to figures from history with titles that include a personal attribute."

"Like Ivan the Terrible?" Qadirah typed, and Arik responded with a laugh out loud emoji.

"That's one example," he replied, "but when I think of myself, I love the truth, which brings me back to your name. If, as it happens, Daisy is what you call yourself in real life, then there's no further discussion and I am in the wrong, but if you've named yourself after the flower in your hand for privacy's sake, then you would be mistaken. That is an aster you're holding, my sister, not a daisy."

Qadirah considered what he wrote and folded her arms. Until that moment, there wasn't a single person she'd met on the platform that interested her, though a few keystrokes was all it had taken to feel drawn to this new presence. It must have been his adherence to the etiquette, not pushing her to violate the rules of modesty and video chat like all of the others, in addition to his unwillingness to be swayed or fooled—traits that reminded her of herself. In this recognition, she felt a likeness that warranted more forthrightness than she had previously shown.

"It's Qadirah," she replied finally. "That is my real name, if you must know."

"Qadirah! The Capable! The Powerful," he wrote back. "A very nice name, al-Hamdulillah. I understand why you wouldn't tell me outright. The internet can be a dangerous place. Things are not always as they appear online. One must take caution."

Over the next several weeks, Qadirah kept in touch with Arik every day. It was always late at night and early in the Kosovo mornings that they held their instant messenger conversations. She read with great attention as Arik shared tales from his past, of the wonderful early years growing up on a farm outside Pristina, and the horrible times that befell them in the final years of Yugoslavia. He said that in 1998, when he was twenty years old, the Serbian police forced them out of their home, separating Arik and his father from his mother and sisters.

"If I knew what was going to happen to us," he typed, "I would have held them, told them how much I loved them, but I was young and foolish. I didn't know anything about evil men; they always arrive bearing good intentions, then show their true colors when your defenses are down."

They were among the lucky ones, he said.

"Many people died, others were permanently disconnected from their families," he typed, "but we were reunited. We were able to return to our property, but arrived to see our home burned down and our farm supplies stolen.

"This is how I became interested in horticulture. For a long time we lived in tents, but there were fields available to us and we could grow things, vegetables and all kinds of flowers. I spent my time in the garden. Other times I scavenged for books, trying to perfect my English and learn more about the struggle of my people.

"The Serbs look to history. They are concerned with events from the fourteenth century involving the Ottomans. They focus on this to avoid discussing the crimes of Milosevic. They think these ancient matters justify the murder, rape, and destruction of property that were carried out at his behest."

Arik led a disciplined life, he wrote, dedicating at least ten hours per day to his studies. He dreamed of becoming a politician, fighting for the rights of the Albanian people in Kosovo.

He was attentive as Qadirah shared her family story—how it was her parents' immorality, even more than questions over doctrine, that pushed her out of the church. "If I had come from a better family," she wrote, "I probably would have stayed." She told him about how they threatened to take her out of their will in order to come back into the fold.

"People with money are the worst," she wrote. "They think everyone in the world is chasing after it, just like them, so they treat people like pawns, then try to cover their dirty conscience with charity. And people are so intoxicated with the money, they completely absolve the rich despite their rotten insides."

"We have this problem in Kosovo, too," Arik replied. "We fought so hard to achieve statehood and so many lives were shattered. Then the men who were chosen to represent our interests in Pristina betrayed the cause of the people to enrich themselves, the *mashtrys*, we call them. One takes it very personally. They make us appear shallow, like we don't care about principle, but just because the leader is without morals doesn't mean that morality ceases to matter or that our cause is unworthy.

"It was a mistake," Arik continued. "Your parents assumed you would follow them. You found a different way. They should have had more children. Parents have realistic expectations when there are many children to feed. Like me? I want to have at least five. It will keep them humble. I want to see them marching into the mas-jid like soldiers going to battle—my own little brigade."

"Your poor wife," Qadirah typed.

"No, sister," Arik replied, "my happy wife. Paradise lies at the feet of the mother. That is a position of power and prestige."

Arik typed this, and for the first time since they'd been in touch, Qadirah felt a small, shimmering hope grow inside her—a feeling that she truly liked this young man and that she could envision her-self in the scene he just painted, shepherding his children through the masjid, her head held high as the matriarch of a large family of true believers.

THE BRIDAL SHOWER was held at the Taj Buffet—an onion-domed eatery in the West suburbs of town. Qadirah and a few of Ihsan's friends had rented one of the private rooms for the occasion and decked it out with balloons and streamers in pink and gold, with an abundance of flowers to match. The crowd of seventy women, most of them Temple attendees and women Ihsan met in college, arrived in due order. They were dressed like high-end fashion models in designs tailored for a modest runway, their delicate, billowing fab-rics swooping as they entered the room, which pulsated with the intricate rhythm of Amr Diab's "Amarain." They milled about, pil-ing curries, chutneys, and popadum's onto their plates as they spoke in joyful tones, eager to begin the celebration.

Many of the women were familiar to Qadirah, though other faces were new. Whoever she was speaking with, however, the con-versations were all the same. Whether it was a woman from the Temple or a work colleague of Ihsan's, they would comment on the lovely couple and then, inevitably, they would ask whether Qa-dirah was married, then if she had met anyone promising.

Qadirah would nod that yes, she was talking to someone, though she would not elaborate. She hadn't even told Ihsan about Arik, much less that they were in regular contact. She hadn't shared anything about him with anyone, not his prodigious intellect, his passion for the deen, or the depth of his knowledge about plants. He could tell the story of any and all blossoms—using both the common and scientific names—and tell their scent and the time of year they would bloom, so sensuous in the rendering it was like having him near.

Qadirah knew not to mention any of this, certain that Ihsan would be concerned. She didn't want to hear the endless stories to follow, of women who'd ventured into the world of online romance and come out of it disappointed and financially depleted. She didn't want to fight their subtle disapprovals or feel compelled to defend the fact that, in the short time since she'd met Arik, she'd already begun to develop feelings for him—tender, romantic feelings, feelings she hoped would never fade. She tried to imagine the sound of his voice in the moment, divining, in the instance of the bridal shower, just what he would have to say about the festivities of that night. He'd told her all about the Serbian forces starving his people, how they had to eat rodents and dandelion leaves just to survive. She knew he would scoff at the amounts of food that the women, in their jollity and banter, failed to consume, mentioning how their waste was connected to the suffering of others.

"If only we had food in such quantities," she could hear him say, "there would be thousands more among us, and we would thank God for every single grain, not letting a single one fall to the ground."

"It's all so festive, isn't it? With the colors and the loud music, there's almost an atmosphere of Mardi Gras or Halloween."

Ihsan's co-worker Eileen was seated next to Qadirah—a plump, middle-aged Caucasian woman with grayish-blond hair styled in an excess of long curls, who bore a striking resemblance to Miss Piggy. She spoke with a biting sarcasm that mirrored Qadirah's own budding criticisms—her eyes darting about the room as if she were not attending a bridal shower but had instead found herself trapped inside a holding pen.

The only thing that seemed to shake her from her apparent unease was Qadirah mentioning, mistakenly, that she grew up in Bedford Estates.

"Now that's a nice place, certainly a long way from here. I once went golfing out that way. Absolutely beautiful, and you know that famous pastor lives out there," Eileen said, and Qadirah sighed, relieved at the very least that she hadn't been recognized.

Eileen looked Qadirah up and down with new interest.

"Why would you . . . ?" Eileen did not finish her thought, but shifted her eyes from Qadirah and looked around the room, the sides of her mouth downturned.

"Somebody cared enough to help you get ahead and this is where you want to be? This is definitely a step backward. A step backward indeed."

Qadirah shared the details with Arik later that evening.

Over the messenger, she wrote about Eileen's haughtiness, how she condescended to all the women there, and tried implanting the idea in Qadirah's mind that there was something retrograde about her association with Ihsan, given where she was raised.

"I was annoyed, but more so I felt bad for the woman," Qadirah typed. "Another part of me can't help feeling that she only spoke to me that way because she is white and I obviously am not. Oftentimes in this country, white people think their opinions are superior and then, given our history, they just assume you're eager for their approval or too powerless to disagree."

Qadirah waited more than twenty seconds to receive Arik's

reply, and when she felt that one wasn't forthcoming, she typed again, unsure if he had gone away.

"Hello?" she wrote. "Are you still there?"

After a brief moment the gray ellipsis appeared.

"Yes, I am here," he wrote back. "I am trying to understand what you have said."

An ellipsis appeared, and Qadirah awaited the long reply.

"It doesn't seem very logical to me. A woman who is a friend of your friend comes to a party and she upset you with her comment. While I agree that her tone was inappropriate, this analysis doesn't seem correct.

"I'm quite confused," he continued, "when you mention she is white. I do not understand, why does her skin color matter in this case?"

Qadirah had not considered that he might be unfamiliar with the term, and though she found it an odd exercise to have to explain something so foundational to her reality—spelling out for Arik the power that came along with being white in America, she did so anyway.

"There's a whole history. Slavery, segregation, voter suppression, redlining, and white people always come out on top," she went on. "That's why I say, because I'm not white, because the majority of us in the room were not white—I felt that she treated being there at Ihsan's shower differently than she probably would have if it were the same place but filled up with other white people. In that scenario, I'm pretty sure she wouldn't have behaved that way."

"I'm sorry, I still do not understand," he replied. "I suppose I just do not see color. That is why we have Islam, anyway. To take away class and color, to make us all equal in Allah's sight."

The bouquet of flowers Salahudeen gave her a month earlier sat at the end of her desk—brown and wilted, most of the petals having scattered at the base of the glass vase. Qadirah had failed to gather the debris and put it in the trash, so it had remained there, forgotten and untended. In the moment Arik had typed those last words, she imagined herself just like the petals, completely undone and withered. For all the things she came to accept about Arik, she was stunned by his ignorance of the meaning of skin color and how it had impacted her life. She couldn't imagine being able to endure a lifetime of such misunderstandings, of having the person nearest to her doubt the validity of her own observations—someone who made her feel that her sense of reality was off, or worse, that it didn't matter. He wrote in the lull, asking if she was still present.

"I'm here," she wrote back. "But I'm very tired. Goodbye, Arik." He replied in kind, though she meant this in a way that was conclusive, knowing their banter was finished, as she could never bring herself to marry a man like Arik, who didn't know and wasn't curious to learn the challenges she faced as a Black woman in the world.

In the week preceding the marriage ceremony, Ihsan started moving her things from the apartment. All of her personal effects were delivered to her new home, though she would be spending the next few days at a mansion in the Welford Gardens, on the estate where the nikkah would be held.

On her last day in the apartment, Qadirah spent the morning and the rest of the afternoon helping Ihsan deep clean her old bedroom. They played '90s R&B as they dusted, vacuumed, mopped, and scrubbed, getting the space ready for Halima, a university junior and an economics major, who would be replacing Ihsan on the lease.

After several hours the two of them sat across from each other on the barren floor of the bedroom, reminiscing over the things they uncovered in the cleaning process—old Erykah Badu concert ticket stubs, a pair of sequined shoes they'd bought from a vendor at the Eid celebration, and which they both insisted were cute at the time, though Ihsan hadn't worn them out even once.

"Remember the day you took Shahadah?" Ihsan said to Qadirah. "How I offered you the shoes? You were so concerned about offending me you almost accepted them, but I knew you even then. I could see it in your eyes that you didn't really want them, you were just being polite." Ihsan chuckled, though she slowed her laughter, noticing that in just a few moments, Qadirah had grown terribly withdrawn.

"Oh no, I'm sorry. I didn't know . . ." Ihsan started, but Qadirah shook her head to stop her from going on.

"Don't worry about me, I'll be okay. I'm just going to really miss you, that's all. It's all starting to feel very real, you leaving and getting married. I'm really happy for you." Qadirah said the words through a choked throat as she patted the tears from her eyes with the loose end of her green cotton scarf.

"It's so romantic, you know," Qadirah said, "and I'm happy most of all that you're marrying a man who really loves you. Just the way Iqbal looks at you, it's so clear that he'd do anything for you. Do you think you're ready to be married?"

Ihsan shrugged. "In all honesty," she said, "I kinda already feel like I am married. I started feeling that way after we moved our things into the new house. At this point, all that's missing is the dress, the ring, then the cake and ice cream."

"You can't be serious," Qadirah pressed on. "It's going to be a whole world of difference from now to when you say your I do's. I mean, there's so much that will be expected of you. So many new ways you'll have to perform."

"Perform?" Ihsan chuckled. "What makes you think I haven't already figured out that part? I know how to perform, Qadirah, if that's what you're getting at."

Qadirah looked confused. She was thinking about the new obligations that were being placed on her—the financial and other responsibilities Ihsan would be expected to carry out, though after a moment she'd finally understood that Ihsan was responding to a question she hadn't intended to ask.

"Do you mean that you and Iqbal have already . . . ?" Qadirah started, and Ihsan blushed, nodding her head.

"It happened almost by accident," she said, laughing. We were unpacking boxes in the house, just getting things ready for when we move in, trying to cut down on the work. I was headed to the linen closet to arrange a few stacks of sheets and towels, and Iqbal was going the other way, headed to the bedroom. He brushed up against me and . . . things happened."

Ihsan was still blushing, her mind filled with the memory of the encounter with Iqbal, and was stunned to notice Qadirah's expression—how in a matter of seconds it had changed from a look of curiosity to revulsion.

"But you're not married." Qadirah's voice was terse, accusatory. "You only had a few days left before it would be permissible, and now look at what you've done."

Ihsan tried to counter Qadirah, but she raised her voice a few decibels, continuing on her rant so she wouldn't be interrupted.

"You could be sitting here across from me pregnant," Qadirah said. "And what do you think your daughter or son would think of you to know that these were the circumstances?"

Ihsan shook her head like she was disoriented, trying to understand how she'd found herself in this predicament, being lectured by one of her closest friends. She was still shaking her head when an idea captured her, steadying her neck. She turned her head toward Qadirah.

"Are you equating me to your mother? Do you think I'm like your mother?" Ihsan grabbed a ring of keys, which jangled and snapped together in her left hand like shattered glass. She stood up from the carpet, towering over Qadirah, who was still seated on the floor.

"I'm going to go now." Ihsan was abrupt. "But I wanted to point out that some mail came a few days ago. I left it in the kitchen, though you never looked through the pile. There's a letter there for you, I think from your mother. Maybe you should get in touch with her, at least hear her out. And as for the wedding," she added, "you can come or not come, it's completely up to you at this point." Ihsan paused like she wanted to say more, though in the end she lengthened the retractable handle of her rolling suitcase and left the apartment without any added words.

Qadirah sat alone in Ihsan's old room for another ten minutes before venturing out. She intended to lay in bed, though passing through the living room—darkened by shuttered blinds—and against her better judgment, she sat on the nearest couch and opened the letter to read the message.

Dear Qadirah,

I hope this letter finds you in good health and the best of spirits. It has taken me a long time to come around to you changing your name from Karen, as it was your great-grandmother's name, but you are your own person— something it's taken me forever to really understand—so I pray that you receive these words, knowing I'm coming to you with a new perspective and an open heart.

I've been trying to reach you and I never hear back. It used to make me so upset, but now I think I understand. I know you've been holding on to some anger against your father and me for some time. The important news I have to share with you, which I would rather have shared on the phone or in person, is that your father was diagnosed with dementia. It's moving fast, so he can no longer tell you what I'm going to share, though I know he wishes he could.

I know you don't agree with the choices we made in our past, but if we had to do it all over again, we would have chosen the same way as long as it meant we could have you. For all that we may have done wrong, your birth made it right. We did it all so we could have you. Does that make sense? I just want you to understand, I waited so long to become a mother and your birth to me was an answered prayer. You were and still are wanted, and my God are you loved. I just hope someday you'll reach out. You may feel all sorts of ways about me, but don't take it out on your father. He needs you now more than ever.

So stunned was she by the news of her father's illness, Qadirah hadn't noticed that she was sitting with her free hand cupped over her mouth while the other held the letter. Immediately the memories of the reverend flashed before her eyes—of him blowing bubbles and dandelion seeds with her on hot summer days, reading her stories, teaching her to ride her bike, of them driving cross-country on long family trips, singing at the top of their lungs along with their favorite gospel songs. Sitting there on the couch, if only for a moment, she could feel what she'd felt as a child—that her parents' love for her was real, though just as quickly as she fell into nostalgia, Qadirah pulled herself up from the depths, the idea crystalizing that the message was just another of her mother's manipulations sent on behalf of the reverend. Their displays of love—their patience, attention, and generosity—had all been a simulation, a close approximation of the real thing. Underneath it all they were hollow and soulless as marionettes, animated by the pursuit of power facilitated by the church, pining for the grace that always eluded them despite their eloquence and knowledge of the Bible. It was a pursuit that necessitated the acting—the painfully wide smiles and fastidious adherence to the rules of decorum, all of it distracting everyone, save her, from their baseness and incurable mendacity.

Qadirah knew if she responded to her mother, that she would inevitably find herself back under the reverend's thumb, and while it pained her to know that her father was suffering, she could not tolerate the risk of losing her Islam for the sake of a man who had rejected her for embracing the religion. She gave it a moment's thought, tore the letter in pieces, then made a short du'a, praying that her supplications for the reverend, alone, would suffice as a contribution to his well-being.

And so it was for men of dominion as it was for David—revered in all of Israel, though God would claim his firstborn with Bathsheba, then give him Absalom—all men with immense worldly power, whose limitations were exposed by the deep malaise that God sewed into their families.

QADIRAH SPENT THE evening lying in bed crying, more overcome with concern about what had transpired between her and Ihsan than the news about her father. After the heaving slowed, she remained in bed looking at the opposite wall, completely ignoring the call of the adhan that played, beckoning her to the Maghrib prayer.

The only thing that captured her attention in the fading light of day was the flashing of the Nikkah Network icon on her desktop computer. There was a constant stream of blips from someone who was trying to converse with her. After several of these had sounded, she climbed out of bed and sat in the chair. It was Arik.

"Qadirah! Qadirah! Are you there? I've been trying to reach you. Are you alright? I feel that I must have offended you when we last were in touch. In fact, I'm sure I did. I was hoping to hear from you in the days since, and when I heard nothing, I started trying to connect with you. I wanted to apologize."

Qadirah sat, wiping her eyes, unsure whether to respond.

"I have always considered Americans to be rather self-important. Not everyone in the world spends their time trying to understand that place and its history. There is enough going on in the world not to be bothered at all with American culture, but that is not an excuse for me. In that context I should have demonstrated more attention. I am not a callous man, though I don't know how to convince you of this."

"I am here," she typed. "Please go on."

"Qadirah!" She could feel his relief through the screen. "al-Hamdulillah! You are there.

"I have taken the time to go over what I said in our last conversation and I realize that much of what I wrote to you was shared in ignorance.

"When you wrote to me about what transpired at your friend's party, you mentioned the other guest seated near you, placing emphasis on her color as the basis for why she insulted everyone in the room that evening. For me, of course, this is a hard adjustment to make. For the Slavic peoples, you see, power is not determined by color as much as other kinds of identities—national identities, ideologies, and specifically religion. The Serbs hate the Albanians;

they starve us and murder our fathers. They prevent us from having our own nation, or at least fail to acknowledge the country we have made for ourselves. Why? Because their earliest and most sacred holy sites are in Kosovo. So it is power, not the particulars of ethnicity, that is at the core of the dynamic. The differences that separate us? We invent those. Sometimes it is the appearance—the color of one's skin, for example—but very often it is ideology that creates the divide, and if you don't mind me saying so," Arik went on, "it seems to me that the same could be true for you, personally."

"I apologize," Qadirah typed. "But I don't know what you mean."

"I am thinking of your parents, the reverend and his wife, your mother. It seems to me that their public pronouncement of their Christian beliefs gives them access to a kind of power, which someone like me, a Muslim Albanian, very demonstrative about my beliefs and unrelenting in my critique of American empire, could never hope to achieve in your country. So, who is more powerful between us, or to use your term, 'white'? It seems to me that, ideologically speaking, at least, they occupy the more powerful position."

Their banter had always been this way, writing back and forth, though in the moment, Qadirah was inspired and, without consulting Arik, she clicked a button to initiate their very first video call.

Arik accepted the call and within an instant he was before her. Qadirah's eyes widened at the sight of him. She regarded his sculpted features and watched his face morph into his own unique expression of delight at the sight of her. His grin quickly turned into a smile, and just as a flash of his teeth showed from behind his lips, he shut off the camera.

"Did I do something wrong?" Qadirah typed.

"No, please," he responded, "be kind to yourself. Perhaps you wanted to see me live at long last. This is a good sign, as I, admittedly, have wanted to see you. I can only ask Allah's help in my prayers that someday I can see you in a way that would be acceptable in his sight, but . . ."

"But what?" Qadirah typed.

"You are too beautiful. It is too enticing looking at you in this way without a marriage contract to make it halal."

"Are you saying you want to get married?" Qadirah asked.

"Allah knows best," Arik replied. "I don't want you to be under any illusions about the man I am and the important work in which I am engaged, though it would be unwise to be very explicit here and now. There are many evils in the world. Such pain and suffering being visited upon the ummah, and such widespread indifference, even among the Muslims. If I am to marry, it must be with someone who understands my commitment to this struggle, my determination to see a world rid of the kuffar. She must understand this and, if need be, take on the burden of struggle for herself."

"And you do not think that I am such a woman?" she replied. "Because I am. The pleasures of this world are but momentary. The Akhirah is forever."

"Al-Hamdulillah," Arik replied. "That is a start. Just one concern. Your covering," he wrote, "it appears to expose your neck. I do understand that you live in America and that has an influence on your choice of dress, it certainly has the same influence here, but we are the true believers, you and I. We must hold ourselves to a higher standard, don't you agree?"

"Absolutely," she wrote. "It was a momentary lapse. It is my prayer that Allah refine my faith, that he may join us together in complete submission to his will."

✳

IHSAN'S WEDDING WAS held on a bright and sunny day, under the large white gazebo on the far side of the gardens where it was a temperate seventy-five degrees. A crew of workers had arranged a marvelous trellis of roses, peonies, lilacs, and several overstuffed bouquets of the same blossoms that lined the passageway. A small chorus sang a chant in Arabic while a gentleman stood alongside them, strumming a darbuka as Ihsan passed down the aisle in a beautiful white gown with a dramatic veil fastened to her head with a golden tiara. Iqbal stood, tearful and proud to receive her at the trellis, and the two clasped hands as the Imam began the ceremony.

Imam Saleem spoke of the prophet Noah, and told of the flood that destroyed all but the believers.

"And in this we see signs," the Imam said, "to guide those of us who are true in faith. Life is full of obstacles. There will be storms of many kinds, but as long as you are among those who remain pure of heart, you shall be spared the worst disasters life may throw at you."

After the exchange of vows, the groom took Ihsan in his arms and kissed her sweetly, daintily, with pursed lips. The audience smiled, but Qadirah looked into her lap, embarrassed, thinking this could not possibly be Sunnah—that the prophet of Islam would never have allowed such a wanton display of romantic love in his presence.

The banquet to follow was even more extravagant than the shower, with heaping mounds of Manti, Dolmas, and Meze served on large antique brass platters. There was a massive twelve-layer cake, ornate with marzipan roses so substantial in proportion that, even with three hundred guests, it was impossible to finish.

Qadirah sat regarding the plates of the guests, scowling with disapproval. They left gobs of food heaped thereon as they abandoned their tables for the dance floor where DJ Smoove was playing all the so-called clean versions of a string of radio hits. There were couples young and old, dancing and gyrating as if they were unafraid of God's wrath toward the wasteful and the frivolous.

"Now it's your turn, ladies," DJ Smoove spoke into the cardioid microphone. "If you're still looking for that special someone, here's your shot at forever!"

DJ Smoove played a thumping rhythm that was the start of Beyoncé's "Single Ladies," and a chorus of female guests screamed playfully as they crowded onto the dance floor. Ihsan stood with her back to the women who had gathered there. She braced herself, then on the count of three, threw the bouquet toward them, and turned at the sound of the tussling that followed. She scanned the huddle of women, hoping to see Qadirah's face smiling at her, the roses having safely landed in her hands. Ihsan frowned slightly when she noticed it was Shantrell, a hospital co-worker, playing a tug-of-war with a teenaged guest over the bouquet. Ihsan looked to her groom and then back to her guests. On what was supposed to be the happiest day of her life, she felt overwhelmed with worry for Qadirah, who had left the party just minutes earlier, though in a sense she was already a long, long way gone.

SISTER ROSE

When Intisar was small, she imagined that Sister Rose made her home in a mist of clouds enveloped all day in ethereal rays of light. She thought so because of the way Sister Rose seemed to float underneath her long abayas across the Musallah floor to the spot where she and five or so other little girls would gather for her Sunday school lessons. What else could explain her litheness, her sunset-peach skin, the way her irises sent threads of gold bounding out from the pupils like a million solar flares?

So that twenty years later, long after passing through disillusion with the Temple folk, Intisar was almost shocked to behold Sister Rose's actual residence. It was a little bungalow with glossy black shutters, a white picket fence, and a neatly manicured lawn—lovely in its own way, save the spring rains that turned the day dreary and made all the white faces of the daffodils lining the front walkway droop to the ground.

On her knocking, Brother Mujaheed, Sister Rose's husband, appeared behind the screen door in a long white thobe. Of an instant, the pages of Intisar's memory flit from the tall, strapping, burnt-sienna man she recalled to the one that stood before her— more stooped than she remembered, with closely cropped salt-and-pepper hair and a faint smile that failed to betray his weathered countenance.

"Now look who it is after all this time," he said. "As Salaamu Alaikum, little sister!"

Intisar bowed at his greeting. It was all she could do to distract from the way that her tongue had grown unaccustomed to the use of such phrases—Masha Allah, Bismillah, al-Hamdulillah. Instead, she raised a gift to his view and Brother Mujaheed's eyes widened.

"Aww," he said. "You really shouldn't have done this!"

It may very well have been his own surprise that upset his expression, though Intisar immediately began to second-guess herself. You should have just given the Salaams, she thought. You should have covered your hair and worn something that did not expose the bottom half of your legs.

He led Intisar to the living room couch and set the gift down on the La-Z-Boy opposite her before disappearing into the back of the house. He made tinkling sounds with cups and plates in the kitchen, but otherwise the house was still. Intisar might have sat contemplating the seriousness of her visit and the fact that she was going to see Sister Rose—the woman she loved best at the Temple—for the first time in twenty years, but she felt inundated by different thoughts. The living room was discomfortingly familiar. On the east-facing wall there was a large photograph of white-clad worshipers making tawaaf around the Kaaba. A hafiz trained in Senegal, Brother Mujaheed had lined the opposite wall with hundreds of volumes of tafsir, and other titles like *How to Believe* and *The Walk of the Sahabah*.

Intisar was still scanning the room as he reemerged with mismatched mugs of peppermint tea and a tray of almonds and dried apricots for them to share.

"Please enjoy this while you wait," Brother Mujaheed said as he sat in the La-Z-Boy. "It should only be a few more minutes before you can go back."

He released the chair latch and it sent his legs up, exposing the pale yellow undersides of his feet.

"Your father has been telling me all about the things you're doing with yourself. It's been a couple weeks since I last saw him at the Temple. How's he doing?"

Intisar lied, telling Brother Mujaheed that her father was fine. She didn't let on that, aside from an occasional phone call and email, the two of them barely spoke, and she was grateful that he carried on talking and didn't ask her to elaborate.

"I would tell my wife all about it and it made her so happy, like it was her traveling all over the world."

Intisar smiled into her mug, Brother Mujaheed's praise offering a silhouette of pleasure.

"Your pops told me that recently you were in New Zealand and Japan. I know that had to be the experience of a lifetime," he said, tilting the golden head of a honey bear upside down, a slow stream flowing into his tea. "You gotta do all you can in this life while you can, you know."

"Yes, sir," Intisar said. "I'm just trying to make my way in the world."

Brother Mujaheed might have thought it immodest had she gone on. It was at the Temple, after all, where she learned the idea that pride—so necessary in the constitution of a man—was unbecoming in a woman.

Before the awkwardness could settle, he picked up the box and examined all its sides, admiring the silver wrapping and white ribbon, which Intisar had carefully tied hours earlier.

He tore the paper, opened the white cardboard box, and marveled at the contents.

"Wow! Now this looks fancy!" he said, turning it over from side to side. "You mind telling me what it is?"

The problem of what to get Brother Mujaheed and Sister Rose had been as burdensome as the idea of her visit, considering the circumstances. Any of the obvious choices, flowers or a teddy bear, seemed to her ill-suited and laden with upsetting inferences. And so she settled on the most innocuous gift she could think of—a work of modern art. It was a small sculpture she found at a favorite gallery downtown—a solid stone of white marble, mostly round but jutting in places with a few holes poking through.

"It's a Gregg Mantis piece; you should look him up," she said. "As far as what it means, I'm sure he'd say it's all in the eye of the beholder."

"It looks to me," he said, narrowing his eyes, manipulating the sculpture from one side to the other, "like somebody that got in a bad fight and lost an eye."

He was about to offer another idea when an older, very stout woman in a sweatsuit, with short, strawberry blond hair, emerged from the back hallway and said, "You can come this way. She's ready to see you now."

Intisar stood, the nerves tingling her spine like a million little ants traipsing up and down her back. She passed through a dark hallway toward an open door which spilled forth a silvery light.

She turned the corner and there was Sister Rose. She sat near the window in a rocking chair amid an assortment of plants so numerous that despite the hospital bed in the middle of the room, the space looked almost like a nursery. Sister Rose smiled, raising her hands from under the granny-square blanket on her lap, welcoming a hug.

"Inti!" she said, bright but gravelly. "It's so wonderful to see you after so long."

Intisar smiled, uneasily. When she first saw her, Intisar tried hard to disguise her alarm at Sister Rose's appearance. She was starvation-thin and her skin, once a glowing and vibrant peach color, had turned sallow and dull. Her eyes, the feature that had most fascinated Intisar so many years before, bulged in a way that turned her gaze from soft and approving to penetrating and serious.

Intisar moved toward the chair opposite Sister Rose, but before she sat, she removed her trench coat, revealing a cocktail-length black dress underneath.

"I'm sorry," Intisar began. "I hope you don't mind my appearance; I'm just feeling a little warm for some reason."

"It's the plants. They need the humidity to survive," Sister Rose said. "But why sorry? Look at those pretty legs! Girl, you look like a fashion model! Iman! Beverly Johnson . . . Give any one of 'em a run for their money!"

Intisar tried to demur, unsure if she was being patronizing, but Sister Rose smiled, then pointed to herself. "You sure look better than I do, can't deny that now, can you?"

In her own home she dressed differently than at the Temple, though Intisar suspected this was more related to circumstance than custom. Instead of the abayas and the triangle-fold scarves, which Intisar remembered she always pinned underneath her chin, she wore a pink crochet beanie to match a noticeably loose-fitting velour tracksuit.

"So, you've been traveling, I hear," Sister Rose said.

"I've been a few places." Intisar brightened. "As much as my schedule will allow, but it's all work. I'll see a monument or two on my way to and from the airport, but not much more than that."

"Alright now! Getting around, doing big things," Sister Rose went on. "Your father told Mujaheed all about Bates and Georgetown. He's been going around town telling everyone about you! When you were young I used to say to myself, this girl is going to do something amazing. It's just wonderful to know you're doing so well."

Then Sister Rose asked, "Have you heard from Abiola?"

For a brief instant Intisar glared at Sister Rose. Why of all people, she thought, did she need to mention her? Sure, there were plenty of happy things to recall about Abiola. They were childhood friends. They skipped rope on the Temple front stoop and spent hours playing hand games after the Jummah prayer. But the relationship had changed in high school and in the years since it all fell apart, nothing had been done to repair things; nothing that altered the fact that, after so much time, the mention of Abiola still had the power to fill Intisar with venom.

"Why do you bring it up?" Intisar's voice quavered.

"Oh, well," Sister Rose came back brightly. "I just think she'd probably like to hear from you. She's got a lot going on, you know. Had four children with one of the Shafiq boys, remember them?"

Intisar nodded.

"Well, she had a lot of promise, just like you. But she decided, like a lot of these girls, to settle down young and start having babies. I'd always hoped she would go to night school to finish college, but she just got bogged down, you know? Maybe you could reach out to her. I know she'd be happy to hear from you."

"Maybe," Intisar said.

She wanted to ask other questions about Abiola but decided against it, knowing it would come off like gloating if she pried any further into Sister Rose's knowledge of Abiola's life.

"Your turn, Inti." Sister Rose said it just the way she would around the Sunday school circle of girls when it was her turn to read a passage of Quran.

"I want to know everything that's going on with you."

"Everything's good. I just bought a new house. Big, beautiful place out in the county, so there's that." Intisar smiled. "I'm trying to get it all decorated. Planning a vacation for the summertime. Simple things, all material."

"I always meant to ask your dad if you ever settled down, but I don't know. Somehow I just suspected he might not be able to answer that question, like maybe you weren't in close contact."

Intisar gave Sister Rose another suspicious look.

"Have you met someone?" Sister Rose asked, and Intisar dropped her gaze, unsure of how to respond.

They shared an awkward silence, then Sister Rose shrugged. "Well, I'm not surprised, honey. It's hard to meet good people these days. It must be even harder to talk when you don't know if there's anyone you can trust with the information.

"I know what happened, Inti, why you never came back to the Temple after your fifteenth birthday. I was standing on the street when I saw you in the alley with Khabir, and then I saw what Abiola did, how she followed you there and ran to tell your father."

"Nothing happened between me and Khabir." Intisar tried speaking the words with calm resolve though her voice was unsteady— a full-grown woman, of learning and means, reduced to the vulnerable posture of her teenage self.

"It was just a kiss. Just one little kiss. She blew everything completely out of proportion. Do you know what she had people saying about me? That I was pregnant! At fifteen! I don't know how you get pregnant after a kiss. A peck, really." Intisar shook as she choked back tears, dotting the ones that fell with the sleeve of her trench coat.

"It's been twenty years since I last set foot in that place; can't even bear to see it in photographs. Abiola is one thing, but my father?" Intisar groveled. "He should have stood up for me, but he stood there scolding me in front of everyone. He made me feel like I was less than trash.

"And I don't know why," she went on, trying not to raise her voice, "but I had always hoped that you, of all people, wouldn't entertain the gossip, that maybe you would understand."

Sister Rose rocked slowly in her chair, her slipper-clad feet dangling with every push, as Intisar wept into her hands. Languidly she pointed to a box of tissues on the nightstand, and once she noticed the gesture, Intisar reached for a few.

"I'm fifty-six next month, Insha-Allah. Spent the whole of my life figuring out what it means to be a woman in this world, and you don't think I understand," Sister Rose said, soft but incredulous, "after all these years?

"Listen, Intisar," Sister Rose's voice deepened. "There's something I want to tell you.

"You ever heard of Sister Jackie?" she asked, and Intisar shook her head no, dabbing the moisture from her nose with a Kleenex.

"Maybe you were too small then," Sister Rose went on, "but she was a fixture back in the day. And man was she beautiful—almond eyes, smooth, even cocoa skin, just like yours. Everybody thought so, but especially Mujaheed.

"He's a really good man, don't get me wrong. Like most people, there was a time when he was very selfish. A few months after Hamza was born, Mujaheed got it in his head that he was ready to take a second wife. Before I could even blink, much less consent, Jackie was moving into my house.

"At first I took it in stride, figuring it was okay as far as the deen was concerned. How could I object to my husband doing something that our faith allowed?

"I soldiered right through it, enjoying my son and watching

him grow, but something deep inside me just could not abide the presence of this woman in my home.

"Late one night, after baby Hamza had fallen asleep, I left the room I shared with him just down this very hallway. I went into the kitchen where I had a big, beautiful bowl of just-ripe peaches. I reached my hand right past them and grabbed the santoku from the wood block on the counter. I gripped it hard as I've ever gripped anything in my life, walking back down the hallway to the bedroom that Mujaheed and Jackie shared. The door was cracked open, and I just stood there, watching their bellies rise and fall between breaths, waiting for the right moment to enter.

"I don't know what it was, mother's instinct perhaps, because I felt my child was about to start crying. I went back to the kitchen, set down the knife, and rushed to my baby."

"But you didn't do anything wrong. You didn't hurt anyone!" Intisar said.

She sat, wide-eyed, trying to assuage Sister Rose's conscience, and yet simultaneously imagined her in that moment—standing behind the half-opened door, santoku in hand, looking for the right spot on Brother Mujaheed's and Sister Jackie's bodies to plunge the knife.

Sister Rose chuckled.

"Sweet girl, still so naïve. I had no intention of merely hurting my husband. I was going to kill him and Jackie, then drive down to the border with my son."

Then she sighed. "The next morning, Mujaheed did notice the knife. I had forgotten to put it back in the block, so it was just lying out on the counter. All he said was, 'I wonder how this got out.' Otherwise, I don't think he had a clue.

"Not long after that, Mujaheed came to his senses and they broke up, and that's when I realized something. All the time I was mad at him for taking another wife, I realized I was really mad at me. He could go on and have any old liaison he wanted, and all anyone would say was "al-Hamdulillah," but what about me? I'd been a mother, a teacher, a wife—always doing for others. When in my life was I ever going to step out? To have my own kind of adventure?"

She lifted her hands, motioning Intisar to come nearer. Sister Rose put her hands in Intisar's and clasped them with all the force she could muster.

"I'm proud of you, Inti. So, so proud of you. I just wanted you to know that."

She became dizzy some moments later, and the strawberry blond lady rushed into the room like she anticipated this. There would be more administering of ointments and changing of gauzes, but before the flurry of work would begin, Intisar kissed Sister Rose's hand and touched the back of it to her forehead.

"I've gotta go now," Intisar said, "but I will be back to see you soon."

Sister Rose gave her the faint smile of one who has learned how to manage hope.

"You have your life, sweet girl, promise me you'll go out and live it."

Intisar nodded. "Of course I will," she said, then turned to leave.

Intisar donned her trench coat on the way back to the living room and made Brother Mujaheed aware of her intentions to return, and he welcomed her back. He talked about his wife and how she'd been looking forward to the visit, but all Intisar could think of in that moment was his body splayed out and bloodied in their marital bed. She imagined what the headlines would have said:

In a Fit of Rage, Woman Kills Husband and His
Mistress, Who He Claimed as Second Wife

"Come anytime," he said, "there's reasonable hope that she'll pull through this one, Insha-Allah."

"Yes . . . Insha-Allah," Intisar said. The words filled her mouth awkwardly, though she said them because in this case, they were the only words that would do.

"Oh, another thing," he added. "I let Ms. Ella look at the gift you brought. She said it looked like a baby dove. It's real interesting, thanks again for bringing it."

Intisar gave a nod and waved as she turned from the walkway to leave.

She walked back to the train in the afternoon silence. With the rain having slowed, the evidence of spring was all around—the bright green budding leaves on the tree branches, the damp earth, birds singing the promise of the new season. She thought about Sister Rose and Brother Mujaheed as she placed her token in the slot and walked up to the subway platform to await her train back into the city, back to her life apart—the one for better or worse that she'd crafted outside the embrace of the Temple folk.

She entered the train where the singsong pleading of a little boy quizzing his mother interrupted her thoughts.

"What's the name of the tallest mountain in the world?" the little boy asked.

"Mount Everest!" his mother said.

Intisar smiled to see them—the little boy reaching for his mother's face, covering her eyes as he asked his questions, and the mother patiently allowed him to explore the curvy places, pointy places, and deep grooves. But deeper, pressing concerns pulled

Intisar into herself. What would happen to Sister Rose? Why had she been so stubborn about reaching out? What might they have explored together and learned about the other if she had only believed in the strength of their bond? By the time she could return to see Sister Rose, would it be too late? More than anything, she wished that her illness wasn't real; wished that the world were different and that she hadn't wasted so much time.

"How much longer do we have to go?" the little boy asked.

"Just two more stops and we're home!" his mother said.

"Mama?" the boy repeated. "What's that lady doing?" He pointed to Intisar, though her eyes couldn't see, nor could she really hear any longer with her head bent before her upturned hands.

"Praying, honey," his mother said. "I think she is praying."

DUE NORTH

It was in the early days after the Imam's death that I started seeing him in visions. In the same way I saw my mother two years earlier after she died of congestive heart failure, he appeared in my dreams, resplendent in a white jalabiya and matching kufi, restored to vibrant health. He stood at my bedside with his arms outspread. No parts of him ever moved, save his blinking eyes, though he spoke to me, soft and gentle in a resonant baritone—a few notes deeper than his natural voice—telling me to set my heart at ease. He had made it safely to the other side where he was reunited with my mother, and that I must find a way to move on with my life.

The visions of my mother resolved within a few days as the brief reassurances were sufficient comfort to help me make it through the early stages of my grief, though visits from the Imam persisted, taking on new and unusual forms. After the first two appearances, the visions changed from dream-state occurrences to my father showing up in the waking hours as a fully reconstituted, living, breathing man.

The first time he appeared to me in this way was on the day of the Salat al-Janaza. I spent the morning with my brother Jabril, from whom I had been estranged for going on fifteen years, greeting the thousand or so worshipers who gathered at the Temple, come to pray for our father, who had been a pioneer and a pillar there dating back more than fifty years. We accepted their condolences, then stood for the four takbirs, praying that God keep us in a state of Islam and, for the sake of the Imam, that he died steadfast in faith. An interment had not been part of the plan on that day and declining any visitors, Jabril and I went back to our parents' home, where we spent all afternoon sorting through endless piles of clothes, books, and medical supplies, trying to figure out what to do with the last of our father's things.

After several hours of work, I found myself alone in the prayer room, having just completed Isha. I was sitting after the salat, finishing the last utterances of the du'a, which I spoke into hands held high before my face. When I was done, I brought them down and rested them on my lap and that's when I saw the Imam. He was seated just three feet in front of me, leaning in my direction, looking me up and down with a disapproving scowl.

My eyes widened at the sight of him, but I wasn't really scared, as the grief had exhausted whatever fear was left inside me, rendering it meaningless. I was more stunned by his realness, as I knew of an instant that I was seeing the Imam with the certainty of sight. He was not a vaporous, wispy presence, but a man of true-to-life gravity—his skin catching the orange-yellow glow of lamplight that cast onto a circular patch of the large Persian rug.

I thought to call his name and it was only then that he went away, standing up from his perch in front of me, a notebook tucked under his left arm, of the sort he always used to write his Friday address, then he walked clear through the oak-paneled wall like it was an open door.

It was all too strange.

I had spent enough time at my mother's and father's knees, growing up around the Temple folk and had heard all kinds of unusual things uttered within those walls, including their talk of specters who came calling, lingering in and around their homes. They came to visit, they said, in the form of friends or family members, recently passed on, with whom they had unresolved business—all stories which I dismissed outright, considering it haram and completely incompatible with the deen to believe such outlandish things.

Seeing my parents in my dreams was an entirely different matter as far as I was concerned. I saw it as the mind's way of trying to comfort me, smoothing out the peaks and valleys of my grief. The Imam appearing to me—all flesh and bone—should not have been possible and challenged everything I knew, and that my parents had taught me about my faith—my rock in this life, the one thing after their deaths I felt I had left to hold on to.

I never bothered thinking about which came first—whether I simply loved my father and by extension believed the things he believed, or if it happened that the things he had to offer me in that respect were tailored to my needs—but for as long as I could remember I had always poured myself into the deen.

It was, in part, the beautiful way he put things, forgoing textual explanations that were the substance of his daily study and his work at the Temple, instead directing Jabril's and my attention to nature, pointing out the hand of God in the unfolding of all things. We could not sit near a window and watch birds in flight nor look up at the night sky without his commentary, always inviting us to belief.

"And we see Andromeda over the spiraling arms of the Milky Way, knowing they are approaching each other, though among the billions of stars in their makeup, no two shall collide. Such is the vastness of the universe; the vastness Allah wants us to perceive in him—the vastness not just of his power, but of his love and his mercy—so great it fills up time and space. Who would not bow to the creator of such magnificence, who turned elements of hydrogen and helium into great fiery spheres to shine above terrestrial skies, pointing the way for all humankind who are guided by their light?"

It was a presentation of ideas that made every day feel like magic. The Imam had always told me that he saw the love of God inside me from the moment of my birth, but it was his words that led me to my earliest devotion. My parents didn't force me, and questioned my desire to live this way, though I started donning a hijab on a daily basis from puberty and adopted the chador at the age of nineteen, when I was a freshman in college.

I remained in the city during those years, though my parents, wanting me to pursue my independence, insisted I get a place of my own when I graduated. I moved to the Eastside Towers, just two blocks away from the all-brick Victorian where they raised my brother and me, though I always made myself available whenever they were in need.

It was a few years later, when Mom's heart started to give out, that they welcomed me back. I was all too eager to help them out, cooking and cleaning and sharing expenses to make sure they could live out the remainder of their years with relative ease.

On her deathbed my mother told me, mustering what breath she could, that I had been a good and righteous daughter. "God knows I named you right," she told me—the final confirmation that my sacrifice to her had been understood and accepted.

I shared similarly tender moments with my father after his late-stage prostate cancer diagnosis. In the past he could be quite demanding in the home, ordering my mother and me about when we hadn't done things to his standard, though in his final months, he never complained about the care I gave him. He even told me I was a gift to him sent straight from Allah, a gift that he felt he didn't deserve.

There had been one confusing conversation near the end of his life. After a visit from the home health aide, I sat at the Imam's bedside, patting his head with a cold compress, praying aloud that Allah be pleased with him, and assuring him I would continue on, abiding by his example long after he was gone.

That's when the Imam looked at me, his eyes welling with tears.

"But I," he said with a rasp, struggling to get out the words. "I misled you. I completely misled you, honey. Someday I hope you can forgive me."

I frowned when he said it, placing the straw from a tall glass filled with ice water near his lips, dismissing his self-flagellating talk as either a side effect of his medication or the thoughts of someone who saw his days drawing to a close, living them out with nervous anticipation of the final judgment.

I knew it was nothing to do with me but his own conscience that made him say those words, as I never saw my father as a man with faults and never saw myself as owed anything more than what he already provided.

While he was alive, I always made a point to show my gratitude, and so I sat on the carpet, wondering why the Imam would appear to me in this way and why he seemed so angry. I knew better than to think of myself as an innocent, feeling in my heart that a Muslim might earn hellfire for holding on to such a notion, though I had to give myself credit for conscientiousness. I was by no stretch a perfect human being, though I told myself, come the day of judgment, I would be standing before the creator of the heavens and the Earth, some part of me assured that I had done my best to live out the letter of his commands.

I was thinking this as sounds of laughter filtered into the prayer room from where Jabril was watching television, just a few feet away in the den. I was mildly disturbed those first few minutes, grappling with the ghost and why it had shown itself to me, but hearing him in that moment so full of gaiety was like a thorn in my side. The discrepancy was too obvious, as it was clear to me that if anyone between the two of us deserved a haunting, it was surely Jabril.

It had been fifteen years since we resembled anything close to a real family unit—a reality that back in those days of togetherness I could not have predicted, taken as we all were with the talents God had placed within Jabril, namely the sparkling elegance of his mind.

Jabril had shown an early aptitude for the hard sciences and was entranced by mathematics, "the purest, clearest language in the universe," and he would perform all kinds of experiments that helped make useful the formulas and theories that were always dancing around in his head.

And perhaps this was the major difference between us. In assimilating lessons from the Imam, they dwelt in my heart where I could feel entranced by the idea that an invisible, merciful being had comprised all of reality, from the mountains to the seas, though Jabril's affinities with the scientific method made him more parsing, examining the mechanics of the Imam's claims, his mind always seeking to uncover a more perfect explanation of the workings of things.

The Imam always encouraged his capacity for abstraction. He liked to keep an eye on me all the time, though he allowed Jabril to spend hours and hours alone, as he could always be found seated at his desk, absorbed in study. I wonder about the exact point when our father started to regret this choice—when he realized that, in encouraging Jabril's habits of mind, he raised a son who would grow up and only bring him heartache and trouble.

I was twelve years old the first time I sensed things headed south between Jabril and the Imam. We were seated at the dining room table one summer evening, about to eat the roast chicken and potatoes our mother had prepared for dinner, when there was a clap of thunder, followed by heavy rainfall, and the power went out, submerging the house in darkness.

I remember my fear, my voice shaking as I pleaded for my mother, who had stepped away from the table to light several candles, when the Imam tried to calm me down.

"Don't worry yourself," the Imam said, his face illuminated in the faint orange glow of the tapered candle Mom had set before him. "It's just Allah replenishing the earth. The rain is charged with blessings. Never be afraid of a storm, honey. That's just nature following God's command."

It must have been the darkness and the sense of dissociation that comes along with doing things unseen that made Jabril cut the Imam's words with laughter.

"The rain is charged with blessings," he echoed the Imam, mimicking his tone. "Nonsense," Jabril added. "We have rain because there's this thing called the water cycle. It evaporates into the air, condenses into clouds, then falls back to the earth. That's water following the commands of nature, not God. I don't know why you teach her these things; it will only confuse her later on."

It may have turned into one of those things that just got swept under the rug if the lights hadn't cut back on only moments after Jabril had spoken, so that he was immediately revealed, his face still bunched with contempt for the Imam.

"I guess we won't be needing these," Mom said, blowing out the candles, trying to lighten the mood, pining for a sense of normalcy that would evade us for the rest of the evening and for months to come.

That was around the time, when I was twelve and Jabril was sixteen, that the Imam decided to enroll us in a twelve-week course

in modern Arabic at the home of a man named Aziz Al-Hassan—
an adjunct professor at the university where our father worked a
day job for many years as a tax accountant.

He took us to the Al-Hassan home on Saturday mornings—a
forty-five-minute drive from the city into the county—where we sat
for two hours straight learning simple phrases and how to write short
paragraphs, filling reams and reams of writing pads with bulbous,
elementary attempts at the Arabic script, tugging our hands across
the page, trying to get accustomed to writing from right to left.

"It was something that was underemphasized in the Nation
days and that's partly why that whole thing came to an end," Dad
told us on our first ride out to Cattysburg. "And then you've got
these brothers that go to the opposite extreme, making their kids
learn all of this classical Arabic that won't be useful to you when
you're not in prayer. Standard Arabic will help you connect with
real people. Getting to talk to people across cultures will do more to
help your deen than anything else.

"He's a good man," the Imam said, "and promised me that he
would push you a little bit so that you'll have some proficiency
when it's all done. I think you'll be happy by the end of it when you
see how much you've learned. Here's something you'll find interesting." He looked to Jabril, who was next to him in the passenger
seat. "He and his wife come from Damascus, Syria. He's finishing
up his postdoctoral research on the early trade routes that helped
spread Islam beyond the Arabian Peninsula into West Africa."

I was sitting alone in the back seat, nodding as the Imam spoke
those words, looking at Jabril, who was staring out the window,
eyeing the shoulder of the road as if he might open the door at any
moment with the car still in motion and throw himself over the
railing.

He didn't want to be there, away from his books and his

formulas, and it showed from the minute Dad dropped us at the Al-Hassan family home and we walked into the front door to the dining room where we could begin our lessons.

Mr. Al-Hassan did not waste any time, nor indulge Jabril's standoffishness, and he immediately launched into the lessons, making very few gestures at getting to know us beyond learning our names.

I was somewhat put off by his approach at first, though I learned to love his teaching style as my facility with the language started to grow. It must have appealed to Jabril as well—Mr. Al-Hassan's methods broke through his aloofness and soon he seemed as absorbed in his learning as I was.

It was on the fourth week of classes that we started to see Mr. Al-Hassan as something more than our teacher, the day that we finally met his family. There was a jangle of keys at the front door, and he stood from his chair as his wife, Bassma, walked into the entryway. He went out to greet her and they spoke in emphatic Arabic, going back and forth, I assumed, about why she had come home early, interrupting his class before our lesson was through.

While they went back and forth, there were two small bodies that passed from the front door to the kitchen—Ayyub, their curly, blond-haired, eight-year-old son and a girl who looked my same age whose name was Zainab.

Mr. Al-Hassan and his wife were wrapping up their argument while Ayyub and Zainab poked their heads from behind a wall into the dining room where we were sitting. They did this like it was a game, and while it seemed to annoy Jabril, something inside of me wished they would come into the room and say hello. Zainab wore her hair covered in a long black scarf that draped loosely around her neck, exposing straggly auburn curls that poked out from underneath, and I remember wanting to get to know her—the girl from Syria with the big bright smile, who carried a spirit just like mine.

The argument between Mr. Al-Hassan and his wife must have ended with Mrs. Al-Hassan as the victor, because at the following week's class, Zainab and Ayyub were there in the house, standing several feet away from us in the kitchen, helping their mother prepare madlouka as we began our lessons. I tried my best to focus on what Mr. Al-Hassan was saying, but frequently made eye contact with Zainab, who was smiling in my direction as I struggled to assimilate what I was learning.

The lesson that day was focused on food. I was having a hard time with the tenses and was nearly at the point of tears trying to arrange the sentences and speak them aloud. Mr. Al-Hassan tended to be relentless in these moments, but noticing my exasperation, he gave us a ten-minute break. He walked outside to place a phone call and Jabril carried on, writing out the conjugations, as Mrs. Al-Hassan and Zainab entered the dining room with a plate of sliced apples and mandarin oranges.

Mrs. Al-Hassan uttered some words in Arabic to Zainab, who sat in the seat next to me. She shifted my writing pad and moved it closer to her and began jotting down notes as she spoke the phrases aloud.

"'Ana aakulu' means 'I am eating,'" she said in accented English, "'aakalatu' means 'I ate,' and 'sa'aakul' means 'I will eat.' Do you understand?"

In those moments I developed an impression of her as very studious and kind, with the same dedicated focus on learning as her father. I rehearsed the phrases with her until Mr. Al-Hassan returned, and as she left, she nodded with satisfaction, "You are getting clearer and clearer," she said before returning to the kitchen. "Keep it going!"

* * *

OVER THE NEXT few weeks, I came to know more about Zainab. Her family had moved to Cattysburg from Damascus only three years earlier, and in that time she taught herself English by listening to the radio and watching television. Her favorite show was *Jeopardy!* She was middle-school age like me but had tested well enough to land in the tenth grade at Cattysburg High, where she was at the head of her class. On top of her studies, her mother hadn't learned much English since their arrival, so she spent most of her days translating for Mrs. Al-Hassan.

"It isn't that I'm smart, I simply had to learn. America is not kind if you don't know the language. It is harder for you because you don't need Arabic the same way we need English to survive."

I asked if she ever felt burdened by leaving her homeland and her mother's dependence, and she laughed.

"It means I am capable and strong. I'm proud I can help her. Insha-Allah, someday I will be rewarded."

INTERACTING WITH ZAINAB helped me grow my interest in the lessons, and I became a more ambitious student, though Jabril grew bored of them.

Two weeks before the end of the Saturday sessions, Mr. Al-Hassan asked Jabril to try correcting his own work, using a red marker to circle his errors. Jabril had done as Mr. Al-Hassan asked, and when he was through, he turned toward me, placing his hands under the table and coloring his nails with the crimson ink.

He did it while Mr. Al-Hassan had his head bent down, going over Jabril's work. I didn't know what to think of what he was doing, but our eyes met—giving me the distinct impression that

Jabril had wanted me to notice. I felt relieved when he got up some moments later and went to the bathroom to wash his hands of the ink. He got most of it off, and I hoped for Jabril's own sake that Mr. Al-Hassan didn't notice, though my hopes were not enough to make it so.

Mr. Al-Hassan didn't let on for the rest of the afternoon just what he saw. He simply waved goodbye to us when the Imam pulled up to take us back to the Eastside, not providing any clue in the moment that it was the last day we would be allowed into his home.

Over breakfast the next morning, before I left with the Imam to attend the Sunday T'aleem service, he was unusually stern, confronting Jabril over his comportment at the Al-Hassan residence, mentioning some inappropriate behavior he had committed, reported to him by Mr. Al-Hassan that prohibited our return.

"I try to give you a bit of freedom, but not to violate standards of basic decency. What's for men is for men and what's for women is for women, and there's no room for anything in between."

Jabril rolled his eyes at the Imam, reaching new depths of contempt that shifted from open protest of his ideas to outright and constant displays of condescension.

"Well, if a white man said I did something wrong," Jabril uttered sarcastically, "then it must be the truth. So many years in the Nation, but what did it teach you about standing up for your own kind?"

Something about that combination of words made the Imam erupt in a fury. He had never raised a hand to either of us, though immediately he stood and balled his right hand into a fist. He stayed there for a long moment as if contemplating whether or not to hit Jabril, who sat nonplussed, waiting for the blow. The Imam relaxed his hand but commanded Jabril upstairs to his room—marking the rocky start of Jabril's final year at home.

OVER THE NEXT eight months, the household was troubled by constant eruptions between the two. The Imam had no proof but what Mr. Al-Hassan had told him about Jabril painting his nails, though he interrogated Jabril constantly about his notions of men's versus women's roles, how it was okay for him to present himself, and who he could love. Jabril seemed endlessly amused by how it all disturbed the Imam and loved egging him on, until the day that our father's anger reached a fever pitch, and my brother decided to leave home just one week before his high school graduation.

Jabril slammed the front door as he went, and the Imam tried to play like he was relieved to see him go.

"Good riddance," he yelled, as Mom started to cry, cupping her face, her back sliding down the vestibule wall before her bottom hit the floor.

"Just let the boy go," the Imam told her. "And I don't want to hear you speak the name of that broke-wrist devil in my house ever again."

And that's when I began to understand Jabril in a way that I never had before, finally grasping what his aloofness and his inclination toward his studies had been all about—a way to distract from the deeper passions of his heart, knowing that being himself—a young man with amorous feelings for other men—would never be tolerated in a family like ours.

The Imam had only ever said the worst things about people like that, and it made me feel for Jabril, knowing he was stifled in this way for his entire life. After he left, Jabril would occasionally send me messages as some evidence of his concern—informing me when he graduated magna cum laude from the college he attended up in Boston, and when he got his first job as an engineer—but it was watching time go by with no word from him to our parents that turned whatever sympathy I had for him into contempt.

It was a full eleven years into his estrangement from the family before he even reached out, sending Mom a card and flowers after I informed him in a brief email that she was diagnosed with end-stage heart disease. He made his first appearance at our mother's funeral, though he disappeared all over again despite promises to the Imam that he would try to keep in touch.

In the last few months of our father's life, Jabril started to come around more regularly, making the drive down from Boston every odd weekend to sit with the Imam, and then stayed a full five days leading up until he died—a late and paltry show of love that in no way repaid the Imam's investment in his life.

If anyone deserved to be haunted by the Imam it was Jabril, though he came to me as if I was the one who left, only showing up in the dreadful circumstances of our parents' deaths.

The thought stayed with me and would have bothered me all night, though remaining there on the carpet made me feel an inner ugliness—that, and the simple fact that I didn't know if the ghost preferred me in the room by myself, and would use my aloneness as a pretext to reappear.

I finally got up and entered the den where Jabril was sitting in the dark, save the blueish-white light of the wide-screen TV, laughing along with the live audience as he watched a stand-up comedy special.

Jabril adjusted himself, lowering his legs from the couch and sitting upright, his eyes following me as I sat in an adjacent armchair.

"Hey, little girl," he said, stretching his arms, "just wake up from a nap or something? I know packing those boxes almost had me beat."

I listened to him but didn't reply. I didn't want to have to remind Jabril about the obligations of the faith that he once knew and practiced for many years of his life—that it was well past nine thirty on a summer evening, the time appointed for Isha prayers.

"Something the matter?" Jabril finally lowered the volume of the television and leaned in my direction. Since I had been in the prayer room, he had used the time to repaint his nails the same black color he removed hours before the Salat al-Janaza, and rested his chin in his right hand, showing off the glossy manicure.

I shook my head at his question. I didn't want to talk about the ghost, nor express my upset that it had come to visit me while leaving him unperturbed.

He composed himself. "I know today was hard. Trust me, I feel it too."

I thought that was a strange construction, an interesting tell— his compelling my trust, as if anticipating that I might have my doubts about how the Imam's death was really impacting him.

HE HAD COME down the final time while the Imam was still talkative, albeit resigned to his fate. On that occasion, Jabril had been a mess of emotions, weeping at our father's bedside, asking his forgiveness for all the years of distance, and for resisting the overtures Mom and Dad had sent through me to try to reconcile. Only a few days later, before the Imam had even died, the worst manifestations of his grief had already begun to subside, and Jabril was starting to regain the buoyant demeanor that must have become his normal disposition in all the years away. It made me wonder if it was true that, for lack of love, Jabril had already processed the Imam's death and filed it away as another of life's obstacles, which he managed to overcome.

"If you thought the janaza was hard, do you think you'll be up for the funeral?" he asked, and his words sent a chill up my spine. "We're headed to Ossacola, girl—gem of the American South!"

His words put to the side for a moment my concerns with him and the ghost, and made me focus on another of the troubles that had been weighing me down since learning the details of our father's last will and testament.

As had been stipulated—the same as the Imam had done two years earlier for our mother, deciding not to bury her in Elysian Fields Cemetery like the other Temple folk—he wanted to have his remains transported south to the town where he and Mom had grown up, asking to be buried in the cemetery of the old St. Peter's Baptist Church—the place where they met, fell in love, and were married.

The Imam had first told me about his plans just a few days before Mom died.

"When the time comes," he told me, "we're going to carry her on home, send her off the Ossacola way. I wouldn't think to leave her up here, away from our people."

I always understood the significance of the church in their lives. Before my father became a minister in the Nation and then an Imam, he had been a youth pastor at St. Peter's, though, as far as I knew, it was all part of their past. "Our people" were the Temple folk, so while I understood the history, it bothered me that he did not want to bury her in the North, with the people who had embraced him as their leader, in the faith community he chose as his own.

The plan disturbed me for more pressing reasons that were only clarified in the execution of Mom's interment. Aside from the fact that the transport and delay contradicted the Prophet's advice to hasten the burial rites, I realized in the cemetery that the tombstones were facing south, so that the right side of Mom's body was oriented to the west, and not toward the holy city of Mecca.

"Allah knows best how things will happen in Ossacola," I finally answered Jabril, "though I do have some worries about Aunt Lottie running the show."

"That was the one thing that made me scratch my chin," Jabril said. "Like, why wouldn't Dad trust us, or at least you to carry out the funeral rites ourselves?"

When Jabril and I were young, the Imam rarely spoke about Ossacola in a favorable light, owing to the evil that had been visited upon them there. In the khutbas and other speeches he delivered at the Temple, the Imam was prone to repeating the story about the night when he and our mother decided to pack their things and leave town.

After he and Mom were married, they were granted residence in a parsonage, less than a quarter mile away from St. Peter's—close enough to hear the thunderous sound of the blaze and see the funnel of gray-black soot rising into the air, the evening St. Peter's was set aflame.

"Me and Donna," he told the Temple folk, "ran all the way down there to join the others who were already gathered on the roadside, standing in the distance, looking up at the trail of smoke as years and years of memories were reduced to ashes in a matter of minutes.

"I didn't need nobody to tell me who did it, as by that point, I had already spent my life watching gangs of good old boys—who were anything but—terrorizing the people in our community.

"It was then and there that I decided that I had enough of begging for crumbs of respect from white men when I could try to grow my own damn grain somewhere else."

It was the single worst thing that happened during his tenure as youth pastor and enough, just weeks later, to send him and my mother out of town, headed north. The second worst thing was the torment he endured in those years, meted out to him by his sister Lottie.

The Imam was sixteen and Aunt Lottie was fourteen when their parents died and, with their much older siblings having moved far from town, my father was charged with caring for his little sister. He dropped out of high school in order to earn a living, taking a job at a paint factory—sacrifices, the Imam had always said, that Aunt Lottie never appreciated.

"I felt a headache coming on almost every time she came in the house," the Imam said. "I always knew I was going to hear some kind of complaining or something else despite my best efforts to give her what she needed. There we were, having just lost our parents, and she was looking at me like a full-grown man, like I had the whole world figured out and was supposed to just give it to her wrapped in a big, shiny bow."

The only time she would "behave herself," as Dad liked to say, was when they attended the church.

"She liked to stand there, hands in the air, singing praises to God at the top of her voice, then seemed to forget everything she learned by the time we went home. That's when your mother came into my life in a serious way, and as far as me and my sister were concerned, it was a wrap from then on out."

The Imam talked about Aunt Lottie's escapades with the local Ossacola boys, whom she sought out despite his best efforts to keep her in the church or at home.

"Then she ran off with a man almost twice her age," Dad said.

"Almost killed me when she did it. Lottie was so furious about me having married your mother that she decided she was going to find a man of her own."

It was a tension that persisted between them through the years and that Jabril and I had witnessed ourselves on the rare occasions our parents took us down to Ossacola for visits.

I always believed my father's stories about Aunt Lottie, as they were in keeping with the few experiences I'd had with her on the phone and in her company.

She was a woman given to grandiose displays of her Baptist faith—addressing Jabril and me on the Imam's monthly calls, always greeting us sardonically, "in the mighty, mighty name of Jesus Christ!"

These indications of her pieties tried but failed to disguise resentments she held against the Imam, though it seemed unfair to me that Aunt Lottie would go so far as to extend her personal grievances with him and take them out on Jabril and me as we had nothing to do with their dispute.

Jabril was twelve and I was eight the first and last time our parents left us alone in her company. That afternoon she made our lunches, serving us cold cut sandwiches with a side of potato chips. We were hungry, and I remember us tearing through the food, though just before we finished eating, Aunt Lottie announced her mistake.

"Dear Lord, forgive me," she said. "That wasn't no smoked turkey. Dear God, that was ham!" Aunt Lottie yelled the words with feigned shock, staring into my eyes, awaiting the sounds of Jabril's and my disgust at having just ingested food she knew we were forbidden to eat.

Only time and circumstance—several hurricanes; Danielle, her eldest daughter, slain at the hands of a distraught ex-lover—had subdued the fire inside her, giving her a more laid-back demeanor on the family phone calls. Granted, she had been the picture of grace and civility at our mother's funeral two years earlier, though it didn't seem evidence enough to prove that Aunt Lottie had changed in a deep way. None of her newfound mildness allayed my fears that with the Imam "gone from the flesh," as she liked to say, her anger at our father would resurface—that in orchestrating the interment, Aunt Lottie would fail to honor the path he chose in life and turn the occasion from a solemn tribute into a raucous tent revival.

"It's weird," Jabril said after a long silence. "I know she came out to Mom's funeral and all of that, but I had no idea that she and Dad had grown so close that he let her handle the burial. Aunt Lottie is a piece of work for real. How much did he have the accountant send her again?"

"Over ten thousand dollars, I think it was," I replied, "but I'm not bothered by the money. I just don't understand." I hesitated, recalling in the moment a Hadith reported by Ibn Umar. He overheard the Prophet enjoin the Muslims to only mention good things and refrain from discussing the foibles and contradictions of the departed.

It might have been the ghost frowning at my prayers or the talk of Aunt Lottie that triggered it, but a long-repressed thought—one I tried to deny—came forward. Long before my father's illness, I began nursing suspicions that something had fundamentally changed in his relationship with the deen.

In the five years since he retired from the Temple, I began to notice subtle shifts in the way that he went about his daily life. On the afternoons where he wasn't working or gone fishing out in the county, he always spent the time at home in quiet contemplation, reading Quran in the prayer room or listening to the khutbas of his peers on an old CD player. He became more interested in music after his retirement, specifically gospel. I discovered this despite his attempts to hide it from me, stumbling upon him listening to quartets and mass choirs, which he would play at low volume and shut off completely whenever I came into his office to deliver his newspaper or mugs of hot coffee doused with cream and sugar.

Then there was the Bible that was always perched on his office desk, opened next to the Quran, which I had a niggling feeling he left there just for show, as the headings of his notebook scribbles changed from "Al-Nisa" to "Leviticus" and "Revelations," not to mention that he began inserting Bible quotes into everyday conversation.

They were things I had noted while my father was alive, though they remained disjointed in my mind; but sitting in the den with Jabril, the ideas were coming together inside me and made me fidget with anxiety in a way that my brother was starting to notice.

"What don't you understand?" Jabril's voice was soft as he leaned in closer. "You know it's safe to talk to me, right?"

Jabril was staring at that point, making me feel that he was less concerned about my well-being than that he was starting to look at me like I was a lever or a screw—some component in a laboratory device that had just come undone.

"I know it's the grief; it makes it hard, but I wonder if some of your suffering may be self-imposed. You're just—" Instead of finishing the thought, Jabril made a hand gesture like there was a mass of some sort in his lap and he was trying to contain the weight of it, then press it down.

"All I'm trying to say is you can find some relief even in the midst of all that's going on. I wondered if it would make you feel any better if you felt connected to more people, you know? If you put yourself out there a bit more."

Jabril's words were startling, uprooting me from my meditations on the Imam. While my brother rarely spoke with me about matters other than our parents or his engineering work, I could only imagine that he had no difficulties of his own in that arena. Over the years he would sometimes send me photos of himself and his friends, dancing in parades, waving their colorful flags, and pumping their fists in the air without the slightest bit of shame. I didn't want to imagine the extent to which Jabril had put himself "out there," and was more than a little appalled that he was so comfortable recommending his risky exploits to me.

"What are you even talking about?" I felt the sharpness in my voice, like I had just been pricked with a needle, genuinely taken aback by the direction of Jabril's probing. For the past seven years I had sustained myself, working as a student resource assistant at the Beverly T. Ferguson Elementary School and made myself a regular presence at the Jummah, even after the Imam stepped down. "My life is full and I'm more than content with the kind of people in my orb—"

"But are you dating?" Jabril cut me off. "You've never talked about any suitors? Any crushes? I mean, when's the last time you thought about spending your life with some—"

"I'm sorry," I interrupted my brother, standing from the armchair, "but I just remembered I forgot to perform my dhikr. If you hadn't noticed, it's something I always do before I fall asleep."

I could see in Jabril's eyes that he was stunned by my sudden departure, and he looked at me in a manner not dissimilar to the ghost as I left, then turned his attention back to the television.

It left a cloud of awkwardness that would hover until the next morning when Jabril packed up his SUV on the way back to Boston. I stood on the curb as he loaded the car and told him to drive safe. He shut the trunk and then approached me for a hug, which

I indulged, though there was a coldness in our embrace. We stayed this way for a moment, then I was first to pull away.

Jabril registered this and the smile that had started surfacing on his face faded of an instant.

"I'll see you in Ossacola in about a week," he said, businesslike, matter-of-fact. "Pack as light as you can. I don't have that much room in the trunk and I don't want to be overcrowded on the long drive back."

I nodded at his advice and watched my brother climb into his car and drive down the road before he turned at the stoplight. I sighed as he left, then walked back into the unlit foyer, grateful, despite the ghost, to be left alone, in silence.

AFTER JABRIL WAS gone and it was just me in the house, the Imam started visiting regularly enough that I began to make out some of his habits. He never bothered me in the mornings, I guess owing to the fact that those were my saddest times. In life he always called the adhan to wake us, and the early silences in that first week and a half without him were almost too much to bear. In those moments, not even his spookiest maneuvers—walking through walls or secreting himself through the floors—could extricate me from my sorrow enough to even register his presence.

The afternoons were the times he preferred to announce himself. That week before the trip to Ossacola, I was sitting in the breakfast nook, preparing materials for the school year to begin in the coming weeks, and didn't even have to look up to know he was there—his folded hands appearing at the edge of the table where I was working.

He didn't like when I ignored him, so whenever I moved, he followed me, and while I never looked him in the eye, I could see

his reflection in the office mirror and in the sliding glass door leading to the backyard.

I was cleaning the house on Thursday, trying to get it ready for
my departure the following afternoon. I was vacuuming the living
room floor with the TV on when I heard the weight of his footsteps
behind me in the kitchen. I pretended not to notice and continued
with my cleaning chores, hoping he would disappear, but he lingered there. In the mirror above the mantel I could see him leaning
his back on the countertops and folding his arms until I got up the
nerve to finally ask him what he wanted from me.

I turned around and there he was, his face a little stunned,
almost contrite, when his gaze moved away from me and toward
the television. His eyes widened for a second, looking at the screen,
and before I could even pose the question, he disappeared. I looked
at the TV and saw what it was that made him go—footage of
Naomi Campbell scantily clad in a bikini, striding down a long
catwalk.

It made me laugh out loud, and with the laughter I felt a slight
relief, as it was the first moment of true levity I had felt since his
passing. It helped me know the ghost was really the Imam and not
an evil djinn appearing to me in his form. I laughed at the continuity,
that in death, my father had retained the same prudishness—shying
away from the sight of any woman that wasn't my mother—that he
always demonstrated in life and had passed down to me. I couldn't
say I was scandalized by the sight of Naomi Campbell dressed the
way fashion models dress, though I never made a habit of gawking
at women and so I didn't feel compelled to watch. I reached for the
remote like I was about to change the channel, though just before I
pressed the button, I felt a moment of clarity, realizing that if I left
it on, maybe the Imam wouldn't bother me as much, trying to push
me to the point of alarm.

I left the television on all afternoon, into the evening, but the Imam, being slick, sought me out when I was away. I saw him again, in the hallway mirror, standing behind the closet door where I went to grab my carry-on suitcase. With no television upstairs, I did the next best thing, opened my laptop computer and navigated to a website that advertised women's underwear. That's when I knew, once he left the second time that day, that this was the trick— keeping the images nearby. At the airport I purchased a thick magazine and left it open to a La Perla advertisement, holding it to my chest and resting it on my lap over the entire journey south, lest he appear in the next seat or come walking down the aisle, staring me down but still refusing to let me know what he was after.

There had been thick cloud cover throughout most of the flight, though it dissipated on our approach, exposing large rectangular tiles of green and red earth etched into perfect rows—the cotton and the indigo plantations coming more and more into relief as we landed.

I became entranced by the sight of this place that I had been a few times before, but whose beauty I had never perceived, perhaps because I only ever visited in the company of my parents, and without them around, I was finally seeing it with my own eyes. The undulating, uninterrupted landscape, the slowness of life unfolding on the ground—all of it so pleasantly distinct from my life in the city that I was consumed in the moment, trying to comprehend how such awful things could have happened to my parents in a place of such natural beauty—fascinated to the point that I had completely stopped thinking about the ghost.

I ordered a car at the airport, and a young man by the name of Avon a.k.a. "Da Realest"—who looked about twenty-years old— pulled up a few minutes later in a decked-out Cadillac Seville. He was kind enough to help place my suitcase in his trunk and engaged me in a brief conversation, telling me how he went about installing the colorful LED lights inside of Southern Comfort—his name for the Seville—though I spent most of the thirty-minute drive from Tolston staring out the window at the columns of pine trees that lined the two-lane highway headed south—trees grown up in a locale I was finally starting to see as my own, in a sense, and not just the coincidental someplace that my parents had left years earlier.

Avon stayed in the fast lane, though another car, a four-door Chevrolet Colorado, pulled up to us, catching pace at our right side. I looked over as we maintained speed and caught eyes with a child in the back seat. He was blond with freckles and could have been no older than nine. I smiled at him, trying to make the eye contact feel less awkward, but the blankness of his face turned into a hardened stare. The pickup truck gained a bit of speed, overtaking our car and merged ahead of us into the fast lane.

I watched the truck barrel over the hill on the horizon, noting, as it became small in the growing distance, the Gadsden banner on the tailgate and the Confederate flag that was fastened in the place where the rear license plate ought to have been.

We made it to Ossacola by dusk. I almost didn't notice once we passed the incorporation limits, preoccupied as I was for the duration of the ride by the kid and the Confederate flag, but the driving slowed and I uncrossed my eyes enough to see the Piggly Wiggly on Olston Road, and that's when I knew I had arrived.

Jabril and I had made plans to stay with our mother's people, though I had the driver take me to Aunt Lottie's, on the far side of town. She asked me to head that way as early as possible so we could go over a few details related to the interment scheduled for the following day, and so I paid the extra fare to have the driver pull into the driveway of her brick-front rambler, which sat a long distance off the main road.

There were three vehicles lined up under the car porch and it startled me to see Jabril's Jeep Wrangler among them, as I had assumed he would head directly to the Cliffords'. I neared the house and saw past the cars to the open screen door leading to Aunt Lottie's illuminated kitchen, and Jabril was there in silhouette. He opened the door and came toward me, his head no longer clean-shaven, as he was clearly trying to regrow his Mohawk, and he had left his nail beds a natural pink. He raised an eyebrow when he got close, and I wondered what it was that had triggered his interest until I looked down at the magazine in my hand and saw the image that was facing him—a photo of Liya Kebede in a one-piece bathing suit, perched on the beach, staring at the camera like a leopard ready to pounce.

I immediately folded the magazine under my arm and gave him a little hug before he took my bags and placed them in his trunk for the drive out to the Cliffords', then he led me inside.

Before I even stepped over the threshold I was hit by the unctuous smell of chicken frying in the kitchen.

"You made it right on time," Jabril said, rubbing his hands and licking his lips. "Auntie made us a whole spread." I looked over and saw a golden mound of cooked chicken lying on a thin stack of paper towels. I walked closer and saw the collard greens, candied sweet potatoes, black-eyed peas, and cornbread arranged in various lidless containers.

"Everybody else ate already," he said, "but I wanted to wait until you got here before I grabbed myself a plate." I looked from the food back to Jabril, knowing as good as it all smelled, that I was uncomfortable with the idea of eating anything at Aunt Lottie's, and in just that moment she appeared from behind my brother, her stout caramel frame striding into the kitchen. She didn't look the way I always saw her in public. Her hair was wrapped in two-dozen pink rollers and prominent dark circles—which she usually hid with makeup—showed about her eyes, though there was a customary air of fierceness around her that was softened by the winding down of the day. Her eggplant-colored housecoat caught the slight breeze of her swinging arms as she walked toward me.

"Don't worry," Aunt Lottie said as if she had just read my mind. "There's nothing here you can't eat. I did my homework; went out of my way to make everything halal—at least, I tried my best."

She looked me up and down in that moment like she was waiting for me to respond, then she pointed to Jabril.

"Go ahead and get yourself a plate," Aunt Lottie said. "And Taqwa"—she spoke to me without looking up from her pots— "go to the back and get yourself washed up a little. I know you've been traveling all day and must be a little damp up under all them clothes."

I did as I was told and walked from the kitchen through the dining room and the den where my cousins Winston and Christine were seated on opposite couches watching *Wheel of Fortune*. I immediately recognized Winston by his high-top fade, though I had just assumed the person to my left, as I passed down the hall toward the bathroom, was one of his friends. It was only once I washed my hands and face, then doubled back toward the kitchen, that I realized it was not a man but a woman, and that she was my cousin, barely resembling the woman I last saw at my mother's interment. Whereas on that occasion Christine wore a mid-length black dress with her hair in a relaxed bob, sitting there on the couch, her hair was cut close to the scalp and she wore baggy jeans and a polo T-shirt so oversized you could barely make out her feminine shape.

I tried my best not to stare at her, immediately lowering my gaze after waving hello to both her and Winston on my way out of the bathroom. I headed toward the kitchen, where I fixed myself a small plate of food and sat down at the table with Jabril, though I couldn't help wondering what had happened to Christine, what had so drastically changed in her life that it would make her want to start dressing like a man.

I was about to take a bite of the cornbread, when I looked up toward the television. Pat Sajak was standing with a large note card in hand, trying to guide the contestant to solve the word puzzle. "I /_ m/ v _ _ y / _ _ y!"

"Well, that's an obvious one," Winston said, chuckling, then looking at Christine. I turned to look at her as Winston spoke, but noticed her ignoring him, as she was clearly staring at me.

Winston managed to regain her attention as the contestant successfully solved the puzzle—"I am very sly!"—but I was more than bothered by her attention. The last time I saw her, I was dressed in the exact same fashion, in a voluminous all-black shroud, with my hijab fitted tightly about my face and neck. It made me look around, unsure of what it was about me that had so captured her attention when there was nothing new in my appearance, but Aunt Lottie interrupted my speculation, shouting at the two of them from the dining room.

"Alright now," she said. She set down three full glasses of lemonade iced tea on the table for herself, Jabril, and me, then raised her voice a few degrees. "Turn that television down right this minute and, matter fact, y'all two should probably find your way up out of here. You been sitting on that couch while I been working all day and I don't think I heard neither one of you speak a word to your cousin when she came through the den. Go head on," she said, waiting as they rose, shutting off the television and stretching from the couches. "That's why you got your own apartments anyway.

You done eat up all my damn food like you ain't even concerned that I'm living on a fixed income. Get yourself on out of here and leave me in peace!"

They went out of the side door before Aunt Lottie had even finished her lament. An engine vroomed in the driveway, and I turned to watch the plumes of dust from the kitchen window as Winston and Christine drove down the driveway and onto the main road.

"Goodness gracious!" Aunt Lottie said, completely miffed as she settled into the chair at the head of the table. "Well, I raised the little crumb snatchers," she went on, her tone more self-reflective than she had been just a minute earlier, matching the calm that had begun to settle over the house. "Can't be too hard on 'em. They must have got some of their antics from me."

Aunt Lottie had a planner laid open next to her lemonade and put on a pair of glasses to read it while Jabril took a bite of the candied sweet potatoes. I merely sat, staring at the food, still unsure of whether or not to eat, though more than food, I was overwhelmed by the temperature of the kitchen and dining room. I reached to the far side of the table to tear a sheet from a roll of paper towels and brought it to my face, patting the beads of sweat that had started pearling on my brow.

Aunt Lottie was still looking down at the planner, though she started talking to me.

"Taqwa," she said, "I already told your brother, now I ought to tell you that the car is coming to pick y'all up at ten o'clock in the morning, which will get you to the graveyard at around ten thirty. I don't know how long it takes you to get yourself together, but we can't afford no delay. These undertakers nowadays? Make you want to feel it's asking too much seeing your family off to the grave. They'd rather have you leave them at a mausoleum than let you see the final resting place. That's all to say, they been giving me a hard time, so we got to keep to schedule. Buford and Lewis? Now, my brother knew better than to go with them folks, but he insisted on that company, and who am I to go against him? Say," Aunt Lottie went on, "speaking of your father's wishes, how's it coming with the eulogy? Have you had a chance to get it all down?"

As I had learned a week earlier at the reading of the will, the Imam had requested me to offer a brief reflection at the interment service—an assignment that was constantly on my mind over the past several days, though I couldn't bring myself at any point to write a single word.

I shook my head at her question and thought she was going to ask why I hadn't finished, but she furrowed her brow at me instead.

"I don't remember Donna ever wearing her scarf like you doing—I mean, all tied up around your neck, fitt'na choke you or something. I always saw hers wrapped up in a neat little bun. Keep dressing like that in this heat," Aunt Lottie went on, "and you'll catch yourself a haint, I can tell you that much.

"Do she always eat like this," Aunt Lottie turned to Jabril, who was already half done with his food, addressing him like I wasn't sitting in their midst.

"Don't worry about her, Auntie," Jabril cut in. "You know they're going to have food waiting for us over at the Cliffords'. I'll make sure she gets something in her before she goes to sleep."

"She going through it," Aunt Lottie said of me. "Trust me, I know how it feel—like a room with no windows and no doors, a deep, dark hole with no light coming from nowhere. That's how it do. Grief is quite the messy companion, but it do fade away a little with time."

Aunt Lottie's eyes drifted away from the table to the buffet, where there were several photos of Danielle arranged in silver frames—one doing the split in her red-and-white high school uni-

TEMPLE FOLK

form, another of her standing in a long, black satin dress with her first boyfriend, a corsage of baby's breath on her wrist. Aunt Lottie made a deep sigh and shook her head.

"What helps is having people around who love you," she said. "Are you dating anyone, got a serious boyfriend or something? Child, often as I hear from y'all, you could be married, as far as I know."

I turned from my plate and looked at Jabril, who received my glance and then he looked at Aunt Lottie.

"It's just one of those things she doesn't talk about—you know how strict Dad was. I, on the other hand, may have the opposite problem." Jabril raised both eyebrows. He took a paper towel and patted the sides of his mouth clear of grease.

"Alright now!" Aunt Lottie's voice was bright, finding an outlet for the banter that she wanted with me but that I couldn't supply.

"So you're dating but no one special has appeared on the scene?"

"Well, not quite," Jabril replied, a sly grin spread across his face. "I've been with this young lady, Brandi, for just over a year now. It's going pretty well so far . . ."

"But you can't pop the question yet, can you?" Aunt Lottie smiled. "When you find a good thing, you gotta make a move. Plus, how old are you now—thirty-two? And Taqwa's, what? Twenty-eight? Ya'll getting up there in age. Time to start thinking about making a family of your own. Having your own family can help you out in a time like this, that's all I'm saying."

Jabril and I looked at each other, though I was first to turn my face back to my plate so that he wouldn't see me roll my eyes. While he was visiting from Boston I had heard him on the phone, talking in low tones to someone, but I remember him calling them Brandon and not Brandi. It seemed like such a strange choice for someone who had spent his whole life bucking authority, who would sit in the home of Aunt Lottie—a woman who was only a few drops of blood away from being a stranger in a sense—and evince such cowardice by not coming out and simply telling her the truth of who he was.

"Well if it's any help," Aunt Lottie said, "I just want you both to rest assured that everything is ready for tomorrow. I checked and double-checked to make sure that everything is just the way your father said he wanted it. I know you're still working on the eulogy, Taqwa, but I trust that you've got it under control."

I had taken a small chicken drumstick in my hand, though I set it down at her statement.

"I've been trying to think of something to write," I started, "but for whatever reason I haven't figured out what to say. It's like." I paused, trying to gather my thoughts. "I'm not really sure if the picture I had of my father is true to who he really was."

"Well, you were his little right hand." Aunt Lottie looked surprised. "Aside from Donna, can't nobody know him better. Plus, it's just a minute or two. You can think of something to say for that long, even if it's just some pleasantries—"

I cut her off. "I've tried that, but nothing feels right." I almost spoke about the ghost and my growing worry that the Imam would pop up just as I found the right words, but I only sat there, staring from her back to my plate.

She adjusted herself in her seat. "It's some things I supposed he never got around to telling y'all . . . well—" Aunt Lottie stopped herself and took a sip of lemonade, the ice making sloshing sounds inside the glass. "I ain't trying to start no whole heaping mess with your father already dead. All in all, your father was a good man and did everything he could to make amends for what happened back in the day."

"We already know about the church," Jabril interjected. "He

used to mention it all the time when he gave his Friday sermons. How the Klan came and burned it down, and then the preacher went on, telling the whole congregation to turn the other cheek. He always said it made him so mad, what the preacher said, that he and Mom left for the north in the middle of the night, saying he would never have been able to get away if he told anyone about his plans. It was a pretty awful situation, but it wasn't a secret he tried to keep from us."

Aunt Lottie stared at Jabril for a long moment, then shook her head.

"Everett . . . my word," she said, calling our father by his birth name. "Guess some things never change. That's really the story he told you?"

Aunt Lottie was still shaking her head, and when neither Jabril nor I had a reply to offer, she cleared her throat and looked up at the ceiling fan spinning overhead.

"I don't know how the two of you get on, but coming up, your father and I were very close—the youngest of five children, with the next in line over ten years older than your dad. That's why you never knew your grandparents. They were in their early forties when they had Everett and they died when we were in our teens. It was hard for us, but we always had one another.

"Mama was the last to go, dying just a few years after our father, and it was around that time that Everett started getting interested in the ministry. He was always in the church, that's where he met Donna after all, but I think it was Mama's death that made him more interested in taking on the cloth.

"He was nineteen when he gave his first sermon, if you can believe it, preaching about holding on to God even when he seems far away. I'll never forget it—how good he was up there. I mean, from where I was sitting, I didn't have to be convinced that your

212

dad was the real thing, and it wasn't just me. After a while people started to catch on, and he got a reputation as a young man of
God—completely filled up on the Holy Spirit. It wasn't long before
the church took him on as pastor. They let him conduct the Bible
study and deliver the Sunday message about once a month.

"His name started getting around, and people would travel from
long distances just to come and hear him preach. I just wished my
parents had been around to see him like that—a good man, married, spreading the good news; they would have been real proud to
raise a son that went on to do something so wonderful.

"Your father had a friend named Michael. I call him a friend,
but the two of them were more like brothers. They used to do
everything together—hunting and fishing, whatever it was we got
up to in those days, they did it. They only stopped spending time
when Everett married Donna, and since I was still technically a
child in his care, I was around to see how the two of them wasn't
really talking no more. He was just in the house all the time, boss-
ing me this way and that like he was my father. I think he just
wanted to be alone with Donna, you understand, and there I was,
his little sister, still needing his help. It was frustrating for him, I'm
sure, but more so for me 'cause I was just as uncomfortable. Don't
nobody like feeling like the third wheel. Anyhow, that was around
the time when I started dating Billy, Samuel's father. We started
getting pretty serious pretty fast, and even though Everett didn't
approve, he let loose of me a little 'cause it gave him more time to
spend with your mom.

"It was a Saturday, and I was sitting in the little living room,
waiting on Billy to pull up and take me on a drive, when I saw Michael walking up to the front porch. I was the one who answered
the door, but Everett was close behind me, and so I was right there
when Michael asked—this big ol' smile on his face—if the two of

them could go out fishing. Your dad talked with Donna about it and after she waved him off, I watched the two of them walking down the long driveway, then turn onto the main road, headed to Lake Nicodemus.

"Billy came a short while after to pick me up, and I remember feeling nervous about it because your father had a rule that I had to be back in the house by nine o'clock at night, and I didn't get home until nine thirty. I had expected him to really lay into me, but when I got in the door, all I saw was Donna sitting at the dining room table, stressed out because y'all's father was still gone.

"We was both worried that the worst might have happened to him, but he finally came home, stumbling up the stairs around an hour after I got back. Both me and Donna was so relieved to see him, but he wasn't in no mood for us expressing any kind of happiness for his return. You know how your father had these narrow eyes, like he was always halfway squinting to see you? Well, not that night. His eyes were big as saucers, and he was sweating like crazy, like he had just seen a ghost. He was clearly terror struck, but full of anger at the same time, and didn't tell me or Donna nothing about what happened to make him that way. All he said was we needed to go to bed so we could be ready for church the next day.

"We carried on the next morning, trying to pretend like nothing was wrong, then got to the church, come to find out that only half the folks was there. And that's when word started to spread, and me and Donna finally heard the news that Michael . . ." Aunt Lottie looked down at the table, wrapping the fingers of her left hand around her neck. She shook herself of the memory, trying to bring herself back to the story.

"Anyhow, all the folks in the congregation was talking when the choir came out and started to sing, and when that was through, your father, who wasn't assigned to speak that week, walked up to the pulpit to deliver that Sunday's message.

"Everybody was real upset as you can imagine, but watching Everett stand up there filled us with a sense of calm, like despite what we'd just heard happened to Michael, we was in good hands and everything was going to be okay.

"He got up there and started talking, his voice less sure than it usually was. That's how they used to get started—all calm and slow. I was waiting for the message to build, to take all of us somewhere, we was so in need of a good word, but there was my brother standing in front of us, with all the energy of a garden snail, talking about turning the other cheek. That we had to forgive the men who did what they did to Michael, as Jesus forgave those who betrayed him. He stood up there preaching that message and walked away from the pulpit, looking just the way we all felt—hollow and defeated.

"Your father became real mean after that; it seemed like the smallest little things could set off his fuse, you know, 'cause he was there to witness what had happened to Michael. He couldn't help him then, and he didn't help us with the pain we was feeling around Michael's death. The problems I was having with your dad before wasn't nothing compared to what came later. We was practically fussing every day, and it got so bad that I decided to move out of the house and settle with Billy, which I regret to this day. I was just an impressionable girl and didn't see the little signs they tell you to look out for, but when I moved in with him, I started noticing things—the drinking, the hiding out on the weekends, all the things he was doing to show I meant about that much to him." Aunt Lottie pinched her fingers together, leaving space enough for a gnat to fit in between.

"I lasted about two months in the house with Billy before I decided I couldn't take any more of his ways. Now Billy had me out in Camden, which is about an hour from here, so it was quite an ordeal for me to pack my little suitcase and move back in with Everett— far enough away that I didn't hear a peeping word about the fire. All I remember was having my friend drive up to that little house where they was staying. I walked up there early one evening and remember feeling stunned that the car was gone and there were no lights on in the house. I knocked a few times, but no one was there. Then I looked through the window and saw all the pictures taken down from the walls, and that's how I found out—standing on the old porch by my lonesome—that your father was gone. It was a bit later that I learned what they did to the church. And that's how my life began—I moved back in with Billy and became a mother, holding on to the scary thought that the child in my arms was the only family I had left, as my brother had disappeared into thin air.

"After Samuel was born—one year later to be exact—Everett finally contacted me. He sent a letter under an assumed name, and the lead pastor at St. Peter's delivered it to me. I could tell from the handwriting who it was, and then I read what it said, letting me know that he and Donna had made their way to the north and he wasn't ever coming back home. There was a ten-dollar bill inside and a phone number to reach him. I called the first time a few weeks later, but it took him several months after the call to tell me the whole truth of what had happened. He and Michael had gone to the far side of the lake, when they were confronted by a gang of good ol' boys. After they did their business with Michael, they made a move on Everett, when one of them recognized him as a "famous preacher" from St. Peter's Church. They decided to let him go on the condition that he not say anything about what happened at the lake. That's why he preached that god-awful sermon, and even when he did what they told him to do, they still burned down the church. I think your father was just disgusted at that point—disgusted with the Klan, with the South, and with hisself—so he decided he couldn't stay here no more and didn't tell a soul when he left.

"I wasn't surprised in the least when I found out he had joined the Nation, fed up like he was with the state of the country. I always wondered if saying all he said in them suits and bow ties was enough to clear him, to release the weight and the guilt of how he left. I guess it's just some things that's not for us to know, but it was your father preaching about turning the other cheek. For him to put that message on someone else, claiming it wasn't him talking that way, tells me what he must have been carrying over all those years. Now you may feel you have reason to not believe me, but that is the God's honest truth. He tried to make it right, and God is merciful, so it's nothing to hold on to, just gives you a little perspective, that's all."

We sat in silence for a good long while after Aunt Lottie stopped talking. Jabril was first to dismiss himself, getting up from the table to go wash his face in the bathroom. Aunt Lottie was next, wordlessly gathering our plates before heading into the kitchen where she turned on the tap to make a sudsy pool of soaking water.

I was overwhelmed with everything that Aunt Lottie had said, though something compelled me to walk over to where she was standing, sending ripples down the back of her housecoat from the motion of her scrubbing the dirty dishes.

Aunt Lottie must have felt me behind her, because her dress went slack as she stopped scrubbing. She turned to face me, looking me up and down until I had fashioned the words I wanted to speak.

"Auntie," I began, "you mentioned something earlier and I just wanted to ask, is it just the heat? Is that what brings on a haint?"

Her face had been severe with worry as I asked the question, though she relaxed a little when I was through.

"A haint?" She laughed a little as she sighed. "Child, I was just talking. That's something I always heard the old folks say around this way: 'You'll catch a haint...' It's just one of them things, something to make conversation, not nothing no serious people really believe. But why are you worried?" she asked me. "Is there something bothering you?"

I didn't know how much to tell her without eliciting a strange reaction, so all that came out were my concerns about delivering the eulogy the next morning. Aunt Lottie dried her hands of the dishwater and brought me in close for a hug.

"Oh, girl," she said, speaking into my arm. "You'll do just fine. He made his choices, but at the end of the day, your father was a good man. He cared for you, raised you up good and stron—" Aunt Lottie stopped herself before she finished the word, and just held me for a minute. "He was a good man, Taqwa. Whatever you write in your eulogy, be sure you mention that."

A SIX-DOOR LIMOUSINE from the Buford and Lewis Funeral Home arrived to the Clifford family residence at ten a.m. the next morning. The house belonged to Aunt Pam, my mother's sister, who considered herself the worldliest woman of Ossacola and filled her house with trinkets from her frequent travels. In the guest bedroom where Jabril and I stayed, I had to pull the curtain back from behind several wood carvings she'd bought on a trip to Kenya, to see the car pulling up and watched as the heavy-set driver emerged in a suit and tie, walking awkwardly—taking a half second longer on every odd step—on his way to the front door. I eventually realized it was a prosthetic leg that had altered his stride, when I saw the metal pole poking up from the thin sock hovering above his black patent leather shoe. I was so entranced by the sight of the man that I hadn't noticed Jabril hovering over me with folded arms, saying it was time for us to leave.

"And don't forget to bring your remarks," he said, walking out of the bedroom door, pointing at the leather-bound notebook that I had left on top of the black lacquered drawer Aunt Pam had bought on a trip to South Korea.

We had to share a room on the night before the interment, and Jabril had gone to bed to the sight of me sitting on the floor, pen and pad in hand, trying to write the eulogy. I remained in that position for several hours, though I hadn't gotten down a single word, as I was overwhelmed with everything Aunt Lottie had shared earlier in the evening.

I got past the question of whether or not Aunt Lottie was to be trusted and believed, at least on the matter of our father's past, and so the revelations, which I took to be true, had disturbed me. I didn't know why, when he shared so much about the circumstances of his departure from Ossacola, he would leave out his having witnessed a lynching or that he had been the one to preach the sermon forgiving the men who killed his friend. It struck me that this might have been the substance of his apology before his death, knowing that in the aftermath, the facts would emerge and that Jabril and I would be left grappling with the truth of how it was not some other preacher but his own shameful cowardice that had made him abandon his hometown.

The thought made it more possible to feel that, perhaps, there had indeed been other levels of his deception in our interactions, and it had the odd effect of making my suspicions more potent that he had abandoned Islam without explicitly telling anyone. After some hours I finally lay down, with the notebook still empty. Noth-

ing appropriate to the occasion had come to mind, as the words
I fell asleep wanting to write down portrayed a version of myself
that I had never shown, of which I never thought myself capable
to access—the growing feeling I had that the Imam was a liar and
a fraud—words that felt awful to hold on to and that I knew I
couldn't commit to paper, much less bring myself to speak at his
memorial.

It was in this state of mind that I awoke in the morning, and
where I remained as I got ready, then sat hovering at the bedroom
window. It showed in the way I pulled at the fabric, tightening the
headscarf atop my head, refastening the pin at my chin, before I
grabbed the empty notebook, stomping on my way out the door.

A new St. Peter's had been rebuilt closer to town and would
have taken just a few minutes for us to drive to from the Cliffords',
though the journey to the old burial grounds was much farther,
taking us beyond the two-story federal-style buildings and shops
that circled the town square. After a twenty-minute drive out of
town, through the cotton fields, the limousine slowed and rocked as
it turned off the highway down a long, graveled road. I felt my eyes
welling with tears. I turned to Jabril, who was facing out the opposite window, and saw him raise a Kleenex to blow his nose. I knew
he was thinking of our mother, and how we'd traveled the same un-
even roads just two years earlier to lay her in her final resting place.

I doubted that he could be thinking about the Imam in that
moment, and for the first time in many years I felt allied with Jabril
in his assessment of our father. I emerged from the car and walked
alongside my brother, into the green tent, down its center aisle toward our front-row seats, feeling a kind of emptiness that contradicted the solemnity of the occasion.

Aunt Lottie and fifty or so other guests, most of whom I didn't
know, were already seated inside at the time of our arrival, speak-

ing low against the hum of the generator that powered the two microphones that were situated a few feet away from the shimmering gold of the Imam's flower-draped casket.

I felt the people quiet themselves as we walked along and met eyes with a few of them, noting the intensity of their stares toward me, wondering if anyone among them had been informed that the Imam was a Muslim with Muslim children, and that it was only correct for me to be dressed in the way I was. I tried not to feel I was being overly scrutinized and so I walked with my head pointed to the ground, trying my best not to make out their curious expressions, and to deflect from the fact that the noon hour hadn't even arrived and yet I was boiling hot underneath the chador.

Only a few minutes passed before the crowd was completely settled and four men dressed in white suits, noted in the program as the Tolston Tenors, greeted the crowd before launching into an arrangement of "Nearer My God to Thee."

The music was pleasant enough and did indeed remind me of the Imam and the barbershop quartets he played at low volume in his study—the music he tried to hide but was so comfortable showcasing in death. They finished their tune to great applause and shouts of "hallelujah" before Tyrell Buford, assistant pastor at the rebuilt St. Peter's, stood from his seat in a voluminous purple robe, the white fringe of his clerical stole swinging back and forth as he walked to the flower-draped podium to speak.

"Good morning!" the pastor began, and the crowd responded in kind. "This is the day that the Lord has made. I shall rejoice and be glad in it," he said, and several "amens" went up from various points in the crowd.

"We thank you, oh Lord, for waking us up, for putting clothes on our backs and food in our bellies. We thank you for giving us the strength to gather together on this day, to celebrate the life of one of our very own, Brother Ahmad Saleem, known to many in this crowd as Everett Walker."

The pastor grabbed the chord of the microphone and stepped from behind the flowery podium into the center aisle where he continued to speak.

"I received news of the passing only a few days ago, and then came word from his sister, Lottie, that he wanted me to deliver the address on this occasion. I recalled the address he gave at his own wife's interment just two years ago and thought, in that spirit, of what I myself would say at his, though Lottie quickly informed me that Brother Saleem had already, in a sense, planned my remarks for today.

"I'm more than twenty years his junior. Point being, we were not contemporaries, but I'm a Buford," he said, and the crowd gave a unanimous "umm hmm."

". . . And the Bufords, same as the Walkers, helped build the original St. Peter's, so we've got some shared history. When I thought about Brother Saleem, I considered what would be appropriate to share with those in attendance. Maybe I would talk about the prodigal son, gone a long way from home, or maybe I would talk about King Nebuchadnezzar and the long exile of the Jews from Judea—the years they spent in Babylon and their eventual return to Zion. But Brother Saleem had given specific instructions that, on the occasion of his interment, he wanted me to speak about Sarai, the wife of Abram.

"As the scripture shows us in Genesis, there was Adam and Eve and the fall from Eden, there were Cain and Abel and then Noah and the ark, sent to restore the earth to righteousness—showing us the cyclical nature of man's disobedience and God's redemption."

"Alright now," someone—a man—uttered in the crowd, lightly stomping his feet and rocking his head side to side with inspiration.

"Then we see the story of Abram, who came along with his wife Sarai, who left Haran for Shechem and then, when there was famine, they moved to Egypt. Sarai was a great beauty—one of the most beautiful women anyone had ever seen—but her womb bore no fruit, that was despite the fact that the Lord had spoken to Abram, promising him land and many offspring. Sarai was trying to understand how Abram could be the father of nations when, after ten years in Canaan, she still hadn't conceived a child. But she had an idea. She went to Abram and offered him Hagar, her hand-maiden, who gave birth to Ishmael—someone whom the Holy Bible describes as an ass of a man."

There was another scream of "hallelujah" from the crowd.

"Ishmael was a man whose hand would be against every man," the pastor went on, "because it wasn't Hagar who was destined to fulfill the covenant, but Sarai. She followed a false word of inspiration and found herself seized by the spirit of jealousy."

"She had become very old before the Lord blessed her with Isaac, who was the fulfillment of God's promise to Abraham, and this, my brothers and sisters, is what the Bible has to say about Sarai.

"Now I asked myself," the pastor raised his voice a notch, "why it was that Brother Saleem, in all his wisdom, would want me to tell that particular story on this day? What was it about the story of Sarai that made it so important to share on the solemn occasion of his burial?

"And then I started to think a little bit deeper," the pastor said, more animated and with more volume. "I started to think about the promises we keep, and the promises God makes to us that we forget, trying to make our own plans when God has already showed the path.

"Now I don't have to tell anybody here today the circumstances of our brother's departure from this place, leaving the folks behind, who were his flock, to rebuild this church without his help. But he found a life elsewhere and made a family, his two beautiful children are here with us today. But the calling God had placed on our brother's life and his life in this church was too strong to keep him away," the pastor said, and the people started shouting, "Amen! Amen!"

"All of us who call this place home, who know its history, can't help but be aware of the horrors that have been visited upon this land and this church. Our brother made the decision for the sake of his own family to leave it all behind and seek a different kind of life in the north, but like Sarai, he fulfilled God's promise. Our brother came back to the church. It was fifteen years ago that Brother Saleem reestablished a relationship with St. Peter's. He reached out to us, trying to be helpful where he could, and then it was five years later, when we started building our new campus, that he lent his accountancy talents to help us fundraise."

I looked over to Jabril, knowing I must have appeared confused or angry or some combination of the two, and saw some version of my own sentiment in his expression.

"He even came down for the breaking of the ground, then he made himself a regular at the church, donating money and helping us out whenever he was in town," the pastor said, and the crowd continued with their applause. Their celebration never quite met the fever pitch I had anticipated, though they were undoubtedly jubilant at the pastor's glowing praises of my father, who had been financially supporting the church—another fact I was only just learning.

"Let it be some evidence," the pastor went on, "that God's word is true. That we can forget his promises and go our own way, but when he's put a call on your life, there will be an answer!

"We thank the Lord today for our lost-and-found brother,

Ahmed Saleem born Everett Walker, and thank him for the family who are our family—his sister, Lottie Jenkins, and his children, Jabril and Taqwa Saleem. We pray God comfort your hearts in this season of loss, and as you make your way back home, that you remember to come and visit this place, because this here is also your home." The pastor blessed the crowd to warm applause and shouts of "hallelujah" before someone in the back of the tent began singing an old gospel hymn.

"Amen!
Amen!
Amen!
Amen!
Amen!"

He sang a few "Amens" before the rest of the crowd joined in, adding syncopated rhythms and harmonies that turned the atmosphere truly jubilant, though there was no such feeling coursing through my body, as I was overwhelmed with the newest revelations of our father's secret church life, in addition to the fact that I was becoming increasingly sweaty and faint due to the heat.

The crowd eventually quieted before Aunt Lottie, acting as the mistress of ceremonies, finally invited me up to deliver the eulogy.

There was polite applause as I rose from my seat and stumbled behind the small podium, opening the empty notebook, looking down at it like a security blanket as I repeatedly wiped the sweat from my brow.

"Good morning and peace be with you," I said, off the top of my head. "It's truly an honor to be with you on this wonderful occasion . . ." I paused after saying that, hearing the inappropriateness of the expression, before continuing, "celebrating the life of my father, Ahmed Saleem."

I looked at my Aunt Lottie, whose face was tied in a knot of concern, though she was nodding her head slightly, encouraging me to go on with my speech.

"My father," I said, "wanted me to speak a few words about him, so that you could know how I saw him as his daughter." I took a few deep breaths before I continued, and the air was thick and heavy with each inhale.

"My father . . ." I felt myself searching my thoughts like chasing birds through the skies. "My father . . . was a good man." I looked down at the blank interior of the notebook and turned the page like I was really reading. "He was a really good man . . . A man who taught me everything I needed . . ."

I said this and then I stopped. I could hear myself breathing into the microphone, then took another swipe at the sweat on my brow when I heard the voice of an older woman in the crowd reply, "It's alright baby, take your time."

I briefly looked up, trying to make out who had just spoken, when at the opposite end of the center aisle I saw a man in a heavy shadow, standing at the edge of the tent. My eyes went wide as I saw him gliding down the aisle in my direction, a notebook open, hovering between his hands, and all I remember after the moment I recognized it was the Imam rushing toward me, was an enveloping shadow that turned everything black and the feel of the left side of my body falling hard on the grass.

WHEN I REGAINED consciousness, I found myself laying supine on the guest bed at the Cliffords', a doctor and my mother's niece

Velma hovering over me, looking me up and down like a science experiment.

"She's going to be fine" were the first words I heard the doctor say as he glanced up at my cousin, then over to Jabril, who was standing near the door. "Just make sure she drinks plenty of water, and she should stay out of the sun if possible. I'm just relieved for you, ma'am," the doctor said, turning to face me. "The situation could have been so much worse."

I tried sitting up, and Velma helped me, propping my back with several pillows as the doctor packed his stethoscope to leave. Velma exited the room, escorting the doctor to the door, and Jabril sat at the edge of the bed near my feet.

"He's already been laid to rest," he said, nodding his head like he was trying to convince himself of something. "I threw a few roses into the grave for you. I figured you would want that.

"Did you want to see for yourself?" Jabril asked. "I can take you and—" He stopped at the sight of me shaking my head.

I told him I didn't want to go back to St. Peter's. I was ready to leave Ossacola and get on the road for the long drive home.

Jabril didn't need much convincing. He packed our things as I continued recovering my strength, and in less than an hour we were off.

We drove in silence for several miles, until we passed the Ossacola incorporation limit and all there was ahead of us was the endless highway, hugged by dense conifers on both sides.

I stared out the window, trying to gauge just what I was feeling, when I turned toward Jabril and saw him hugging the wheel. I asked him how the ceremony ended, and he shrugged.

"Aside from laying him in the ground, you didn't miss much. People wanted to be sure you were okay, but after a couple of us carried you to the car, the service kept going. Then Aunt Lottie got up to speak."

He shook his head. "You know, this whole time I was so proud of her for not showing out, but the closing invocation . . ." Jabril tightened his lips, his head ticked toward me like he was trying to get a kink out of his neck, though his eyes were still narrowed at the road. "Everything was fine by me until she ended everything, 'In Jesus's name.' In Jesus's name? I don't know," he said. "There was something about it that got under my skin. When we came down to memorialize Mom, she knew good and well Dad kept it very neutral, and he certainly wasn't praying 'in Jesus's name.' That's not what he would have wanted, so for her to say that . . ."

Jabril left his thoughts unfinished, sighing heavily, though after a moment's silence he perked up.

"You know, we could always have our own memorial. There's no reason that service has to stand as our final commemoration of his life."

I hadn't been present to hear Aunt Lottie pray "in Jesus's name," and was still nursing my upset with the Imam, but I listened without interrupting.

"You know how Dad loved the outdoors," Jabril said. "Why don't we stop and go fishing? Remember how much he liked going to the pond as a kid? See there!" Jabril pointed his right hand away from the steering wheel toward a brown sign with white lettering that read SILVER LAKE PARK AND CAMPING GROUNDS, located another twenty miles ahead on our journey.

"We can go to a big box store, get some poles, and set up shop for a few hours to catch some fish, throw them on the grill. You'd assume at a campground they have facilities for that sort of thing. Whatcha think?"

I wasn't particularly interested in fishing, but the idea of us heading out into nature pleased something inside me, reminding me of the times when we were young and the Imam would take us out to the county for hours and hours of catch and release. It must have been in that moment that I started smiling, because Jabril smiled back at me, then sped along, veering toward the next exit, where we stopped to get our gear.

Jabril pulled into the green zone parking lot of the Silver Lake grounds by two thirty in the afternoon. We walked a solid half mile with our poles, a bucket, and other materials in tow until we found a private spot on the lake—a little pebbled beach with a few sitting logs arranged around an ashen firepit, secluded from the path by a large thicket of swamp grass.

Jabril let on that, in our years apart, he taught himself all there was to know about roughing it in the great outdoors—a claim that was quickly disproved over the hours it took us to sort the fishing poles and thread the hooks with earthworms before we made our first catch. We stood side by side on the rocky shore when I finally felt a tugging on the line, and after an effort, reeled up a shimmering white bass that must have weighed five pounds.

I yelped with glee when it came flopping out of the water, and Jabril set his pole down to remove it from the hook and place it in the bucket for the grill.

"That's going to make for a delicious dinner," he said, taking up the pole again just minutes before he retrieved a white bass of his own. It didn't take very long once we got the hang of it, and by the end of our fishing expedition we recovered six in total—among them two catfish, which Jabril agreed, with some prodding from me, to throw back into the lake.

He was actually quite skilled at cleaning and descaling the fish, so that they were beautifully filleted by the time I got the fire going. We had bought a simple campfire grill, burying the stakes deep in the ash pile to accommodate the fish and several ears of sweet corn that I seasoned with butter, salt, and pepper before wrapping them in large sheets of tinfoil.

It was strenuous work, though not oppressively so, as the sun sank lower and lower in the sky—work that was made lighter by Jabril's recounting of stories that the Imam used to tell us when we were kids.

"Do you remember the legend of Harukkal?" he asked me as we served each other the corn and fish we'd just finished roasting.

"King of the Manasee—a tribe of loggers and fishermen who lived for centuries in the Shona Valley. They were fearsome warriors and masters of their trade, though Harukkal was known as a kind and just ruler. He had a beautiful wife named Telukki, who gave him two smart and obedient children, and she minded them with love and care." Jabril smiled at this, taking a bite of the corn, and I smiled, too, as I started to remember the Imam telling the tale, and wanted him to go on.

"He was revered among his people and renowned far beyond the valley, except for Mortakai, who was king of the Lomen tribe. He waged a series of wars in the mountains, proving himself in battle many times over until the Lomen territory stretched from the sea to the foothills leading to the Shona.

"It was early in the morning and Harukkal was out tending to his sheep when he saw, on the horizon, a cavalry of over one hundred men coming over the hills in the distance. Mortakai was at the helm galloping at breakneck speed toward Harukkal, who stood alone with no one but the sheep to witness what was unfolding—that the king of the Manasee was under siege and defenseless before the might of the Loma.

"Mortakai led his horse so that he was just feet away from Harukkal, towering over him. He had muscles like an ox, bulging eyes and thick black hair that grew all around his face like a lion's mane, with large tusks draped around his neck—much more fearsome than Harukkal, with his relatively slender build and the ordinary dignity of his demeanor.

" 'So you are Harukkal,' Mortakai said, 'king of the Manasee!' He said the words, turning to his men, and they laughed, their horses rearing at the sound—loud enough to stir the Manasee people so that they came streaming from their huts, trying to make sense of the commotion. 'You are but a peasant, a worthless and lame excuse of a man whose rule derives from the weakness of your tribesmen. We will not make war with you and riddle your people with our arrows and swords, but give you the chance to save yourselves by agreeing to pay tribute to me.'

"The Manasee were all gathered around with Telukki and their two children at the front of the crowd as Mortakai commanded Harukkal to bow to him—the new king of the Shona Valley. Harukkal stared at Mortakai, looking deep into his eyes, though he did not respond to the command, which infuriated him. Mortakai asked again, his voice booming for all the people to hear, for Harukkal to bow and when he refused, in a flash of rage, Mortakai drew his sword from its sheath and slayed the king of the Manasee, the blade cutting through him from the base of his neck, tracing a diagonal all the way to his left thigh.

"Mortakai withdrew his horse several feet as the Manasee circled around the dying king. 'We will camp in the hills, leaving a few of our soldiers to lay claim to your weapons before they, too, shall leave. We give you one full day to mourn your king, but come the dawn, you will hear the sounding of the Oliphant, and when we return, I shall rule the Shona Valley and you will become slaves of the Loma!'

"Mortakai rode off with his cavalry and Telukki fell upon Harukkal, cradling his face as he stared into her eyes before exhaling his final breath. The Manasee did not immediately bury their king but laid him in a hut to rest, covering his body in rich fabrics and flowers, surrounding his lifeless body with stones.

"Telukki stayed with Harukkal through the night, praying to undo the horrible fate that had befallen the Manasee, but the more she prayed the more hopeless she became, and by morning she had resigned herself to the fate that she and her children would be subjects of the brutal Mortakai.

"The sound of the horses' hooves came soon after the sounding of the Oliphant and at the break of dawn the cavalry were upon the Manasee, ready to lay claim to the Shona Valley. Mortakai dismounted at the hut, demanding that Telukki present herself, without her children, so that he could take her as his consort, and feeling unable to challenge him, she exited at his request with her head lowered toward the ground. Mortakai laughed with an unnatural resonance, which echoed through the valley and shook the trees, sending the plovers and ptarmigans flying from the branches by the thousands, but there was another reverberating shock, coming not from Mortakai, nor the trees, but from inside the hut. The Manasee and Mortakai and his men all looked on in shock as a strange, colorful illumination poured out of the opening, and stood gape-mouthed as they watched Harukkal emerge, growing larger with every step, his eyes emanating a searing white light. He stood before the paralyzed cavalry and inverted his hands until the sky went dark, summoning the lightening that pooled, growing brighter and stronger, dancing about his palms, then grabbed the bolts like daggers and threw them at the Loma, incinerating them all, including the fearsome Mortakai, until they were reduced to ashes."

I sat in suspension as Jabril shrugged his shoulders, reaching, finally, for a few more bites of the fish and the corn.

"That is how that story ended, isn't it?" I asked. "I could have sworn I had forgotten all about it, and he told it all the time when we were little. You would think I would have remembered."

"You didn't forget, Taqwa," Jabril said through bites of the corncob. "It was just one of the memories you've suppressed. But it all came back to you; it just took you a moment."

"Do you think Dad was secretly Christian?" I blurted out to Jabril, and it made him pause to look at me, the half-eaten cob hovering just inches from his face.

"I mean, all of this stuff with the burial, the sermon, that story even . . . I didn't tell you half of what it was like living with him over the past few years. Like, he started quoting the Bible and listening to gospel music in the house with the volume low, like I couldn't hear it. All of it just makes me think that he was hiding who he really was all these years, and honestly, I just don't know what to think anymore."

Jabril finished the last of the corn, wiped his hands on the sides of the jeans he changed into after the interment, and leaned forward the way he always did when trying to focus.

"Dad was a Muslim." Jabril said the words like setting down a heavy weight. "He may have had an affinity for the Bible and gospel music only because that's the way he grew up; it was an important part of his life. I don't understand how any of that means he died a Christian."

"Then how do you explain that sermon? Sarai gives birth to a son after many years of wandering behind Abraham, connected to Dad's return to the church? So Dad going back to the church, donating to them—behind our backs, mind you—was the fulfillment of God's plan? Like Islam was a deviation from his true path?" I folded my arms, and my entire body shook a little, a feeling of contempt growing inside me the more I thought about the day we spent laying the Imam to rest and all the unsavory revelations about his secret life.

"I don't think the preacher preached the message the way Dad had intended," Jabril said. "Then, you've got to imagine the amount of guilt he must have been feeling over the years. I mean, he was their pastor, with official responsibilities to the people of that church, and he just up and left them, not even giving his own sister a clue about where he was going. It's clear that he felt he was doing the right thing, but it had to have been on his mind all the time. You don't know that weight, Taqwa. It's the kind of thing you can carry forever."

"Do you ever feel guilty about the way *you* left?" I said the words with more ice than I had intended, and felt the mood shift with the dimming of the daylight, the sun having already fallen far past the horizon.

Jabril ticked his head at my question.

"Of course I do," he said. "Every day I feel guilty, you have no idea. By the end of their lives, I felt like Mom and Dad weren't going to fully accept me. I did sense that they were trying to under-stand me at least, and that's the part that makes me feel the worst. I always shut them out. I'm not sure I'll ever forgive myself for wast-ing the chance to reconcile. As one does, you just learn to live with it, you know. You can't change the past. But there again," Jabril looked at me like he felt there was something I hadn't fully under-stood, "people leave, Taqwa. That's what we do. That's what we all have to do. I left home. But Mom and Dad . . . they left Ossacola, St. Peter's, and Aunt Lottie. You can't say they did it the right way, but would you say they should have stayed?"

I thought about it and shook my head.

"They made mistakes and they hurt people, but they had to go, Taqwa. And even if they failed and had to go back, they tried to make a difference in their lives—in our lives—by doing something new. That's how you get perspective; it's the venturing out that grows you . . ."

Jabril was getting worked up, like he was trying to prove something not just to me but to himself, and so he stopped, taking a few moments to breathe.

"What I'm trying to understand," Jabril went on, his voice curled with accusation, "is why my guilt, Dad's guilt, or his beliefs—why any of it matters to you so much?"

It felt like a trick question, and so I stared at Jabril like he was being simple.

"Because he was my father, and I was his daughter—a very good and dutiful daughter. I did everything he said was right to do because I knew the punishment I would suffer in the hereafter if I didn't honor my parents. If it turns out that Dad was a Christian after all of these years of pretending to be Muslim, what does it mean—"

"What does it mean about you?" Jabril interrupted. "You don't know where it leaves *you* if it turns out that he didn't really believe the things he taught. Do you think it leaves you stranded, like you don't have your own road to travel, like there isn't something just around the bend waiting for you to find it?"

Jabril was staring at me, when a flash of genius traveled across his face. He raised his left brow.

"I didn't know you were so into fashion magazines," he said with a curious tone. "Is that something new or have I just been too distant to notice that magazines were your pastime?"

"It's for the ghost," I said, and then froze, looking up at my brother, then back to the campfire whose light had become our primary illumination with the fading of the day.

I had done so well disguising what had been happening to me since the janaza, that I didn't want to have my brother probing for details. I knew he wouldn't accept my experience of the ghost as something real, but I broke down, not wanting to hide the secret any longer.

"The Imam has been visiting me since the day of the janaza— like really menacing me—but the only thing that keeps him at bay are fashion models, but not just any models, they have to be in bikinis. I keep the magazines around and when I do that, he leaves me alone. When I fell over at the interment it's because I saw him coming down the aisle, and without any pictures on hand I was defenseless, so I passed out."

Jabril chuckled a little.

"So he knew," he said. "This whole time he knew. Everybody knew but you, girl."

I didn't know what Jabril was trying to say, but before I could ask him to clarify, he pressed me. "I just don't understand, why won't you let anyone love you? What would be so bad about that? Meeting someone can be exciting. I mean, you're beautiful and smart. Someone would be really lucky to—"

"I don't need your advice," I interrupted. "I have a good life, Jabril—a good, clean life with plenty of people. I don't need to pursue any dangerous relationships to be happy. You and Brandon can go about your lives doing whatever wild things you do, but I'm more than content—"

"Who's Brandon?" Jabril smirked, his head tilted as he tried making sense of my words. "My girlfriend's name is Brandi. I don't think I even know a Brandon—wait . . . is it because I paint my nails? Just because I paint my nails you think that I'm . . . ?"

Jabril looked to the ground and shook his head for a moment, then, still leaning forward, he glared at me, the red-orange flames of the campfire dancing in his eyes.

"Remember when we were kids, just before I left home?" Jabril asked. "After we stopped going to the Al-Hassan's, did you ever keep in touch with Zainab?"

As soon as he said the name I froze.

"I take your silence as a no, which is strange to me because you seemed to like her so much in those days. I don't know your impression of me when we were kids, but I was paying close attention to you, Taqwa. I never once saw you so taken with somebody, not ever.

"Remember how Dad always made us carry those notebooks with us to class, even though Mr. Al-Hassan gave us writing pads to use at his house? It was on a really harried Saturday morning that I remember grabbing yours from your room. I didn't want Dad to get mad at you for not bringing it along. I promise you, Taqwa, I wasn't tying to violate your privacy, but I reached for the notebook on your desk and it fell open, and what you wrote in that notebook didn't have anything to do with Mr. Al-Hassan's lessons."

I shook as he spoke, trying to will myself out of my body, to black out as I had done at the interment, but there was Jabril, reciting the words like he had the notebook right in front of him,

"'Ana aakulu ma'a Zainab. Ana uhib Zainab. Zainab hiya habibti.'"

"And how did you love Zainab? Did you see her as just a friend or was there something more? Have you even given yourself permission to ask the question?"

"I never acted on it." I managed to get out the words. "I never did anything. I didn't want the Imam to reject me."

"And that's the problem, Taqwa. Are you so afraid of who you may become if you let go of Dad as the Imam? Maybe it's better if you start to see him as a man who made his choices, who wants you to make some of your own?"

"I don't want to do anything wrong," I said, wiping away the stream of tears that wouldn't stop flowing.

"There's nothing wrong with you; it's the environment. It's the people around you making you feel that way. You're not safe where you are back home, and finding a way out . . . that's the path ahead of you.

"I kept it to myself, but I always tried reaching out over the years because I wanted you to know that if you ever needed someone as you were figuring it out, I would be there."

I wanted to scream, to send all the birds on the nearby tree limbs scattering in the twilight air, then run off into the darkening woods, but Jabril had disarmed me and I was reduced to heaving cries. I sobbed for I don't know how long, until I perceived my brother on the log at my side, opening his arms to hold me. I fell into his embrace and he held me tight, rocking me back and forth.

He continued holding me as my breathing slowed, and we looked up at the sky, dark enough to see the stars emerge, with Jabril pointing out the asterisms and constellations—Draco, Cassiopeia, Boötes, and Ursa Major—with the Dubhe star, on the upper rim of the Big Dipper, aiming straight at Polaris.

ACKNOWLEDGMENTS

I would like to thank my editor, Yahdon Israel, the rainbow, and Eric Simonoff, my agent. Thank you for your brilliance and the gift of your attention to these stories.

A very special thank-you to my sister, Naimah, and my niece, Araba, who helped me through the storm before the rainbow shone through the clouds.

To the most beautiful woman in the world, my mom—thank you for encouraging me to follow my imagination and to love all good people and things, especially literature.

To my father who, when I was born, whispered the Shahada in my ear, leading me into the world that inspired this book. Thank you for the long talks about the NOI days.

To my family—the Bilal's of Washington, DC— I love us, especially my sweet grandma Ruth Bilal, the photographer, and my grandpa, John Bilal Sr., the gardener.

To Tim Tomlinson, E. Ethelbert Miller, Michelle Garnaut, Katherine Atkinson, and Dr. Amina Wadud—the early supporters—thank you.

I would also like to acknowledge my late beloveds who live in me and run through the pages of this book Imani Abdul Haqq, Rosa Shareef, Devin Heatley, and my sister, Susan Licon-Lewis.

ABOUT THE AUTHOR

Aaliyah Bilal was born and raised in Prince George's County, Maryland. She has degrees from Oberlin College and the University of London School of Oriental and African Studies. She's published stories and essays with the *Michigan Quarterly Review* and *The Rumpus*. *Temple Folk* is her first short story collection.